gianna
TWO
SIDES

Dedication

This book is to anyone who has ever lied and lived to regret it.

Acknowledgements

First and foremost I need to thank my husband Ben Robinson. Thank you for always allowing me to pursue my dreams. Even though I ignore you whenever I am on my computer or my cellphone. I love you.

My parents: Thank you for always showing me what hard work and determination can accomplish.

My sister & nieces: Love you guys!

My family and friends who I ignore all the time…I love you. You know I do.

Rebecca Marie: You never disappoint! Thank you for an amazing cover, as always!

Michelle Tan: Best beta ever!

Heather Harton: You have been with me since the beginning. Thank you so much for being you. My GILF!

Alexis Moore: I love our crazy banter and your support!

Jennifer Mirabelli: I love your voice! And you.

Shannon Franco: Thank you love!!

The bloggers: THANK YOU, THANK YOU, THANK YOU!!

READERS & FANS: THANK YOU!! Without you, I am nothing.

Disclaimer

Two Sides: Gianna is an Adult Dark Erotic Thriller, which contains dark elements that include kidnapping, rape, both physical and mental abuse. Please take that into consideration before reading. If this isn't a problem then welcome and enjoy the ride.

Prologue

Friend: A person attached to another person by feelings of affection or personal regard. A person who gives assistance, a supporter, faithful companion, and keeper of secrets. Someone with whom you can laugh or cry, share your hopes and dreams. Someone who knows all about you and loves you anyway. [1]

Best friend: Someone who you can trust with your life who has seen the best and worst of you and will be there whenever you need someone to talk to. There is a balance in friendship between give and take. You feel so in sync with them that you can comfortably share your innermost feelings and thoughts.[2]

Sister: A person who's been where you've been. Someone you can call when things aren't right. More than just family. A sister is a friend for life.[3]

Broken: Having been fractured or damaged and no longer in working order. Having given up all hope, despairing.[4] Dictionary.com

How do you go from one extreme to another? How do you feel like part of you is missing and you have no idea where to find it? How do you lose your whole life, everything you thought you had, you thought you knew, you thought would happen…how does it all go away as quickly as the wind blows? The secrets, the plans, the dreams, I can't even tell them apart anymore. They all melt together, forming one big cluster of nothing. Which is exactly what I am…I am nothing but a damaged person. I have been since day one.

People can be whatever you want them to be. I am the perfect example of that. On the inside, everything is wrong, all of it is misplaced, and nothing holds secure. I was never pretty enough, I was never good enough, I was never smart enough, I was just never enough. They needed flawlessness and excellence, and on the outside, I portrayed it to a T. But on the inside, I was dying. Damaged goods. At least when you buy something broken you can return it, but what do you do when that's not an option? When you have no choice but to wake up every morning with a smile on your face because that's what people expect. Your family, your social circle, and your best friend– someone you call your sister. McKenzie thought she knew me, everyone did. I told you I played the part perfectly, hour after hour, day after day, year after year.

I am Gianna Edwards.

But the truth is…

I have no idea who I am.

Chapter One

"Excuse me…" I gasped at the guy standing in front of me at the bar.

I had to blink several times because the man before me looked identical to Mr. Nichols. Was my mind playing tricks on me? It couldn't have been him, he had been in jail for seven years. Did he get out? Did he come for me? No, he couldn't have come for me, he was still in prison. This man just looked like him; it was always the same, they all looked like him. It didn't matter, but that's what my eyes would always see.

It was the price I had to pay.

"I've been trying to get your attention for the last few seconds. Are you all right?"

"Yeah. Sorry, what did you need?"

"Well, your name for starters."

I downed my drink trying to calm my nerves. "G," I answered mid swallow.

"That's an interesting name. Is it short for something?" he interrogated.

I laughed. "Yeah…it's short for mind your own damn business."

"You're feisty. Anyone ever tell you what you should do with that mouth?"

"All the time." I snickered.

He grinned. "I'm Nick," he introduced himself, sticking out his hand.

I looked at it and raised my eyebrow. "Of course it is," I stated, laughing at the situation and myself.

"Excuse me?"

"Don't worry about it," I quickly rebutted. "So, Nick," I said, accenting his name. "To what do I owe the honor of your presence?"

He curved his lip. "I actually wanted to buy you a drink, maybe talk to you a bit. Get to know you. You know, the typical guy meets girl conversation among two consenting adults." He reached his hand further and he placed it on my thigh.

I placed mine on top. "And then what? What happens after that?"

He chuckled. "I get your phone number, maybe?"

I opened my legs, watching exactly where his eyes went. "Is that all you're looking for, Nick? Some light conversation and my phone number. Because I'll tell you right now, I'm looking for a hell of a lot more than that."

He licked his lips and caressed my thigh, "Is that so? What are you looking for, little girl?"

I smiled. "I'm looking for a good time, right now. Not tomorrow or next week. And you most definitely won't get my phone number. You're lucky you even got my name."

"G isn't a name, it's a letter," he teased.

"Really? Wow. I hadn't noticed…maybe you could take me back to your place and show me other letters, like O for orgasm, and C for climax. I'm actually quite fond of B for bad girl."

He shook his head and chuckled. "What if I want a good girl?"

I shrugged. "Then you wouldn't still be standing here."

"Let's go," he ordered, placing a bill on the bar and grabbing my hand.

"I thought you'd never ask."

Nick lived in the penthouse suite at a casino nearby. The suite matched the imported car the valet chauffeured up. We didn't talk much on the car ride back to his house, which was fine by me because I didn't care to do much talking.

He punched in a code and the elevator took us up to the top floor. The doors opened to a big open room with a panoramic view of Sin City. What happens in Vegas stays in Vegas.

"Can I get you something to drink?" he whispered in my ear from behind me.

I curved my neck to feel his breath on me. "Of course, what kind of girl do you think I am?"

"Exactly the kind of girl I'd like to put over my knee." He spanked my ass, making me yelp.

The smile that appeared on his handsome face before he walked away from me made me ache. It resembled the smile that Mr. Nichols would always give me. I didn't think I could follow through with it anymore and I began to walk toward the door.

"Going somewhere?" he implored, grabbing me by the waist. His tone was arrogant and inviting. I closed my eyes, trying to stay in the present and avoid the flashbacks that had been coming to me at an increasing rate.

The tip of his fingers touched the side of my arm. "Because...I didn't say you could go." He murmured in my ear, "I thought we were just getting acquainted. You look like you could use a friend."

"You don't know shit about me," I angrily replied.

"You're right, I don't." He traced soft kisses down the side of my neck and I subconsciously leaned toward them, wanting more. Nothing was ever enough.

"How about you tell me...not that I wouldn't mind finding out on my own," he enticed as his hand moved from the curve of my ass to my pussy from behind.

"You're wet."

"No shit."

He groaned and the thoughts that led as his fingers slipped into my opening were of Mr. Nichols' hands on me. When he rubbed from my nub to my opening, spreading the moisture all over my folds, I bit my lower lip from calling out his name.

"Why is your pussy so wet, G? I've barely even touched you." I jolted when he roughly grabbed the back of my neck, moving me toward the couch.

I should have been scared...terrified even.

He shoved my upper body forward on the back of the couch and I fell over, barely catching myself on the edge. I turned to watch him pull down my dress and panties. He grabbed one ankle and then the other, leaving me completely exposed with nothing on but my heels. He stepped back to admire me and I relished in the feeling of having a man's eyes on me. G loved this. This was where she was confident, and this was where she shined.

He was still fully dressed in his black slacks and blue button down. His index finger caressed my spine in an up and down motion. "You're so tiny, G. I don't want to break you."

"You can't break what's already broken, Mr. Nichols," I mindlessly responded.

"What did you call me?" he roared in a tone that made my eyes roam to the back of my head.

He licked his fingers and placed them on my clit. "That's not my name," he reminded as his other hand reached around and grabbed me by the front of my throat, moving me on his chest. He felt firm, muscular. I wanted so badly to see him naked.

He slapped my pussy, lightly at first, and then he slapped harder until my knees buckled and I whimpered.

"I asked you a question, G, and I expect an answer," he prompted as he made slow circles around my clit.

"Oh God," I sighed, trying to catch my breath. "I called you Mr. Nichols."

"Who is Mr. Nichols?" he interrogated in a patronizing voice, while moving his fingers faster around my nub, making it difficult for me to stand.

"Mmmm..." I moaned in both pleasure and pain.

"Answer the fucking question. Trust me. You don't want me to ask again."

"Jesus...fuck..." My head fell back on his shoulder, as did most of my body weight. His hand squeezed my throat harder as he continued to monopolize my pussy.

"I won't let you come until you answer," he stated, biting my shoulder and slapping my pussy.

I hesitated for a few seconds. "He-he was my teacher," I revealed and he spun me around so fast I didn't even see it coming. He grabbed my chin. "You are a fucking disaster, aren't you?" His fingers moved to the sides of my mouth and dug into my cheeks, making my mouth open.

"You have no idea what you agreed to when you came home with me, G," he warned as he placed me on the edge of the couch.

"Open your legs," he ordered. "Wider." He rubbed and slapped my pussy, taking turns in making me jump and struggle.

His hand found my throat again, but this time he had more leverage to squeeze since he was facing me. "Trust me with your body," he coaxed.

He tightened his hold around my throat and slowly my air was taken from me.

Everything started going dark, darker, black...until the only thing I could see was my life playing out for me like a tragic Shakespearian play. I saw it all, starting from when I was little. I went from being with Nick, with his hands around my neck, to being nine years old and playing hide-and-go-seek with Mack.

"Mack!! Mack!! I'm going to find you...you can't hide from me. Are you behind the bushes? Are you under the slide? Hmmm...where is Mackity Mack?" I roamed around aimlessly looking for her; I had been for

11

the last ten minutes. She was the best hider; sometimes it took me over thirty minutes to find her. I don't know why we continued to play a game where she was always hiding and I always did the seeking. I guess that's what nine-year-olds do.

I saw her shadow behind the big oak tree and I ran as fast as I could before she could see me coming. She screamed in delight as I took off after her.

"You can't catch me! I am faster than you!" she yelled, looking behind her to see how close I was. I saw it before it happened. She didn't see the branch that stuck out of the ground and fell face first into the ditch.

I got down on my knees as soon as I caught up to her. "Oh my God, Mack, are you okay?" She sniffled as the tears fell down her face. "Do you want me to run home and get my dad?"

She shook her head no and brushed away her tears with the back of her hand.

"What can I do?"

"I don't know. I'm okay I think." Her knee looked pretty bad; there was blood mixed with dirt, but I think it was only a scrape. I wanted to make her feel better.

"I know..." I smiled and got up to find what I was looking for. It took me a few minutes to find a stick that was pointy enough. I eagerly grabbed it and ran back to sit right beside her.

"What are you doing?" she questioned, looking at me lopsided.

I grabbed the stick and cut into my skin right across my knee, the same place Mack was hurt. She looked at me like I was crazy. I pushed the palm of my hand over my cut and told Mack to do the same to hers. She did. I grabbed her wrist with my clean hand and brought my bloody one up, then I closed them together.

"There! Now we're blood sisters. Anything you feel, I feel; we're attached for life." The smile that spread across her face was worth the wincing pain in my knee. We helped each other up and leaned on one another, limping our way home.

Mack and I always did everything together. We were both only children and a part of me always wondered if they did it that way for a reason. If they had it planned out that way, was our friendship inevitable since day one? Do families normally do that? I still don't know the answer to that question, but it has never stopped me from thinking about it.

I'd like to say that I was an amazing student and that I caught on quickly to new and old material, but I would be lying...school and I didn't click, not one bit. I always tried my best because I wanted to impress my parents; they had high expectations for their only daughter. That put an immense amount of pressure on me. I never wanted to let them down; I wanted them to be proud of me. Even though I was the only child, it didn't mean that I didn't feel the competition I had to keep up with. McKenzie was great at school; she was quick and clever. She caught on to anything, just seeing it one time. It was inspiring; I wanted to learn like she did. She didn't even have to study half the time. Everything came so natural to her; she never had to try, it was just there.

"Ugh! I don't understand, Mack. This is so stupid. Why do I need to learn this?"

"Ummm…because it's math and you might need to add something."

I rolled my eyes as I heard the garage door opening.

"Hi, girls," my dad said with a huge smile across his face.

He came right over to the dining room table and kissed the top of my head and then proceeded to do the same to Mack.

"Look at you guys. Are my girls studying hard?"

"Of course," Mack bellowed. It made me want to roll my eyes again.

Mack always did this when my dad was around. She always wanted to seem like she was the perfect one. I couldn't really argue with that because she was. She did everything right the first time and never had to constantly keep trying like me.

"What about you, Gia? You understanding the material?" The fact that my father had to ask this further ingrained in my mind that he thought McKenzie was better.

"Yeah…I get it," I lied. I didn't understand it at all.

"Are you sure? Do we need to get you a tutor?" he questioned with an authoritative tone.

"Yes, I'm sure," I whispered, trying to keep my head high.

"Keep listening to what Mack is explaining. She knows what she is doing. Just follow her lead. We don't want your grades to be slipping, Gia. Your mother and I pay a lot of money in tuition to offer you the best and we expect to see results."

"I understand."

"Don't worry, Kyle. I won't let her fall behind. I promise." Mack beamed, looking straight into my father's eyes. He grinned in response and tugged on her hair.

"I know you won't, Mack." He excused himself to go find my mother, and it was then that I noticed I was holding my breath. I let out a sigh

13

of relief when he exited the room. I wanted nothing more than to go running after him and tell him I was smart. I could do it. I didn't need Mack's help; I could figure it out on my own. Just because I didn't understand it right away didn't mean I was a failure.

"I'm smart, too, Mack."

She cocked her head to the side with a confused expression written all over her pretty little face. "I know you are, Gia. There is nothing wrong with how you learn. It takes you a little bit longer, but once you get it, it stays. I will help you; I won't let you fall behind. You're my best friend. We have plans to go to the same college, remember?" she said and I nodded.

We had lots of plans to do a lot of things. Most of the time it was her who came up with them and I followed along with what she said. I was only nine when I realized I wanted to do something different. I wanted to travel the world, I wanted to see things I read about in books, I wanted to go backpacking through Europe and stay in hostels and meet new people. I couldn't tell her that, though...she wouldn't understand. Mack had these big plans for us to go to college, become successful with decorating, and make lots of money.

Her idea of a life was so cookie cutter, like the perfect image of the movies we saw...meet prince charming and have him sweep you off your feet, get married, and then live happily ever after.

Blah! So boring...

I didn't say anything and smiled, exactly how I did every time. We continued as we were.

When we graduated from fifth grade, our parents made a huge deal about it. They threw us a combined graduation party and pulled out all the stops. Both of our families were extremely well off. I guess you could call us high class; we had the best homes, cars, clothing, you know...all the things that money could buy. My mother was probably the most vain person I had ever met, she was always perfectly put together and expected the same exact thing from her daughter. No one would talk about the Edwards; our name would not be gossiped about by people in our town of Shayla Harbor, Rhode Island.

We lived in one of those towns where everyone knew who you were and knew everything about you. Our family needed to appear picture-perfect. I don't ever remember there being any conflict in our home. My parents didn't really fight, at least not that I personally saw. If they were arguing, then they kept it behind closed doors. My mother and father were both beautiful people, they looked like they should be in catalogs and magazines. I often found myself admiring my mother from afar; we always had a great relationship. Sometimes I felt like she knew what I was going through, but she had no idea how to approach me about it. We talked about everything...most of the time. There were things I couldn't share with her, as much as I wanted to, I couldn't find the words to express myself, and I was terrified that she wouldn't understand. I already thought I was a disappointment to one parent and I didn't want to lose another.

Our graduation party had the works–a clown, pony rides, face painting, even a fucking magician. All of our friends were there as well as their parents. I socialized exactly how it was expected of me. I made my way around to everyone, kissing them on the cheek and thanking them for coming to our party. My mom dressed me in the most ridiculous outfit. I hated it, but McKenzie wore the exact same thing. We looked like two porcelain dolls. Mack loved our dresses; she spun around in it for hours before people started showing up. I wanted to rip mine off as soon as I had it on. The pantyhose made my skin itchy and hot, and the black baby-doll shoes pinched my toes. But I did what I had always done, I kissed my mother and thanked her for the gorgeous outfit and spun around in circles just like Mack.

After my mother felt like I had socialized enough for her standards, I was finally permitted to do my own thing. And the first thing I did was run up to my tree-house to take a moment for myself. I don't know how long I was up there admiring the children who looked so happy and carefree. I wondered what they all thought about as they participated in our extravagant party. Were they jealous of me? Did they think I had it all? Was I envied?

I watched Mack get her face painted excited as she picked out the colors and designs. All black and silver, exactly the kind of girl she was. She had butterflies all over her face and glitter was used as the wings. I related to the butterflies that were designed on her face more than I did with the girl that was in front of me. I wanted to fly away and be free. To be myself, whomever that may be. With no judgment or expectations of who I thought I was supposed to be. She ran right over to my dad, looking for praise and admiration I'm sure, and he gave her every last bit of it. His eyes shined as she flapped her arms up and down in the same motion as a butterfly twirling in circles around him. He laughed at her innocence.

I wanted to feel like that. I wanted to feel anything other than the suffocating emotions I felt on a daily basis, like I was being strangled. I didn't breathe the normal air that surrounded me; I inhaled dark clouds and hazy skies. All of which left a bitter aftertaste in my mouth and especially in my life. In a way, I was like the doll I was dressed like that day–absolutely perfect on the outside and hollow in existence on the inside. The portrayal of the perfect girl that only existed to everyone else because I was far from it. We were miles apart, countries really…

"Gianna! Gia! Where are you?" Mack yelled.

There was no way she could find me hiding from everyone. She wouldn't understand. I slowly climbed down from the tree-house, making sure I didn't rip my pantyhose. I walked around the back of the house and came in through the front.

"Gia! Where have you been? Look at my face! It's your turn. Come on! Let's get your face painted exactly like mine. We will be twins!" she exclaimed when she found me in the kitchen.

"Okay!" I replied with the same enthusiasm.

We didn't have to help our parents clean up when the party was over. They hired people to do that. I took off my outfit the minute my mom said it was all right to. Mack stayed in hers, she said she would never have an opportunity to wear it again and wanted to enjoy it. She didn't understand why I wanted to change out of mine.

We made our way to the tree-house with cake and soda. I only took a few bites of mine. I gained weight easily, but Mack could eat whatever she wanted without a care in the world.

"What are you thinking about, Gia? You seem off today," she questioned, stuffing her face with the biggest spoon of chocolate icing.

"I'm thinking about how amazing our party was," I lied.

"I know, right? Oh my God, I can't believe our parents did this for us. We really are very lucky."

I nodded, not knowing what to say.

"Can you believe we're going to be in middle school in a few months? I am so excited! I can't wait to make new friends…and the boys, Gianna! We are going to be with eighth graders, I hope they like us."

"I know! I hope they do, too. I'm kinda nervous, though…I mean, new school and all."

She rolled her eyes. "Are you serious? We're Mack and Gia, everyone will love us. They always do. I bet we will be the most popular girls in school, the same way we are now. I mean, Suzie Jacobs and Carrie Markus were at our party. They are going to be in seventh grade next year! We had sixth graders at our party, and that says something about us. You have nothing to worry about. Stop being weird."

"You're right. I'm being silly," I replied, taking a bite of my cake as I tried to avoid looking at her face. I was scared she would notice how big of a fraud I was if she looked into my eyes. But the reality that I would learn much later, was that no one could see through me. I was a chrome metal shield that no one could break or see through…with the exception of one person.

I wanted someone to call me out on my bullshit, I wanted someone to call me a liar, tell me that I was a fake, a phony, but it never fucking happened. People just nodded, agreed with me, or smiled. I was the epitome of the poor little rich girl and no one knew it but me. How many secrets can one person hold? I would also learn that. I was full of them and that box only got bigger as the years went by.

When you're younger, you are supposed to have someone you look up to–a hero of some sort. I didn't have one. There wasn't anyone that I wanted to be like, no one I wished I could be. I don't know if that set me up for failure or not. Was I destined to be empty for the rest of my life? Was I made wrong?

"What are you going to wear on the first day of school?" she asked, bringing me out of my thoughts.

"Oh I don't know. What are you going to wear?" I replied, not caring about the question at all.

"I definitely want to wear something awesome. We should find something similar, you know, dresses or skirts," she suggested and I nodded.

We both turned to look out at the sky. It was gorgeous with all the beautiful stars and lighting from the moon.

"Oh my God, Gia! Did you see it? A shooting star! Make a wish!"

She didn't have to tell me to make a wish…I had already made one. I made a wish I could never share with anyone. It was another secret I would keep to myself. But like with anything in life, it was only a matter of time until the other shoe would drop. I just had to wait until it happened. I never imagined the repercussions that would come about. I never thought about the consequences to any of my actions. I just went along with everything, thinking it was what was best for everyone. I didn't realize that by internalizing all the wants and desires, I started to mold myself into someone I couldn't recognize.

Someone I didn't respect or want to be.

How could you turn in to someone that you hate? How does your enemy become someone you see every time you look in the mirror? How do you hate yourself so much that sometimes you think the only way out is by ending it all? It's a selfish wish. But wasn't I allowed to be selfish, couldn't I be for just one second? To show the scars that I felt on the inside? If people knew who I really was, they wouldn't like me, they wouldn't want to be me…they would know the truth, and that would be much scarier than the façade.

I could change the inevitable as much as I could change the bright color of the sun or the darkness of the night.

Everything happens for a reason…

Don't do something today that you will regret tomorrow.

Chapter Two

Middle school proved to be much more of a challenge for me and much less of a task for McKenzie. We were in all honor classes, no thanks to me. I found myself constantly trying to keep up with my classes; I would study for hours, even after Mack helped me. As much as I didn't want to do it, I had to get a tutor.

"Dad," I said as I walked into his office. He put a finger up, telling me to hold on. I hadn't realized he was on the phone.

"Yes, I need those files by tomorrow morning. Mmm hmm, thank you," he stated before hanging up.

He turned his attention to me.

"Gianna, you know to knock before entering my office," he chastised me, making me feel more embarrassed for what I was about to ask. I could never do anything right in his eyes.

"I'm sorry." I dropped my head, looking at the clean tile Maria, our cleaning lady, just freshly mopped that afternoon.

"It's all right, no need to apologize, just don't do it again. What do you need?"

"Oh…well…I…" I stuttered, shifting my balance from one foot to the other. "I umm…sort of need some help in my English class."

He folded his arms and sat back in his office chair, disappointment spread across his face just as fast as the words came out of my mouth.

"I thought McKenzie was helping you. She has straight A's in all her classes," he affirmed everything I feared about this conversation. I knew the second I said I needed help, he would compare me to Mack, it was his go-to card.

"She is helping me, Dad, but seventh grade is a lot harder and all my classes just keep piling up. I'm doing pretty well in all of them, but I'm really struggling in English. I wanted to know if you could get me a tutor."

"Hmmm…" he replied, taking in my request I was sure. "I can't say that I'm not disappointed, Gianna. Though I would much rather you come to me and ask for help, rather than sink without me being able to save you."

I nodded.

"Let me make some phone calls and I'll have someone come to the house as soon as possible."

"Thank you. I am sorry, Dad. I don't mean to disappoint you. I would never want to do that," I expressed, wanting anything but the words that would follow.

"McKenzie has always been an amazing student and I hoped you would follow in those footsteps. The fact that you haven't is a little disappointing as a parent. Not because I don't think you are capable of it. I think you're lazy, Gianna. I don't think you try hard enough. I don't think you care. I think you don't apply yourself enough to reach your full potential. I want you to care about your academic achievement."

If he only knew how much I tried to be everything he ever wanted, I tried to be everything everyone always wanted. I molded myself for everyone else…how could he not see that?

"I know, Dad. I will try a lot harder for you. I promise."

He smiled, "I love you, and you are capable of anything you put your mind to. You're an Edwards and we're not quitters. We're leaders."

I wanted to swear and tell him to fuck off. It was the first time ever I wanted to tell my father, the person who created me, who brought me into this world, to go fuck himself. I wished I would have had the courage to do it. It would have probably changed so much of my life if I could have just said the fucking words. However, I didn't. I nodded my head and smiled bright and high. The same smile that made my father's eyes light up. It was the look I knew he adored. It was the Gianna Edwards smile that he was proud of. He loved the illusion that was his daughter. Just like everyone else.

The year went by rather quickly and before we knew it, we were in eighth grade and I had just celebrated my fourteenth birthday. I woke up one morning to McKenzie screaming into the phone.

"AHHHHHH!"

"Oh my God, Mack, my ear," I said, pulling the phone as far away from my face as possible.

"I got my period! I'm a woman! Can you believe it? Gianna, I got my monthly friend."

"Yay!" I shouted, trying to share her same enthusiasm.

I didn't get my period for another six months. I was almost in ninth grade by the time it wanted to show up. That's not the only thing that changed over night; Mack started to become a woman. Her breasts grew, as did her butt and thighs. She had the perfect hourglass figure and I was still rail thin.

I tried everything to get my period to come–drinking herbal tea, jumping backward fifty times when the sunset…yeah, I found that one on the Internet. I was desperate to keep up with Mack and tried to do everything for Mother Nature to catch up. She also started to get attention from boys, and I mean it was everywhere. They left notes in her locker, they called her house at all hours, and she was asked out on dates on a regular basis.

It just further proved that she was better than me.

We sat around one afternoon at Mack's house just hanging out, watching TV.

"Girls, what are you doing? You need to do something other than fry your brains all day watching mindless entertainment."

"But we love mindless entertainment and it's *90210*, Mom. Dylan just cheated on Brenda with Kelly. Ugh! I hate Kelly," Mack groaned as her mom turned the TV off.

"I will not allow you guys to watch any more TV. You need to pick up a sport, something, anything that gets you out of the house and away from being couch potatoes."

Mack turned to me and sighed, making her look much younger than her body appeared to be. "My mom is being so dumb; we don't need to pick up a sport. We're perfect just the way we are."

I laughed; this was her attitude about everything. I envied her confidence.

"She's sort of right, though…we don't really do anything other than watch TV or homework," I said.

"Are you serious? We do so much more than that, Gia. You're selling us really short."

I shook my head and grinned. "Okay, you're right. But I still think maybe we can take up a sport and have some fun." I clapped my hands together. "Oh! I know! We can do cheerleading. I've always wanted to try it. We watch it on TV enough to be able to pick it up."

She groaned in her discomfort of not wanting to get off the couch.

"Mack, this is actually a perfect idea. Everything is indoors, we wouldn't have to sweat that much. Just think about it, we could continue doing it in high school and all games are at night time, so you wouldn't have to worry about your fair skin."

"Okay, I guess that makes sense and it's better than any other sport."

"Yay! Let's go tell our moms."

Our moms were more than delighted to enroll us in tumbling and dance classes. We had six months to get ready before high school tryouts. We were adamant that we would make the team. Tumbling and dancing came natural to me, and it was the first time I felt like I did something better than her. I mean, she was good, but I was better. I learned things much faster as opposed to her trying to do them three or four times. The first time I did a back handspring, you would've thought I cured cancer or something. The adrenaline and pride I felt by learning to do it on my very first try was phenomenal. Our teacher had spotted me, but he said he barely even supported me.

I found my passion, and I know that sounds young and silly, but I found something I was better at than Mack, and I didn't ever think that would happen. My period decided to make its presence known the next day. I thanked my back handspring for that. And just like Mack, my body changed overnight. I grew breasts, 34C to be exact, and a butt. I had a toned figure from dancing and tumbling. My skin glowed when I looked in the mirror and my mom had allowed me to get highlights. It took my plain, brunette hair and made it blond. McKenzie didn't want to dye her hair and she didn't need to, she was beautiful the way she was. I needed it to make me look better. I wasn't a natural beauty like she was. I had to work at it.

I also grew into my facial features and I was able to finally get contact lenses. It made my green eyes grab everyone's attention. Frames of black glasses no longer blocked their view. I had long eyelashes and when I applied mascara, it made them look like fake lashes; the pink blush gave my cheekbones color, and I wore icing flavored lips gloss that made my lips pouty. I was 5'6 and slender, I felt pretty, beautiful even. I learned at a very early age that I could get boys and much more attention with my sex appeal. Mack didn't need to use that, they just flocked to her, but when it came to both of us standing together, they always came to me first. I loved having that one power over her. I know that makes me sound extremely vain, but I couldn't help it. I always came in second place and now I was allowed to be in first, and I reveled in that.

Our eighth grade dance was upon us and almost every popular boy in our class asked me to go with them. I didn't care about any one of them. I found myself being attracted to older guys. That was another reason I was excited to be going into high school. I would be with men and not just boys anymore. But with that, came the expectation of knowing how to do certain things. I still hadn't had my first kiss and I felt like I needed to get that out of the way before I entered into a much different environment. One that I wanted to strive in, excel.

I decided to go with Matthew Smithson. He was held back a year in sixth grade so he was already fifteen. Mack went with Michael O'Neil who was our star basketball player. Everyone knew he would make varsity team freshman year. Our parents got us a limo, of course. Once we got to the dance, we drank punch. Matt pulled a flask out of his pocket and spiked our drinks. He took his drink down like a champ, making me think that he did that sort of thing often. I tried to follow his lead but had to choke it down; it was not what I expected it to taste like. We socialized around our friends. Some of the students danced and when the booty music came on, people were bumping and grinding. I started to feel like my brain was fuzzy and that I could do anything, it was a feeling of freedom and confidence like I had never experienced before. Matt whispered in my ear for us to go out back by the gymnasium, and I knew in my bones he was going to kiss me. I grabbed his hand as he escorted us to a secluded spot.

He stopped when he found one and turned to look at me, he pulled a piece of hair that had fallen out of my up do and placed it behind my ear. My stomach did some flip-flop thing and even though I didn't really like him, I wondered what it would feel like to have his hands and lips on me. Is that normal for a fourteen-year-old to want?

"You're really pretty, Gia." He smirked.

"Thanks. You are too. I mean, handsome." Great, I was already fucking it up. We laughed at our nervousness. He didn't appear to be nervous, though maybe my anxiety was contagious.

"Have you ever been kissed, G?" He was the first guy to call me G and I sort of loved it. It was like G was allowed to be naughty…she was allowed to be free. I shook my head no and waited.

He grinned and grabbed the back of my neck. "That means you will always remember me and I fucking love that." My eyes widened as he leaned in. It wasn't soft or gentle. He was rough and urgent. He pushed me up against the wall the second his tongue made its way into my mouth. He tasted like punch and cigarettes. I wanted to devour that taste. He pushed and pulled his tongue around in my mouth until I caught on that he wanted me to do the same. I mimicked every movement he made and his hand moved from the back of my neck to the top of my cleavage. His knuckles grazed them back and forth. I opened my eyes and moaned. I quickly closed them again when his hand started to move lower. He cupped my breast, and it was then that I felt a tingle in my private place. I had no idea what to do, but I didn't want him to stop.

The door opened and he moved away from me as fast as possible. The last thing we needed was to get in trouble right before school let out. Luckily, no one saw us and I can't say I wasn't disappointed when he grabbed my hand to walk us back into the dance. I remember thinking how far I would have let him go if we hadn't been interrupted. It didn't make me feel slutty or easy, it made

24

me feel empowered, like I had finally found a tool that I could use to get my way. I hadn't realized how big of a weapon I owned with my sexuality and it made me feel free. It was a feeling unlike any other.

I never told McKenzie what happened that night. I didn't want her to judge me. I knew she wouldn't have understood, so I locked away another secret in the box.

It was the summer before entering high school that Mack and I went back-to-school shopping. Our moms permitted us to shop around by ourselves for a few hours. We felt so grown up being able to wander around the mall without having a chaperone. Our moms were still in the mall, but they weren't hanging around us. It was our first taste of freedom. It was one of the best memories I had. I was able to pick out whatever I wanted to wear without having someone tell me I couldn't.

I really loved finding my own independence and style. I bought tank tops in all colors, shorts, jeans that had holes in them, flannel shirts, and wedges. To have the liberty to wear shoes with some height to them was liberating. It was one thing that Mack and I had in common; we bought several wedges to be able to wear with our new clothes. We were similar in size and would be able to borrow each other's things, which made it even more fun. It was like we would have two closets.

We ate lunch and drank strawberry and banana smoothies, waiting for our mothers in the food court.

"I can't believe we are going to be freshman," I said, biting into my Cesar salad.

"I know, right? How exciting is that? I mean, before you know it, we will be driving."

"Has your schedule been mailed to you yet?"

That was one thing I was dreading that I knew she would be ecstatic about. I didn't want anything to do with the classes I was going to be enrolled in. They would be honors classes and hard as hell, and I wanted no part of that. The older I got, the more I realized that I didn't care for school. It's not that it wasn't my forte, because if I put my mind to it I did understand the material. I just didn't want to put my mind to it; I didn't even care about going to college.

My parents had all the money in the world and I couldn't tell if they were truly happy about it. They both worked like crazy, and sometimes, I felt like the things they owned, owned them instead of vice versa. I didn't even know if they were happily married. I mean, I witnessed affection from them but not the kind that I read about or watched in movies. I didn't really see love in their eyes when they looked at each other. It made me wonder about love and if it was real. Which led to me to wonder if anything was real, or if we all fit in Pandora's box of expectations.

Nevertheless, I needed to continue playing the part that I was given. I nodded and told McKenzie everything she wanted to hear. My performance was flawless, just like it always had been. Nobody ever assumed I was anything more than what I portrayed myself to be.

My mother loved all my new clothing. She said it accentuated every one of my perfect features. I would even go as far as saying that she was more excited than Mack and I. I helped her hang all of my clothes.

"Mom…can I ask you something?"

"Of course you can, honey. You can ask me anything."

I sighed and sat down on my bed as she sat down next to me. "Does dad hate me? I mean, does he wish I was different? More like McKenzie?"

She put her hand on her chest in a surprised motion. I immediately regretted the question. I should have just kept my mouth shut.

"Gianna…my God. What makes you think that? Your father loves you."

I shrugged. "I don't know. He just seems bothered by me. I feel like I'm always disappointing him, especially with my grades."

"Honey, your father has built his business from nothing. He just has high expectations for you. He wants you to succeed and maybe it's just his way of showing you he loves you, that he cares."

I scratched my head, completely confused. "Yeah…"

"Listen, I know your father can be extremely hard on you, but from the moment you were born, he wanted nothing but the best for you. It was endearing to see how this big macho man could crumble to his knees just looking at you. I remember the first few months after you were born, I would catch him staring at you in your crib. It was like you were his prized possession." I wanted to understand what she was saying, I really did.

"Okay," was all I could reply with.

"Trust me, honey, you make your father very proud. You make both of us very proud. You and McKenzie both do." It would have been so much better if she hadn't mentioned McKenzie's name. She wasn't my real sister, but I was constantly being compared to her.

Why couldn't I just be G?

"Are you all right?" she asked with concern in her voice.

The last thing I wanted to do was disappoint another parent. I couldn't take the pressure. I nodded and told her it must have been hormones and we quickly changed the subject to more comfortable topics for the both of us.

School was about to start, and I for one couldn't wait. I think G was going to come out a lot more. And I had become so good at keeping secrets, what would a few more hurt…

Chapter Three

High school was a changing time for me. It was also the first time I fell in love. I'll get more into that later...

Mack and I made junior varsity, only because they had some rule that freshman couldn't make varsity. Our classes were difficult, but at least we had a few normal classes and they weren't all honors like they had been in middle school. Mack and I had three classes that were together and four of them that weren't. It was mostly our electives that we chose separately. I lied to Mack and told her they must have been full on my first picks, but the truth was, I ended up erasing everything that we chose together after she left my house. The last thing I wanted to do was take home ec or drama.

Instead, I chose world travel and PE, I really liked being active. I noticed that when we started tumbling and dance. That was where I met him. His name was Jake Henderson, a senior and captain of the football team. We had PE together, seeing as it was open to every grade. The first few weeks of school, we spent a lot of time outside so I didn't have the opportunity to talk to him. It's not like I would have talked to him or anything. He was much older than I was and I didn't think I could pull that off. We had a week that we were going to be working in the classroom and he sat right next to me.

I remember looking around to see if all the seats were taken to explain why he was sitting next to me. I realized that they weren't; the class was nearly empty and he had chosen to sit there. My heart sank to my stomach, but I played it off and just scribbled miscellaneous things in my notebook.

"That's a really good drawing," he said, breaking the silence.

I stopped drawing that instant, not knowing how to respond.

"I'm Jake," he said, extending his hand to me.

I turned to look at him and his eyes were piercing blue. They had a hint of gray in them. His hair was messy and he had the most perfect cheekbones and lips. He looked like he could be a model if he wanted to. He was dressed in jeans and a t-shirt that had *South Park* on it. He smelled like nothing I had ever had the privilege of inhaling, it was musky scented, a mixture of his own pheromones.

"I know who you are," I blurted out and he smiled.

"That's great, because I know who you are, too. Gianna Edwards, right?" he asked, still keeping his hand out for me to take it. I finally did, but I was sure I already made myself look like an idiot. His hand was big and it toppled my tiny hand. He didn't let it go and placed them, interlocked, right on his lap.

"If you don't mind, I think I'll keep your hand in mine. It's comfortable there," he teased.

I laughed. I thought it was sweet that he was trying to make me less nervous.

"So, Gianna, how old are you?" he asked with mischief in his eyes.

"I just turned fifteen."

"That's not too bad, considering the things I'm thinking about," he stated, making me hot and tingly all over.

"How old are you?" I questioned, trying to change the subject.

"Seventeen. I turn eighteen in a few months. I'm actually a Christmas baby." I was sure my hand was starting to get sweaty, and the last thing I wanted to do was turn him off.

"Can I have my hand back, please?"

He laughed. "No. I like having your hand in mine. But…I'll make you a deal. If you go out with me Friday night, you can have your hand back."

I smiled. "Okay, although that sounds more like bribery than asking."

"Yeah…that's how I roll. I mean, I could pick you up and throw you over my shoulder."

"Wouldn't you have to knock me out first? You know, me Jane, you Tarzan."

"You're adorable, you know that?"

I shrugged and could feel my cheeks turning bright red.

"And that shade of red makes you look even more adorable." Of course he would call me out on it. "So, what do you say, Gianna with the pretty shade of red cheeks, will you go out with me Friday night?" he retorted, making me feel more at ease. I smiled, nodded, and that was it.

We started dating quickly after that. One date became two and two became three and before I knew it, we were exclusive and boyfriend and girlfriend. My parents had to spend time with him a few times before they approved and allowed me to start dating a senior. They said that he was responsible and good for me, and they were happy that I found someone so mature and grown up for his age. They thought he would be a good example and positive influence on me.

Mack was surprised when she heard about us becoming exclusive. She had concerns that I was settling down at such a young age, and that maybe I should fish in the sea of high school boys before I reeled one in. I didn't really care what she thought because nothing could compare with the way Jake made me feel. No one had ever made me feel like that; not my parents or Mack…he made me feel special. I was the only girl in his eyes when he looked at me and I had never had that before.

They say you can see a person's depth through their eyes, that you can tell every truth and lie. The eyes are the windows to a person's soul. I wish I could say that Jake really knew me and that I was honest with him and shared the dark corners of myself, but I didn't. I let him believe what everyone else did; it was much easier that way. I wouldn't even know where to start if I wanted him to know the truth. There were so many secrets. Sometimes I felt like a mouse on a spinning wheel going around and around without making any progress.

That didn't stop me from caring about him. He was good to me and we spent every second together. Mack and I were still best friends and when I wasn't with Jake, I was with her. She loved Jake too; he treated her like a little sister. He never made me feel envious or jealous of the attention he would give her. It was the first time that I didn't feel like I was competing with her. It was not needed because Jake was mine.

We kissed...a lot. We fooled around some, but it was mostly on top of the clothes stuff. And it wasn't like we ever talked about it or anything; we would just stop when things started moving too fast. I didn't know if it was for my benefit or his. It just happened that way.

Valentine's Day was fast approaching and Jake said he had something amazing planned for us–that it was a surprise. As much as I didn't like cookie cutter, it didn't mean I didn't fall for cliché situations. I wanted to feel loved and nothing makes an insecure girl feel more loved than those cliché moments.

He took me to a five-star restaurant that my parents and I frequented often. I didn't tell him that I hated that restaurant and all the pretentious people who would go there to order a twenty-dollar baked potato. I took it for what it was and appreciated the sentiment behind it. We talked about the colleges he had applied to over Christmas, he kept telling me that he was more than happy to attend Brown University and stay in town to be close to me, but I knew he was lying. One of the first times I went into his bedroom, he had catalogs for Columbia University all over his room. His dad was an alumni and I knew he had his heart set on getting accepted. As much as I didn't want to dwell on it, I knew he was going to attend Columbia. I was going to pretend that I was thrilled and happy for him, even though I was dying inside and didn't want to see him go.

After dinner, we took a walk on Barrington Beach that was near a cove that Mack and I grew up around. He held my hand the entire time and we even played in the water, splashing each other back and forth. It was super cheesy, but I loved it. I ate it up. The sun started to set and we sat in the sand, watching the stars and the moon make their appearance. I sat in between his legs with my back to his front and he kissed the side of my neck every few minutes, running his soft lips back and forth, giving me chills down my spine.

"Gianna..." he whispered in my ear, making me giggle and hide my neck from him. "I love you." He breathed into the side of my face.

My eyes widened, my heart sank, and my stomach flipped. I turned around to look at his face and he had on the most sincere expression. I had never seen that look on anyone's face before and it was as if I was living one of those moments in the books I read. He was beautiful and he loved me.

"Oh my God!" I screamed. "Are you serious?"

He cocked his head to the side and smirked. "That's not exactly the response I was looking for," he mocked, making me giggle again.

"Of course I love you, too. How can I not? You are so fucking good to me. I have never met anyone like you before, Jake."

"That's a little better," he praised and leaned in to kiss me.

It turned heated fast and we got to second base that night. It was the first time anyone had ever seen me topless. When his hand grazed my nipple, I didn't expect to feel all the sensations I felt below my belt. It made me anxious, nervous, and excited. I wanted to keep going, but he stopped it from going too far. He even went as far as hooking my bra back on and helping me put on my shirt. He always told me he didn't want to rush things and we had all the time in the world to take things further.

As much as I wanted to believe him, I couldn't. He was eighteen and about to go off to college, he would meet other girls. No. Not girls. He would meet other women. I wouldn't be able to compete with someone who he could be sexually active with. He would have his own apartment and the freedom to do what he wanted, and as much as I wanted to believe every single word he told me, my insecurities wouldn't let me. I was tied down to feeling inadequate and not enough; the binds were so tight and consuming that I never stood a chance to break free of them. They were a part of me as much as breathing was.

A few months later, prom was among us and I bought the sexiest black gown I could find. It was backless and made me look older. My mom made appointments to get my hair and makeup done. I looked into the mirror that night, and even though I looked different, I felt the same. I wanted one night where I didn't feel like I was not enough. I honestly thought that the get-up would make every ugly, destructive thought in my mind go away. As if it would magically disappear. It didn't. My presence was altered, but my own manifestation was exactly the same. I felt desolate. Would it ever go away?

The limo picked us up with a few other couples. They were friends of Jake, with whom I was friends with by association. My parents took hundreds of pictures before we were excused to go. They allowed me to spend the night out that night which completely surprised me. They said they trusted Jake with me and that I was old enough to make my own decisions; that they knew I would be responsible and wouldn't let them down. I took it with a grain of salt and was grateful that I could finally give myself to him like I wanted to.

"Gia, here," Chris said, handing me a glass.

"No," Jake said, intercepting and snatching the glass away from me.

"What the fuck, man? It's prom! Let her drink. She doesn't have to go home tonight and maybe you will finally be able to get your dick wet." Chris laughed and Jake glared at him. I was sure if I weren't in the car, he would have swung at him.

"It's fine, Jake," I said, trying to break the tension. "I will just have a little. I want to celebrate, too."

He sighed and handed me the glass. "It's champagne. It will go to your head fast because of the sugar. You only take drinks from me, understood?" he ordered.

I didn't like the tone he was using with me and I really didn't like the fact that he was ordering me around. He made me feel like a little girl and I always tried hard to prove to him that I was much older than my age implied I was. I hated that he made me feel that way. He was the one person who didn't do that to me, and I once again felt like I wasn't good enough. The voice in the back of my mind that had been quiet, reared its ugly head and reminded me that it was still there…and I was still broken.

What goes up must come down…it's the rule of life.

I smiled, nodded, kissed him on the lips, and then grabbed my glass of champagne. The first sip was much different than I anticipated it to be. I was expecting it to taste like the spiked punch, but it was far from it. It tasted sweet and went down smooth. It only took a few minutes before I was requesting a second glass, much to Jake's disapproval.

We walked into prom hand in hand and I immediately needed to use the bathroom. I was definitely feeling a little fuzzy. Jake escorted me to the bathroom and when I walked into the bright room, my reflection in the mirror caught my attention. I slowly walked over to the vanity, and what I saw made my eyes light up. I looked unrestricted; the ties and binds were gone and I was free. I felt it and saw it. Alcohol made everything go away. All the noise, ruckus, expectations, illusions, and thoughts were gone. Just like that.

I smiled a real smile at myself, feeling sedated and confident. Gia–Gianna–was gone…I was G again and I didn't want this feeling to go away. I wanted to capture and hold on to it as long as I could. I decided then and there that G was who I was; she was who I wanted to be twenty-four hours a day, seven days a week, and three-hundred sixty-five days a year.

I laughed at myself so hard that my head fell back as I made my way to the stall. I found Jake outside waiting for me and his eyes roamed my body. I gave him the best seductive look I could muster and he cleared his throat and grabbed my hand.

We socialized and danced with everyone but left an hour before prom was over. We rode in the limo back to the hotel party that the prom king was throwing. It was packed by the time we got there. I knew Jake wouldn't allow me to keep drinking and I didn't want to disappointment him, so I did the only thing I could think of and snuck in alcohol without him knowing, anytime I went to the bathroom or when he wasn't looking at me. I was pretty intoxicated, although I believe I played it off well.

"Hmmm…Jake…I want you to get a room here," I suggested, catching him off guard.

"Gia, you've been drinking and so have I. Let's just go back to my house and you can sleep it off in the guest bedroom."

"I don't want to. I want to be with you, and I want you to get a room." He looked around the party and grabbed my hand. We walked back to one of the bedrooms and he closed the door behind me.

He turned to face me with the most bewildered and confused look on his face. I wanted to laugh and tell him he was overreacting, but I didn't think that would get what I wanted accomplished.

"Listen…we don't have to do this. I told you time after time that us being intimate doesn't matter to me. We have plenty of time for that. You trust me, don't you?"

I looked him right in the eyes and lied, "I do."

I didn't trust him at all, not one bit. But at least this way he would know that I was giving him my virginity, and maybe he wouldn't cheat on me as much in college. That maybe he would come back to me if he knew I was willingly waiting. Guys love that kind of commitment, don't they?

"Baby, I don't want to get in trouble. I'm eighteen, you're fifteen; I could get in to a lot of trouble if we made love," he reminded.

The fact that he said "made love," not sex, or fucking, should have made me feel better. And in a way, it did. It gave me more reassurance about the fact that I was going to sleep with him. Would I have called it making love…probably not. However, the fact that he did, gave me hope.

"You won't. I looked it up and there is this Romeo and Juliet law that if you start dating before one person turns eighteen then there is no problem. I promise. Plus, I won't tell anyone."

"Not even Mack?"

"Especially not Mack," I retorted, not even thinking about it. His face showed confusion that I replied like that, but he didn't call me out on it.

"I love you," I proclaimed, trying to make him change his mind.

"I love you, too," he repeated.

He kissed me, and the second I felt his lips on mine, I knew that I had won.

Chapter Four

I didn't really consider the severity of what I was suggesting until we were already in the room. Jake had gotten our overnight bags from the limo and told the driver he could go home. It was easy to check in to the same hotel the party was at since Jake was eighteen. I grabbed my bag that he placed on the bed and told him I was going to use the shower. He seemed relieved that he would also have a few minutes to himself. I lowered the zipper that was on the side of my dress and turned on the shower, making sure it was warm enough before I got in.

Taking the pins out of my hair ended up being a task, but after a few minutes, I pulled the last one out and stepped into the shower. I took my time while I was in there. The alcohol was still fresh in my system and I still felt buzzed, but my anxiety was creeping its way into my bloodstream. I washed every inch of my body with the hotel soap that smelled like honey and vanilla and then washed my hair. I made sure to apply extra conditioner in case he wanted to run his fingers through my hair. I knew he really loved doing that and I wanted to make sure it was nice and soft for him.

I turned off the shower, squeezed out my hair with my hands and wrapped the towel around my body. I rubbed the steam from the shower off of the mirror with my hand and took a look at my disheveled appearance. I appeared younger without the hair, makeup, and dress. I subconsciously wished that I had kept my attire on, because I didn't want Jake to see me for the age that I truly was. I wanted to go through with this and now I was afraid he would back out. I brushed my hair, leaving it wet around my face, and then brushed my teeth. I applied a little bit of mascara, blush, and lip-gloss. Then I slipped into a pair of lace panties and a white tank top. You could see my nipples through it and it made me feel a little less nervous. My sexuality was my golden ticket.

I opened the door and he was sitting on the edge of the bed, changing the channels on the TV. He turned when he heard the door open. His eyes widened and his mouth dropped. I tried to keep my confidence and sexy demeanor as I paraded to the bed. His eyes followed my composure the entire time. He had removed his tie and unbuttoned the first few buttons of his dress shirt, leaving it open in the front. It was the sexiest thing I had ever seen. I stood right between his legs in front of him. I swear I could hear the drips of water from my hair hit the floor as I stood waiting for his next move.

"You're absolutely beautiful. I love you just like this, baby. You're naturally gorgeous, you don't need anything to make you more perfect than you already are," he praised, not touching me.

I shyly smiled and reached to unbutton the rest of his shirt. He let me, and I removed it from his body and threw it on the floor. Jake had played football since middle school and his body was defined and muscular. I will have the image of him shirtless in my mind for the rest of my life. I went to unbuckle his belt but he stopped me.

"Baby, are you sure?" he questioned. Of course I was sure…why didn't he believe me? I nodded, not knowing what else to say. I thought my actions would speak louder than words, but it seemed like it wasn't translating.

He smiled, showing his perfect white teeth and grabbed the back of my neck, pulling me forward. I thought he would kiss me passionately, but he didn't. It was slow and soft. He was being careful and gentle with me, and a part of me didn't want that. I wanted him to be uncontrolled and uninhibited. I didn't want him to treat me like I would break; it just further proved how broken I was. Could he see it but wouldn't tell me? Did he know that I would shatter eventually?

I tried to kiss him more urgently, more demanding, but he stopped, putting his forehead on mine.

"Baby, we don't have to rush. We have all night. Let me take care of you. I want this to be good for you," he expressed with a sincere tone, making me feel like an asshole.

Why did I want him to take me? Why didn't I want the sweet, loving side of this? Why was this "love making" he talked about so hard for me?

I just did what I always did, smiled and nodded. That seemed to appease him because his hands found the bottom of my shirt and my arms rose as he lifted it off me. I stood there in only panties, feeling completely exposed to him as he took in each and every curve of my body.

"How did I get so lucky?" he admired and grabbed my chin to make me look into his eyes. He wrapped his arms around my waist and I straddled his lap. It was the first time he allowed me to feel like I was in control–he was usually the one on top of me when we made out. I felt his erection immediately, and part of me wanted to giggle. But that would only show my immaturity, so I kept it hidden.

He kissed me, and this time, it was more urgent and I loved it. His hands were still around my waist and on my hips as he started to move them forward and then backward. I followed his lead, and slowly, he let me take over at my desired pace. The more I grinded and slowly moved along his hard-on, the better it felt for me. I had never played with myself before and I had no idea what I was doing. But the tingles in my lower abdomen made my toes curl. We never stopped kissing, and the faster I moved, the more intense our kiss became.

The room started to get really hot and my eyes felt like they were rolling around in the back of my head. I was making noises that I had never made before, but I couldn't control them. They were getting louder and Jake's fingers started grasping onto my hips. I swore he was going to leave marks if he didn't let up. When my legs started to shake, my body just took over and I rode him with enthusiasm to have something happen. I had no idea what was happening but I didn't want it to stop. My breathing faltered and my body just exploded, I shook, moaned, and my head fell back.

I don't know how long I just sat there on his lap convulsing, but when it was over, I felt like I had just run a marathon. I finally opened my eyes and they found Jake's glare; he looked primal. His pupils were dilated and it made his irises look black instead of the piercing blue they normally were. His breathing mimicked mine and before I could say anything, he picked me up and laid me on the bed.

His mouth attacked mine and he groaned. I helped him remove his belt and he kicked off his pants. It was then that I realized he was going commando and didn't have on any boxers.

"Hold on, baby," he said in between kissing me.

He reached for his pants and pulled out his wallet. I took the opportunity to look at him for the first time, and what I saw made me gasp. He quickly looked back at my face and he grinned. I could tell he wanted to laugh but kept it in.

"I'm sorry...I–" I tried to explain, but seeing his erect dick was a bit of a shock to me. I had never seen one in person before and I contemplated if it would even fit inside me. Not only was he thick, he was also long.

I watched with fascination as he opened the packet and rolled on the condom, making a mental note that you pinch the top of it before you roll it down.

"It's okay. I need you to tell me if you want me to stop. I will do whatever feels better for you."

I smiled. "I promise."

He pulled down my panties, leaving wet kisses from my breasts to my lower abdomen. The lower he went, the faster my heart pounded with anticipation.

I was naked in front of him for the first time and he stopped to take a look at me. I wanted to hide under the blanket and shield myself but, at the same time, I loved the look in his eyes. I had never seen him look at me like that and I wanted to cherish the moment. It was everything I wanted to see, and the approval he showed made me want to cry. I had never felt that before, not from anyone.

He kissed his way back up my body and found my mouth again. He positioned himself on top of me, resting on his elbows with my legs spread open. His dick nudged at my entrance and he slowly and carefully eased his way inside me. The pain and discomfort I felt was almost unbearable. It didn't feel like anything that was described in my books.

"Jesus, baby, you are so fucking tight. Tell me if I'm hurting you," he groaned.

He angled my leg a little higher and pushed all the way in. I wanted to scream but I didn't.

"Oh shit. Sorry...baby, I thought it would be easier if I just pushed all the way in. Are you okay?" he blubbered, looking at me with lust and concern all over his face.

"Mmm hmm," I replied, wanting to hide the pain that I was sure was evident on my face.

He started to move, slowly at first, and I could feel the wetness as he slipped in and out. There were no fireworks like there was before when I was on top of him. I didn't want to make any noise or movement, I wanted it to be over and soak in a bath to relieve the soreness that I knew I was going to feel. I didn't understand how girls at school would talk about sex like it was some amazing thing. If it was like this every time, I didn't know how I was going to work up the nerve to do it again.

His movements became quicker and more forceful and I felt like he was tearing me open, I wanted no part of it. He abruptly stopped and shook on top of me, like I had done to him earlier. I also felt his dick stir inside me. He was sweating, as was I. This wasn't sexy or erotic–it was uncomfortable and awkward.

"That was amazing," he huskily stated, kissing all over my face.

Not really...

"It won't always feel like that. I promise it will feel better and you will experience multiples of what I just experienced."

"How many girls have you been with?" I blurted.

He nervously laughed and kissed the tip of my nose. "It doesn't matter, Gia, they were nothing compared to you."

That was a good enough answer for me. He helped clean me up and we asked for another set of sheets to change out from our concierge. I was beyond embarrassed from the bloodstain on the bed, but he didn't even give it a double look when we changed them out. We slept in each other's arms, and even though it was as cookie cutter and cliché as it could get, I wallowed in it.

Graduation came quickly after prom and then the summer was over and he was heading off to college. He reluctantly chose to go to

Columbia; I pressured him into it because I knew it was what he truly wanted. It was the right thing to do. He swore and promised me that nothing would come between us, that we were going to get married one day. He was going to come visit me every other weekend and that it was only a three and a half hour drive.

I wanted to believe him, but I knew everything was going to change. It was inevitable–when the cat's away the mouse will play, isn't that the rule of thumb?

Sophomore year started and I missed him terribly. Mack tried everything to make me smile. We both made varsity cheerleading and I was ecstatic about it. When I called to tell Jake about it, he didn't answer. He barely ever answered his phone and when he did, we didn't talk much. I even tried to have phone sex a couple of times, but he didn't seem interested. I knew he was probably cheating on me.

I missed him walking me to class and leaving notes in my locker. Everywhere I looked, there was a memory of us. After the first few months, I started to get out of my slump and the boys noticed it, too. I began getting attention from the opposite sex again and I quickly remembered how great and empowered it made me feel.

"Gia, you know you have a boyfriend, right?" Mack asked as we walked to our lockers from fourth period.

"I'm not doing anything wrong, Mack. I'm just flirting; it's not a big deal. No harm, no foul. I'm trying to have a little fun and I'm sure Jake is doing the exact same thing," I responded, turning my locker combination.

"What do you mean? What's going on with you and Jake?" she asked, putting in her algebra notebook and taking out her history folder.

I sighed. "Nothing...I mean, not really. I don't know. Things are different now."

She turned and grabbed my hand. "Gia, I know. He's not doing anything wrong, though. I know you may think that, but he loves you. I see it every time he looks at you."

"I know that, but people change and he's far away. I'm trying to take my mind off him and I'm sure he's doing the same. Stop worrying." I laughed, trying to ease her concern. The last thing I wanted was for her to feel sorry for me.

A few more months went by and it was Christmas break. Jake was in town for the entire three week holiday and we spent as much time together as we could. He wasn't lying when he said he was going to make me feel multiples; our sex life was amazing. I had no complaints and he always took care of me, making sure I had an orgasm at least two or three times before he did. I was tired of having to hide it from Mack, so I decided to come up with a plan to make her lose hers, too. We could finally share something together. She had been dating this guy Mitchell Simmons for a few months.

"Mack, we're sixteen now, we don't need to be holding onto our virginities like they are a prized possession. I mean, you don't want to get married still a virgin, do you? That's just weird," I confessed, sitting on her bed, both of us Indian style.

"Of course I don't. I don't know if I'm ready yet. Are you ready?"

"I am more than ready! I have been with Jake for over a year. I definitely want to fuck him." I laughed, making her laugh.

"Fine. What's your plan?" she responded.

"We are both going to lose it this weekend. We will go to The Cove and Jake and I will go for a walk and do our thing and you will do the same." I smiled, extending out my hand. "Deal?"

She cocked her head to the side and inspected my hand, taking in my proposal. "Deal," she answered and we shook on it.

That weekend fast approached and Jake and I did have sex in The Cove, but it wasn't our first time like I claimed it was. When we finished having sex, we sat near the water looking at the waves and waited for McKenzie to call me when she was done.

"How's school going?" Jake asked, breaking the silence.

"It's good, but I really miss having you around. It's not the same without you there." He smiled and kissed the side of my neck.

"I miss you too," he replied.

"How is school for you?" I countered, wanting to see if he would be honest with me. I knew he had to be doing something. There was no way a great good-looking guy like Jake wasn't fooling around on me. Why wouldn't he? I wouldn't find out and he'd still have me as his piece-of-ass when he was back in town. It was a win-win for him.

"It's much harder than I anticipated it was going to be."

"Mmm hmm."

"What, you don't believe me?" he accused with a tone that made me turn around to look at him.

"I didn't say that."

"You're implying that with your response," he said, narrowing his eyes.

"Are you trying to start an argument?"

"Of course I'm not, are you?"

My phone rang and McKenzie's picture appeared on the screen.

"Hey…yeah…we will head back. Okay, see you soon." I hit the end button, got up, and started to walk away. He grabbed my upper arm before I made it three steps.

"Gia, we're not done here," he stated, not letting go of my arm.

"Yes we are," I replied, trying to pull away from him, which only made him grab me harder.

"Why do you do this? Every time we have a confrontation, you avoid it like the plague and pretend like nothing happened. Can't we just have a normal conversation?"

"There is nothing to talk about. Relax," I expressed, trying to calm him down. I never understood how Jake could go from zero to ten in one second.

"Don't blow me off."

"I'm not, but Mack is waiting for us."

"Is Mack more important than me?"

"What the fuck? No. You're acting like a child. I'm not trying to do anything. I don't want to fight. I have nothing to say," I reasoned, hoping that would appease him and we wouldn't have to continue this conversation. The last thing I wanted to do was talk about us. The last thing I ever wanted to do was talk about my feelings. I barely understood them, how could I make someone else understand?

He sighed and finally let go. "You're impossible. When are you going to let me in, Gia? When the fuck is that going to happen?"

I stepped back from the impact of his comment. I had let him in, more than I had with anyone else. Why was it never good enough? Why was I never good enough? What the fuck was wrong with me? I did what I always did and bit my tongue. I smiled and put my arms around him.

"I'm sorry. Nothing is wrong. I love you," I reminded.

When his arms wrapped around my frame, I knew I had won.

Mack stayed the night at my house that night. We stayed up till all hours of the night talking about how our first experiences went. I explained it the same way it happened in the hotel on prom night, so technically it was sort of the truth. It was only half a lie, a fib maybe. Mack didn't go into too much depth about what happened. I could tell she was shy or maybe nervous to talk about it. I could relate because I had felt the exact same way after I had initially lost my virginity to Jake. It took me a while to get comfortable with my sexuality, especially being naked in front of him, so I let her have her modesty. I figured she would open up to me more after she had experienced it a few more times.

A huge part of me wanted to be honest with her that night. I wanted to tell her the truth, but I was terrified she wouldn't understand and would judge me. I couldn't take another disappointment, not from Mack. It wasn't something I could bear. Our friendship was the only thing I had half an understanding about. She was the only thing in my life that made sense. The thought of losing her would destroy me. So I continued to lie and be the person she wanted me to be. At that point, it didn't matter what I wanted anymore. I was too far gone.

By the time I would realize it…

It would be too late.

Chapter Five

My whole world changed senior year. It went from night to day, left to right, up to down; there was absolutely no gray area. Starting at the beginning of the year, there were major changes that occurred–I was chosen by our cheerleading coach to be captain of our squad. It was a complete and utter surprise for me to be picked for such an honorary position. Ecstatic couldn't even begin to describe how I felt. I was proud and determined to lead my team into nationals and it became my number one priority. I practiced day and night coming up with new routines and challenges for the girls.

Since my academic career started, I knew what was expected of me; my father wouldn't take anything less than me receiving a scholarship for college. It didn't matter that we were loaded and my parents could literally afford to send me to any university I desired. It wasn't about that. It was about me once again proving that I had to be the best at whatever I did. If I could get us to win nationals then I could continue cheering in college, and as much as I didn't want anything to do with school, cheerleading would become my salvation. There would be less pressure for my grade point average to stay a 3.5 because universities would take in to consideration my athletic ability and the contribution I could give to the sports department.

I gave it my all. It was everything I needed in order to stay sane for the next four years of my life. Mack was thrilled that we were that much closer to obtaining our goals and plans that we had established since childhood. I was working my ass off and straining my ligaments on a daily basis. I didn't take weekends off and I became consumed with being the best I could be.

There was absolutely no way I was giving up on my only passion. It belonged to me and I was never going to let it go.

The first day of school altered my perception of everything I thought I was supposed to be.

I was Jake's girlfriend.

I was McKenzie's best friend.

I was the perfect daughter.

I was captain of the cheerleading squad.

I was a scholastic student.

I was popular and envied and everyone wanted to be me.

On the outside, you would think I had it all…

On the inside, I was screaming and yearning for it all to go away. I didn't want to be Gianna Edwards anymore. I hated her. She wasn't real. She was an illusion, one that I created and perfected to a T. There were days when I wanted to run away and never come back. I thought about it time after time.

It was the first day of school, the last period of the day, and the moment that changed my life in more ways than one.

"Gia, what are we doing this weekend? Is Jake coming into town?" Mack asked as we grabbed our books from our lockers for our last class of the day. English, my worst subject…the fact that that's how I ended my day was a major disappointment. I didn't recognize the name on my schedule card. I assumed he was a new teacher.

"Um…I doubt it, he was here all summer. I probably won't see him till Thanksgiving," I responded, grabbing my heavy ass literature book and three-spiral notebook.

"Awe! That's a long time to go without seeing each other. Are you starting to miss him?"

"Of course."

I lied. Jake and I had a great summer together, but he was back at school and I'm sure he was back to his old ways. I'm not stupid enough to believe he was being faithful to me. Our calls became less and less throughout the years. Plus, I only saw him on holidays or the summer; he never came to see me like he promised before leaving for college. I hadn't called him out on it because that would appear like I was an insecure girl, and that's not the kind of girl he thought I was. I was confident.

Jake Henderson would never cheat on Gianna Edwards.

We walked down the hall, arms linked together, and made it to room 702. Mack was talking about our new routines that we were going to start teaching the girls that afternoon. The moment I walked into his classroom I lost my breath–and not metaphorically. My breathing stopped, my heart thumped, and my pulse raced. He was striking, dressed in black slacks and a black button down shirt. He wore no tie and the first few buttons of his shirt were undone. Our eyes locked and I swear on everything that is holy that something transpired between us. It was this electric current that made its way from the top of my head to the tips of my toes. This invisible string latched its way into my heart and it pulled me right into his.

He had dark brown hair that was styled back but a few pieces hung around his face; I could tell that he had just brushed them back with his hands, and I knew that he probably did that often. There was stubble on his face and he sported a goatee with a light mustache. His eyebrows were perfectly shaped and he had a strong jawline with perfect white teeth and a charismatic smile.

His bright blue eyes beamed and it was only for me. I saw them go from a normal hue to a piercing one. His intense and penetrating gaze wreaked havoc on my soul. He was leaning against his desk and I observed his hands squeeze the sides in an agonizing and aching burn. He wanted me just as much as I wanted him, maybe more…although I don't think that was possible.

"Gia! Gianna! What the fuck? Where did you go?" Mack questioned, pulling me out of the tunnel that lead me directly and only to him. He shook his head as if he was trying to wash me away from his thoughts and urges and that's when I looked over at Mack.

"Oh! I'm sorry. I was lost in thought there for a second. I think I forgot something to write with in my locker. Do you have one I can use?" I requested, trying not to look anything like I felt.

She rolled her eyes at me and laughed. "Duh. You would forget your head if it wasn't attached to you, Gia. You know that, right?"

I laughed, wanting nothing more than to turn back to face him.

He clapped his hands, making me jump. "All right class, please take your seats," he addressed as everyone went about their business to find their comfortable locations.

I sat in the back and McKenzie sat in front of me. There was no way I could sit anywhere near him.

"The seats that you have chosen will be assigned to you all year long. This is a senior class and I expect you to behave as the adults that you are. I am going to give you the benefit of the doubt in hopes that you will not disrupt lectures or make me change your seats," he announced, placing his hands in his pockets, which made his chest extend.

"I am Mr. Nichols and I will be your English teacher for the rest of the year. I transferred here from Mitchell High School in Maine to take this position for the head of the English department. I am eager to meet you guys and teach you; to get you ready for testing and prepare you for college next year. I have an open door policy, so if you ever have any questions or concerns, please don't be afraid to come to me. I believe very much in having a relationship with all of my students. Do you have any questions?" he asked and a few students raised their hand.

"It's going to take me a few days to learn all of your names, so if you could state your name before asking your question, I would very much appreciate it," he added before calling on Summer.

"Hi." She waved and flirtatiously smiled. I wanted to rip her eyes out. She was such a slut. "I am Summer Graceland." She shrugged her shoulders and grinned. "Are you married?" The class laughed, but I could tell that every girl was interested in his response.

He blushed and smirked. Was he flirting back?

"I am married. Thanks for asking. I also have a daughter, she's three, and her name is Cara."

My blood pressure dropped and I started to sweat. He was married? Had I fantasized all that I had just experienced? Was I going crazy?

He proceeded to answer all the questions from the students. I couldn't help where my mind wandered, but I imagined him naked. I visualized every last muscle and hair on his body. I pictured me riding

48

him on his desk, in his car; fuck, even outside on the grass. He whispered dirty and inappropriate things in my ear as he forcefully took me from behind. He pulled my hair and bit my skin and I met him for every thrust he pushed into me. I squirmed in my seat from the wetness that was pooling in between my legs. I swear he could smell it on me because he looked right at me as I closed my legs.

I didn't cower down. I held his stare as he described what we would be learning in class. I stalked his every movement from his facial expressions to his body language. When he was really excited about something, he would talk with his hands. He didn't like to stay in one place and would walk back and forth across the front of the room in an almost nervous-like pace. His voice was intense and erotic all at the same time. I was in a daze just wanting to learn every last mannerism. He was fascinating to me, like a new species or creature that I had never had the privilege of witnessing.

I had never experienced anything even remotely close to what I was feeling; my impulses and urges felt uncontrolled and I wanted everyone to leave the room so I could have a few minutes alone with him. Even if it was just a taste, for just a second, I was mesmerized by him. Obsessed is a term that shouldn't be used lightly, but Mr. Nichols possessed me. From that day forth…I was his.

Everything went from heaven…to hell in a hand basket.

Rumors started spreading around the school about him. Girls were just as smitten as I was. They all talked about him and what it would be like to be with him. He was the fascination of every adolescent girl that stepped foot into the school. Although he was married, he was very much the flirt that he portrayed on the first day of school. I was jealous every time I saw another female around him; it wasn't limited to just the students, the teachers were also included. He stayed after school almost every day; I would always see his white truck in the parking lot when I would walk to my car after practice.

I couldn't concentrate on class or anything he discussed, and my grades started suffering because of it. I knew it wasn't all in my head; he treated me differently than the other girls. It started innocently enough with a look or a gaze. Then he would find a way to touch my hand or my shoulder, we never stood more than a foot apart when we were around each other. There was an invisible tie holding us together and molding our behavior.

Was it wrong the way I felt? Maybe. But why does something so wrong feel so right?

It didn't take long for me to realize that the feeling was very much mutual. I stayed after class a few weeks after school started. I honestly didn't understand the material and I was staying after to have him further explain it. I waited till everyone walked out of the room to approach him. I must have caught him off guard because when he turned to start cleaning up the room, he jolted and looked surprised.

He cocked his head to the side and I swear I saw nervousness written all over his handsome face.

"Can I help you, Miss Edwards?" he provoked.

Oh...Mr. Nichols, you have no idea how much you can help me.

He leaned back, holding onto the side of his desk as his fingers started tapping. He was nervous...

I arched an eyebrow and removed myself from my seat, making sure to open my legs to give him a view of my bloomers in my pleated cheerleading skirt. His face said everything I wanted to hear. I heard him clear his throat as I made my way to him. I took my time, swaying my hips back and forth to allow my thighs to show through the pleats. I sat on the first desk that was a few feet away from him, kicking my legs in and out in a cute and teasing manner.

It was my turn to cock my head to the side. "Actually, I'm having trouble in your class and I was wondering if you could tutor me. I've already spoken to my parents and they would pay extra if needed. I'm really struggling and I would hate to fall too far behind and not be able to catch up," I stated in a sultry tone.

His Adam's apple moved and I could tell he was swallowing the saliva that had gathered there.

"I mean, don't you want to help me? Seeing as though you want a personal relationship with each of your students. That does include me as well, right?"

He pulled his lips into his mouth, contemplating what I was saying, never letting up on tapping the side of the desk.

"Miss Edwards." He cleared his throat again. "What exactly do you have in mind? I mean, what can I help you with?"

"Everything and anything," I immediately suggested.

He smiled. "How about you give me a few more specifics than that."

I pulled my bottom lip into my mouth. "I'm having trouble understanding Shakespeare, Romeo and Juliet. I mean, I know they had a forbidden love that was taboo, given the circumstances, but isn't love supposed to prevail? Doesn't every fairytale tell us that?"

"Fairytales are just that, Miss Edwards...they're tales, not reality," he explained.

"So what you are saying is that love doesn't exist...it doesn't conquer all?"

He raised his hand and grabbed the back of his neck. "No, I'm not saying that at all. Romeo and Juliet is a love story about two different people who aren't allowed to be together."

"But that doesn't stop them from being with each other. It encourages them, even if it has to happen behind closed doors. What do you think about that? Do you think it's wrong if you want to be with someone you aren't supposed to?"

My question intrigued him as much as it enticed him. His eyes screamed lust from across the distance between us. He licked his lips and I couldn't help but gawk. My breathing hitched and my chest heaved, his eyes went from my face to the cleavage of my cheerleading top.

"They loved each other. They were soul mates," he asserted.

"Does that make it okay? Do you believe in love at first sight?" I paused. "I do."

He massaged the back of his neck, trying to relieve the tension that I'm sure was forming there.

"I...I mean-I..." he hesitated. "I do."

I smiled wide and my eyes gleamed with joy, I was radiating.

"Good to know." I jumped off the desk. "When can you start helping me?"

"Miss Edwards, I believe it would be better if I found a classmate who could tutor you."

I shook my head no. "I don't need another student to help me, Mack helps me enough and I still don't understand. I need your expertise, Mr. Nichols. Don't you want to show me how to do it?" I teased.

His eyes widened and he nervously chuckled. "Let's talk about this tomorrow, shall we? Let me think about it tonight?" he snapped.

I nodded and walked toward the door. Before I stepped into the hall, I turned around, hanging onto the side of the door. I caught him staring at my ass and he quickly looked up, pretending like I hadn't just caught him in the act.

"Mr. Nichols?" I smirked.

He groaned, "Yes."

"Call me G."

Chapter Six

I felt tingles run through my entire body, and my mouth had a metallic taste to it. Suddenly, I gasped and realized where I was. I was with Nick. Nick from the bar. The same Nick that looked and sounded just like Mr. Nichols but I knew it wasn't him. It was never him and it never would be.

I had fucked all that up.

His four fingers found the inside of my mouth and he pushed them as far as they would go, causing me to gag at the intrusion, fully bringing me back to the present. He did it a few times, each time the gagging became louder and heavier. He pushed them in one last time and rapidly pulled them out with a trail of my spit following behind as he placed it all over my pussy. My eyes watered and I hacked and coughed, but that didn't stop my body from responding to his touch. The more pressure he applied to my clit the closer I got to release. I felt his hard cock on my leg through his slacks.

"You want to come?"

"Yes…" I shamelessly begged. He slapped my pussy a few more times and that's all it took for me to shake with release. My come dripped down my inner thighs and all over his fingers, he didn't stop until every last drop was out of me. My head swirled with aftershocks and he crudely grabbed the back of my neck, pushing me down onto my knees. His fingers raked through my scalp before he grabbed a handful of hair and pulled my head back. I watched him unzip his pants and release his hard, thick cock.

"Look at me. Let me see your eyes." I did as I was told. I stared into the eyes of the man that reminded me of everything that went wrong in my life.

He coated his dick with the residue of my arousal that was left on his fingers. It was slick and wet with my juices and I instantly tasted myself as he plunged into the back of my throat with not so much as a warning. I gagged at the sensation; he pulled his dick all the way out and then thrust it back in. He repeated this process a few more times before I was completely at the mercy of anything he wanted to do to me.

I deserved it all and much more. I surrendered my body and mind to what he wanted to do, and I would allow anything.

"Push out your tongue. I want my cock all the way in, don't fight me," he groaned and pulled his dick all the way out. I expected him to thrust it back in. I was confused when he plugged my nose with his fingers.

"You breathe when I fucking let you," he demanded. "Nod your head like a good girl." I did.

Once again, he shoved his cock to the back of my throat, not letting go of my nose. My head hit the back of the couch and I couldn't move. He didn't stop until my lips met his groin and he held me there for several long seconds.

"Look at me. How am I supposed to know when to let you breathe if I can't see your eyes, G?" He pulled out and I gasped for air while an uncontrollable amount of drool slid down the side of my mouth. He repeated this process for what felt like hours until he unexpectedly pulled out and pushed me onto my back. The hardwood floor made my landing hurt like a bitch. His mouth found mine and he kissed me with intensity and impatience. I tasted nothing but the scotch on is breath and our come entwined; it was my own special cocktail. His teeth nipped at my bottom lip as he stroked his dick back and forth.

"Play with yourself," he insisted in between kissing me.

My fingers went into the opening of my pussy, pushing them toward my g-spot. He pushed my fingers even deeper and slipped in his middle finger along with mine.

"Are you on the pill?"

"What?" I moaned.

"The pill? I'm clean. Are you?"

"Yeah…" I got tested a few weeks back, and by some miracle from God, I was clean.

"I want to fuck you raw," he huskily stated as he removed his finger and wrapped them around my neck again. My eyes widened as he applied much more pressure around my windpipe. At least it felt that way from the angle and him being above me. Once I was fully sedated, his hand assaulted my clit and then my pussy, and my eyes effortlessly rolled to the back of my head as my body arched off the ground.

He clasped harder around my neck each time my inner walls contracted around his fingers.

"Don't come," he commanded, making my eyes open wide. "Stroke my cock."

His hold around my neck tightened when I didn't move fast enough for his liking. The moment I did, he released his hold a little.

"Harder; stroke me harder, G."

The tighter my hand got around his dick, the more he let go. He nudged at my opening, teasing me. I removed my hand and he finally pushed in. He growled as he slipped inside me. He perched his upper body on his left hand, not letting up on my throat. He growled and grunted the entire time he fucked me. The closer my inner walls wrapped around his shaft, the tighter his hold around my neck became.

"Ahhh…" I breathed out, trying to catch air.

He loosened his hold. "Breathe." I did. "Don't close your eyes; keep your head level with mine." Again, he tightened his hold, making me lose air.

He held it there for a few seconds and then he let go. "Ahhh…" I gasped again, trying to take in as much air as possible. He continued this process until I couldn't take it anymore and came with such force that my entire body shook with spasms. His hold tightened, making it almost impossible to catch my breath, with an intensity that I had never experienced before. Seconds later, he thrust deep within my core and my pussy milked his cock of every drop.

He lay on top of me, both of us trying to catch our breaths.

"You're a good girl," he praised.

I turned my head and shifted my gaze to his eyes.

I saw Mr. Nichols and smiled.

Even though I knew it wasn't possible to have spent the last few hours with Mr. Nichols, in my head that's who fucked me.

I woke the next morning in my own bed. I had no recollection of how I had even gotten home. But I didn't really care. I just lay there, thinking about Mr. Nichols. I didn't think about Nick. It was Mr. Nichols that ran through my head as I touched my tender neck, and felt the delightful soreness between my legs.

He'd been in prison for seven years. It has been seven years since I sat in the courtroom and heard gavel slam down on the podium before hearing the word, "Guilty." I could still hear the crowd outside the courtroom making an uproar, news cameras everywhere, microphones in my face, and being shoved all over the place. McKenzie and I just held each other as tightly as we could while our parents shielded us from the mayhem of the press. It was a nightmare; the whole thing was a horrific experience that I wouldn't wish on my worst enemy. We could barely see a foot in front of us from the sea of people.

Mack and I cried the entire way home as we sat in the limo. Her sobs tormented my dreams for seven years. I could visualize everything that transpired in the course of three months. Our days consisted of the courtroom, debriefings, mediations, taking the stand, and mindless hours of interrogation from both sides. My wardrobe consisted of nothing but black, so did Mack's. We didn't plan it, it just happened. We burned all the clothes once the trial was over. It didn't make any of the turmoil go away; that only intensified as time went on.

It had been seven years since my heart stopped beating. I stopped living. The irony of it all was that I didn't start living until I met him. I lived my "true" life for seven months.

It was beautiful, it was chaotic, it was crazy…it was us.

It was love.

He was up for parole and I didn't know how I felt about it. I hadn't felt anything for years, so I didn't think I was capable of emotion anymore. I had turned cold, a shield, a stone…I was nothing. There was no depth to me, just a hollow existence. I was a shell of a person who walked, talked, and moved about like a zombie. I didn't care about anything or anyone, especially not myself.

I had to get out of bed. I needed a drink. I needed to stop thinking about that day.

It rang five times before it ever went to voicemail; I know because I counted. I hadn't spoken to Mack in seven years. In my autopilot state of mind, I didn't realize I was calling her until I heard her voice.

"Hello, you've reached McKenzie Perry with York Fancy. Sorry I missed your call. Please leave your name and number and I will get back to you as soon as I can. Thank you, and may your day be painted with images of York Fancy."

She sounded the same but different, if that made any sense at all. It's amazing how life could change overnight. You go to bed one person—an image of yourself that you have had your entire life—and then in a split second, you wake up somebody you don't know. Somebody you don't want to know. Someone you don't recognize. You can't even look in the mirror because you have no idea who's looking back at you. The reflection is someone with cold eyes and no soul.

I gave that away a long time ago—voluntarily.

After the trial, Mack and I started slipping apart. The connection that held us together slowly became altered and transformed into something different. We were no longer best friends–sisters–we were on two opposite ends of the spectrum. We didn't laugh, we didn't smile, and we didn't share things any longer. Our friendship took a drastic turn, like everything else did. It was a landslide of one thing after another. We said we were going our separate ways because we were older. We wanted to experience new and different things, and it was the furthest thing from the truth. We reminded each other too much about that day.

The day that changed the lives of more than just two teenage girls.

I didn't try to live the life I was raised to live–the life Mack and I mapped out. I was supposed to walk away with a fairytale that every teenage girl dreamed of. Jake and I were the perfect couple, always had been. He stood by my side throughout it all, every step of the way. He blamed himself for what happened; he told me that often, and the morbid thing about it was I never told him otherwise. I let him take the blame; I didn't care enough to not have him carry that burden.

I drank too much and took whatever was handed to me at any point in time. I'd go home with whoever would pay attention to me. I had slept with so many different men that I'd lost count. I couldn't even remember their names. I couldn't hold a job to save my life, and I barely remembered to pay my bills. I fucked men to feel something other than hatred for myself. I took drugs to think of anything other than wanting to kill myself.

I drank to forget.

I was completely and utterly alone. I had no friends–just random people I partied with. If it weren't for my parents taking care of me at the ripe old age of twenty-seven, I am damn certain I would've died. My parents felt sorry for me, for what I went through. They felt responsible. They said they didn't protect me enough and failed at doing a parent's job. I used that pity when it was convenient for me–to pay bills, to buy booze, to party, or whenever I needed or wanted some cash. They gave it to me every single time. No questions asked. I couldn't feel any fucking worse than I already did, so I'd take it, every fucking time.

There were mornings where I'd wake up and had no idea where the hell I was. I had no recollection of the previous night or whom I was waking up next to. There had been times I would wake up in my car. I could only go a few hours without taking a drink, and that started when I was about twenty-three. It began with cold sweats and nausea. In four years' time it had gotten to the point where my hands would shake and if I went too long, my skin felt like it was trying to eat itself alive. My vision would get blurry and I experienced drunken hazes where I had little recollection of what was happening or where I was. By the time I'd get a drink, I'd binge and couldn't stop myself. I ended up in the hospital for alcohol poisoning four times, which led to having my stomach pumped. I had only experienced a seizure one time, and it scared the living shit out of me.

I was a fucking mess.

I deserved it. All the darkness that I created was exactly what I wanted. It was what I craved. There was no light in my life; I said goodbye to that the moment I stepped into the hospital. Gianna Edwards didn't exist anymore; I was G. She had completely taken over my life in every way, shape, and form. I looked nothing like I did in high school. There were days I forgot to eat, or the alcohol in my system didn't allow me to. I was tiny…rail thin, even.

My eyes were still green, but most days my pupils were so dilated I couldn't see the color anymore. They weren't vibrant and alive; they were bottomless and lost. The dark circles made my appearance look tired. I made myself look presentable when I went out, and I would often catch myself staring at my reflection in the mirrors of the restrooms I found myself in. I didn't see anything anymore, and it was crystal clear when I looked in the mirror. I couldn't hide from my reflection and the person looking back at me. It always showed the truth. It was strange to see how much I had changed in seven years.

Depression and anxiety hit me hard after the trial, I didn't want to go out or be seen anywhere. I was terrified that someone would recognize me and would ask me questions or worse, ask me how I was doing. Our town was small and it was a given that I would run into someone I knew. Jake spent every second with me during the time of preliminaries. It took a year before the trial got started. The prosecution hired the best possible coaches to make sure Mack and I didn't crack on the stand. Jake said he couldn't leave me, and that he loved me, that his place was to stand right beside me to make sure I made it through it all. If he could have walked through the gates of the prison, he would have killed him with his bare hands.

He transferred from Columbia to Brown University to finish his senior year and to see me through everything. To add insult to injury, it was then that I realized he never cheated on me. He was the epitome of the perfect boyfriend who worked his ass off in school to come back to me. He worked hard and took heavy class loads because he wanted to provide me with the life I was accustomed to, and the one he said I deserved. I tried to attend Brown University with him, and I made it a semester before I had to drop out. I couldn't take the preliminaries of the trial and still function normally; throw school into

59

the mix and it was just too much. It took a year after graduation for the trial to start and then three months later he was gone.

Placed behind solid bars and away from me.

I couldn't contact the love of my life.

Mack had been accepted to Michigan State and left right after we graduated. She was going back and forth during the preliminaries of the trial. Jake asked me to marry him a month after the trial ended, and it was around the same time that my parents put the house up for sale. They said they couldn't live there anymore and they needed a fresh start. The house sold in three weeks and they decided to move to North Carolina. They were ecstatic when I told them about our engagement and said it came at a perfect time.

The burden of guilt and remorse weighed heavily on my decision to say yes because I felt like I owed it to him. I married him because I thought I had to. He was the only thing that made any sense to me back then. He was my rock, the very foundation that kept me going on a daily basis. Jake did the best he could for us. He studied hard to graduate with a business degree and make a name for himself in pharmaceutical sales. He traveled all the time, leaving me alone with nothing but my misery and self-loathing. The hatred I felt for myself was overwhelming; there were days I couldn't even get out of bed and when I did, I cried the entire day. I didn't know how it could be possible for one person to shed so many tears, but I was drowning in them.

However, that was only on the inside; I was still Gianna Edwards back then. After the trial, people expected to see me relieved and grateful because justice was served, the good guys won and the monster was gone. Placed in a cell where he couldn't hurt anyone ever again.

I did everything I was expected to do; I got excited for my upcoming nuptials, I planned with my mom, I went dress shopping, ordered the right food, and picked out the most perfect four-tier cake. I prepared for a day that I was dreading, and no one knew it but me. The day every girl dreams about became my nightmare. My parents invited everyone they knew and then some. McKenzie was my maid of honor, but we barely spoke throughout the entire wedding process. By that time, we were barely speaking at all. Her speech was short and to the point, but no one thought anything of it. I knew better. We got married fairly quickly, three months from the day he proposed to be exact. Our parents insisted that we have a honeymoon, and I came up with every excuse in the book to not go through with one.

He was starting a new career and needed to stay focused, I wanted to prepare our new home and make it comfortable for us, it was a better idea to put that money in savings…and the list went on. Thank God it worked and I was able to avoid going on a honeymoon with the man I was supposed to be madly in love with. Lying and pretending became my profession, and it was an art I had perfected. The thought of being alone and feigning romance, love, and all that other hocus pocus made me want to slit my wrists.

Everything was going according to plan and I had become numb to it all. It was easy to say "I love you too," it was easy to let him touch me and pretend his caresses were by someone else in order to reach an orgasm, it was easy being Betty fucking Crocker when everyone was looking. It made it that much easier to lie and deceive everyone with their expectancies of the perfect Gianna Henderson.

The woman and wife Jake deserved.

All of that went to shit one afternoon when he was away on a business trip.

We'd been married for six months and my mundane routine was to take care of the household and provide my husband with everything and anything he ever wanted. We all pretend to be something we're not, that's life, and that's how we get by. People's perceptions of you are whatever you want them to be, and I was a Stepford wife.

I cleaned, making sure the house was immaculate and spotless, not one thing out of place. Jake was due back in the evening and I made sure to have all his suits dry cleaned, the bed sheets were ironed, and all of his clothes smelled fresh and were put away precisely the way he liked them. I started to cook his favorite dinner–beef stew– knowing it would take five hours until the meat was tender and held the perfect flavor. Crying had become my outlet from my reality, it was my source of comfort, and I needed to find that elsewhere because Jake could never know about it. I went into his office, hoping to find anything that took my mind off of where it wandered when I wasn't focused on a task to distract my thoughts.

My eyes found it immediately, as if it was calling to me. My feet moved on their own as I walked to the bookshelf of literary works that Jake had organized when we moved in. There, before my very own eyes, was the collective masterpiece of Romeo and Juliet, a gift he had given me. I assumed it was thrown away with the move or I had carelessly left it behind and it got lost. My finger traced the border of the book, feeling the rough edges of the old hardcover. The memory of when he handed it to me quickly made its way into my bloodstream.

"What is this?" I asked, taking the book into my hands.

"It's a gift," he responded.

"You got me something?" The emotion was evident on my face.

"I did."

"Why?"

"Because it made me think of you and I wanted you to have it."

"Oh," I replied, confused.

I opened the book to find a passage written in pen on the first page; "What's in a name? That which we call a rose by any other name would smell as sweet."

I looked up at him as he stood above my desk watching my every move.

"Did you write this?" I questioned, trying to read his expression and what it all meant.

"I did."

"Why?"

He sighed and bent down so that we were at eye level. "Because, Gianna, Gia, G, you are the same person, you don't have to pretend to be something you're not. Let the world see you the way I do, the way you allow me to."

I frowned and my head fell forward; I felt ashamed. He grabbed my chin and made me look at him. "You don't hide from me. You don't ever pretend with me. Do you understand?"

I took in his words and what he was demanding. It was the first time I allowed myself to feel free and accepted. It was because of him.

I nodded enthusiastically, hoping that he could feel as much as I was. He smiled, took my hand, kissed it, and stood up to remove himself away from me. I felt something silky and smooth that he left behind in the palm of my hand. I turned it over to find a single red rose pedal.

I shyly smiled, closed my hand and placed it on my heart, right where it belonged.

Chapter Seven

I found myself in the kitchen, crouched down in the corner with a knife in my hand as I came out of the haze from my memory. I didn't even remember how I got there. The last thing I remembered was looking at the book I thought I had lost. My mind was swarming with different thoughts. I needed to get dinner on the table, I still had a load of laundry in the dryer to fold, was something burning?

"To thy own self be true," I said aloud as I watched the sharp knife slice across the delicate skin of my wrist. The blood was red and warm, exactly like the rose pedal. I continued to cut at my wrist in slow movements, wanting to capture the beauty of the color red that was exposed with each swipe of the blade.

I didn't hear the door open, nor did I hear Jake yell when he saw me.

"Oh my God, baby! What did you do? What are you doing?" he exclaimed, taking the knife out of my hand. He sounded concerned and something else…panicked?

I cocked my head to the side and smiled. "I wanted to see the color red. It's so pretty. Isn't it pretty, babe?" His eyes widened in fear as he tried to make sense of my rambling.

He stood up fast and slipped on my blood as he reached into the drawer for a hand towel.

"Let me see your arm, Gia," he ordered, wrapping the towel tightly around it. He grabbed his cell phone from his suit jacket. He looked so handsome. I really was a lucky girl. I should've appreciated him more, I should've loved him like he loved me. What was wrong with me?

"9-1-1 operator," I heard the lady on the other line say.

"Yes! I need an ambulance...my wife...my wife tried...she tried...I don't know...I need an ambulance. She's bleeding! There's so much blood. Please hurry."

I smiled and caressed the side of his face and his eyes immediately found mine.

"Calm down, everything is fine. I'm fine. I made you beef stew, your favorite, but I have to go take the load out of the laundry." I tried to get up, but he gripped my leg, making it impossible to stand.

"Don't move," he ordered in a strained and demanding tone.

He was mad at me? What had I done? I tried to be the perfect wife; I was Gianna Henderson. Could he finally see the lies? Did he know I wasn't perfect...would he leave me now?

I was transported to the nearest hospital where I was placed in psychiatric evaluation for seventy-two hours. The psychiatrist called it a mental health breakdown; she told my family it was due to the trial and everything I had gone through. She said she was surprised it took that long for me to have a psychotic break. It was far from the truth and now yet another added lie to the ever growing pile.

I was put in therapy and my counselor told me I was a "survivor." Jake swept it under the rug, thinking I was getting help and everything would return back to normal. The root of the problem was solved but it was far from my actual issues. I was prescribed anti-depressants and anxiety medication and for a while, I felt okay. It tamed the beast and it was once again quiet and silenced. Jake started discussing having a family, and my therapist believed that it could be good for me to have something to look forward to and to take care of. I agreed with her, hoping that a child could redeem and save me.

My salvation.

We had been married a little less than a year when I found out I was pregnant. It only took us two months of trying for that little white stick to show a plus sign. I prayed every single night that I would feel half of what I felt the first time I got pregnant. I wanted it so badly that it consumed me. I was overjoyed with my first pregnancy; the possibilities of us being able to be together were endless. We were expecting a child together and it was made from love and passion. No lies tainted it, it was all truths and that's all that mattered. We would make everything work, at any cost. I desired those exact reactions with my pregnancy with Jake, but it wasn't even close. It wasn't even on the same wavelength.

The moment I read the bright pink plus sign, my heart dropped, I had to catch my breath and I felt like I was going to pass out. The bathroom walls crumbled their way into my space, leaving me suffocated and unable to move. I was frightened and scared and I wanted no part of it. How was I going to bring a child that I didn't want into the world? How could I pretend? I crossed the line and had involved an innocent child into my charade of lies. I slid down the wall in shock, staring off into space. I wanted to cry, scream, and run away. I contemplated getting rid of it; nobody would ever know except me. I could go back on birth control and not tell Jake, there were couples that took years getting pregnant.

We could be one of them.

I grabbed my forehead and frowned, how could I be thinking this? Going to hell didn't even faze me because I lived it every fucking day. I touched my stomach and rubbed it back and forth, I had no choice but to continue with my pregnancy. I made my bed and now I had to lie in it. Jake was overjoyed to learn that I was pregnant. He was planning names and wanted to start decorating the baby's room before my first doctor's appointment. I went along with everything he wanted to do, trying to be the perfect wife and soon to be mother. I was ten weeks along when I went to bed with extreme cramping; I figured it was from stress and exhaustion. The intense abdominal pains woke me up in the middle of the night and I ran into the bathroom. I turned on the light and stared at the blood that was staining my panties and running down my legs in the mirror.

It was the most surreal feeling ever. I wanted to feel the loss of my baby, the sadness and darkness to devour me whole, but I didn't. I breathed out a huge sigh of relief because it was gone. I didn't have to involve anyone else in my dishonestly. I didn't have to worry about ruining another life that wasn't mine. It was a blessing to me.

I walked back into our bedroom and what I saw broke my heart. I didn't think my heart was capable of beating anymore. Jake was lying there, rested on one arm while the other was lying in the pool of blood.

"It's gone isn't it?" he whispered, not taking his eyes off the blood stained sheets.

"Yes."

My heart broke for him. He didn't deserve that and he didn't deserve me. I could never offer him what he truly was entitled to. My heart didn't belong to me, it belonged to the man behind steel bars, the man who was locked away for my sins. The man I would never see again. Jake threw himself into work and that was when our marriage started to show its cracks in the foundation. Its true colors made itself present; they were bright and blinding. Anything that is broken will eventually shatter, even if you think you've glued it back together. And all you will be able to do is stand by and witness its demise.

Two months after the miscarriage, Jake called me from Houston, where he was at on business. I will never forget that phone call. I could recite it all by memory. Closing my eyes, I could remember the entire night.

"Hey baby," he said on the other end.

"Hey."

"What are you doing?"

"Not much, just reading."

He paused for a few seconds, and call it intuition, but I knew what he was going to say, I knew exactly where this conversation was going to go and I was dreading every minute of it. I pushed my nail into my skin to relieve the anxiety that was building.

"So I've been thinking, babe. It's been a few months now and I thought maybe we could start trying again?"

My heart sank and I swear the room started to close in on me. How the fuck could this keep happening? Was it ever going to be over?

"Jake, I don't...I mean–"

"No, listen. I think it would be great for us. Most first time pregnancies end up in miscarriages. I have been doing a lot of research on it. It's actually really normal," he reasoned.

I should have been thinking how lucky I was to have such an amazing man in my life but I wasn't. I thought that he sounded needy and I hated myself more for thinking that.

67

"I guess we can talk about it some more when you get home."

He laughed from nervousness. "Really? That's awesome, babe. Oh my God, I'm so glad you feel the same way."

I wanted to hang up on him and pack my bags and disappear. I couldn't take it anymore, the years of pretending to be someone I'm not.

"I have to go, baby. I love you. I'll be home in two days and I can't wait to start trying again."

I hung up before I had to say the words back to him. I wanted to curl up in a ball and cry. I sat there in a trance, trying to re-evaluate my life. The thoughts were too much to bear and I couldn't stand to be there anymore. I had to leave. I went to the nearest bar and downed drink after drink.

And just like that she was back again.

G.

That was the beginning of the end.

"I didn't order that," I told the bartender.

"I did," said a voice from behind me. I turned to find a good-looking, older man standing behind me.

We talked for hours about nothing and he made me laugh. I mean really laugh. G just took over and all the noise in my head just disappeared, it was gone like it didn't exist, like it had never been there. I can't explain how liberating it was to feel free and not tied down from all the lies that buried me.

She didn't stop him when he pulled the hair out of my face and placed it behind my ear. She didn't stop his hand when it touched my knee and slowly made its way up my thigh. She actually smiled at him, provoking him to keep going. When he grabbed my hand and escorted me to his car, I knew exactly what we were going to do. She let him take me back to his house, she let him touch and caress me. She let him bring me to orgasm and it was the first time since he had been sent away that I didn't have to pretend it was "him" to reach climax.

Not one time did I think about Jake or what this would do to him.

For the next few hours, I lived in a bubble of lust and desire, where I let my body do the talking. It was then that I realized that alcohol and sex made everything go away. Alcohol locked it up and I personally threw away the key.

I was...am...a selfish person.

I went home the next morning and dialed Mack's number ten times. I dialed the first five numbers over and over again before hanging up. I wanted to come clean and finally tell her everything. She deserved to know the truth. But I couldn't do it, and every time I got close to dialing the sixth number I would start to shake and get a nauseous feeling in the pit of my stomach. I would hit the end button before I could change my mind. The last thing I wanted was for her to judge me, to be disappointed in me, I already did that enough for the both us. A part of me felt like she knew exactly what I was going through because she was going through the same thing. The lies we shared together would forever bind us.

Months went by, moving at a slow progressive rate. And with each day that passed, I placed my own nails around my coffin, one by one. I tried to stay faithful to Jake, but every time I looked at his sorrowful face, the face of the man who blamed himself, I couldn't help but run in the opposite direction. It was the face of a man who loved me but had no idea who I truly was, he loved Gianna Edwards and she wasn't real. I didn't deserve his kindness, his respect, his adoration, and most of all, his love. I never had...even before that night. He was too good for me.

My friendship with Mack also drastically changed and we weren't the same girls anymore. We didn't talk or hang out at all. Her eyes mimicked mine; she was as empty as I was, and there was absolutely nothing either of us could do about it. It was too late. She left for an internship in Detroit two years after we graduated and it was the best decision she could've made. We needed to get away from each other; our friendship was no longer healthy for either of us.

I filed for divorce two years into my marriage. It wasn't fair for me to continue running around on Jake. He had always been my safety net and it was time for me to set him free. The affairs were getting too much and I was enjoying being G; I didn't want to pretend anymore. It was the only time that I felt like the Band-Aid wasn't on and drinking and being with other men allowed that. I was allowed to show the darkness that I felt harboring inside. I let it take over the day we signed the papers. Jake never found out what I did when he wasn't around. When I told him I wanted a divorce, he didn't fight me on it. He didn't even seem surprised when I handed him the papers. He kissed and hugged me and told me that everything was going to be okay. That we would still be in each other's lives and that he would always love me.

I cried that night, but it wasn't because we were no longer tied to each other. The tears that fell down my face were from happiness. I was free. I could do anything I wanted and wouldn't have to lie about it anymore. The years that went by slowly began eating away at me. Like with anything that's new, the first few years were fun, but all good things must come to an end. And it became about survival...

It was nearly four days of partying before I made it back to my apartment where I slept for two straight days. I woke, dry heaving, looking around and trying to figure out where the fuck I was. I reached for my ringing phone, realizing that was what had woken me.

"Hey, Mom," I moaned.

"My God, Gianna Skyler Edwards. Where have you been? I've been worried sick. Your father was going to call the police if I didn't reach you today."

I stumbled to the bathroom, squinting my eyes. "Yeah, sorry. I've been busy," I mumbled, rubbing the sore spot on my head. I had a bump, where the fuck did that come from? I walked to the kitchen and opened every cabinet in the house, looking for coffee.

"That is no excuse to not call your mother after she has left voicemail after voicemail." I put the phone down on the counter and hit speaker, just allowing her to bitch and complain as I looked for Baileys to put in my coffee. By the time I was done with my first cup of "coffee," she had finished yelling.

"Mom, I get it, okay. I'm sorry." I poured myself another cup trying to take the edge off.

"Ugh...honey, I know you do. I'm sorry for yelling at you. You have been through so much. My little girl is such a survivor." I rolled my eyes and downed my cup.

"Did you send out the letter?"

"No. Mom, I don- fuck- mom I got to go." I hung up before she could get another word in.

I hadn't even realized that I drank half a bottle of whiskey until someone knocked on my door. I opened it to find a FedEx packet on the floor. I grabbed it and ripped it open as I closed the door behind me.

Gianna,

Since you seem to be too busy for you own mother, I have taken it upon myself to write the letter for you. We cannot let this man go free. He has put all of us in shambles for what he did to you girls. There is no way he can be let go and possibly do what he did to you and Mack to some other poor, innocent girls. The letter is attached in the packet; all you have to do is sign it. There is also an envelope all ready to be mailed out. Just put it in your mailbox. I think you can handle that. I know you have been through so much, baby. I am so sorry this happened to you, you know if I could switch places with you, I would do it in a heartbeat. I have to live with knowing that I didn't protect you. I didn't do my job as a parent.

I love you, Gianna.

Mom

I found the attached letter.

I didn't even read it.

I ripped it in half and threw it in the garbage.

Chapter Eight

I woke to a splitting headache and a blinding light in my eyes. I opened one eye at a time, hoping it relieved the pressure that was building. It didn't work and I immediately grabbed my temples and squeezed as hard as I could. It was then that I took in my surroundings, and found that I was lying in a bed that wasn't mine, in between two men, one on each side. Both their backs were to me and the sheets hung low, which exposed their muscular forms. *Fuck me.* I silently prayed that we used a condom; I would have to get tested again. Third fucking time in the last six months. I quietly crawled toward the front edge of the bed and slipped one foot in front of the other on the hardwood floors. I tip toed around the room trying to find my clothes that seemed to be scattered everywhere. I didn't find my bra or panties; I put my clothes on without them. Another pair lost in the land of one-night stands.

How the hell did I get there? My head was pounding, my eyes burned, and my stomach was churning with nausea. What the hell did I take? I was becoming a human garbage disposal…at this rate I wouldn't make it through the year. I found my clutch in the living room and made sure all my contents were inside. The condoms were gone so we must have used them. I grabbed my cell phone as I gently closed the front door behind me.

"Fuck!" It was dead.

I walked outside and looked around, the main road was a few hundred feet in front of me. I recognized where I was on the Vegas strip. It took about forty-five minutes for me to find the first breakfast diner. The pay phone was inside and I called a cab before I went into the bathroom. I looked in the mirror to inspect the damage. My hair was a mess and I pulled it up to an even messier bun. I rinsed my mouth with mouthwash that I kept in my purse and put my aviator sunglasses back on. It covered my bloodshot eyes and the disaster of my appearance didn't seem so bad. I found the first vacant table and ordered some coffee. My fingers started to twitch and I placed them in my lap; that didn't stop my knee from bouncing up and down, though.

The waitress stood above me waiting for my order. "You guys wouldn't happen to have any alcohol would you?"

She looked at me with shock and disgust and I couldn't really blame her.

"Darlin, you look like you need some food. Let me get you some tomato soup, I just made a new batch."

"I'm fine," I responded and she cocked her head to the side, giving me a stern look. It reminded me of my mother.

"Whatever. Soup is fine."

She nodded and made her way back to the kitchen.

I grabbed my stomach in pain and I knew I was minutes away from starting to get sick and dizzy. I quickly looked in my purse to find anything to take the edge off. I found a white pill that appeared to be a pain pill. My phone was dead so I couldn't research it.

"Fuck it." I took it down with nothing but the saliva in my mouth.

I took a deep breath, trying to calm my anxiety and nerves. I needed to do something to take my mind off the withdrawal as I looked around at the other tables. There was a newspaper and I reached for it, bringing it back over to me. I avoided newspapers like the plague, but I turned each page wanting to find the comics section.

Right there on the seventh page was the headline news that I tried to avoid seeing at all costs.

Parole hearing for James Nichols, who was sentenced to ten years in prison, causing uproar in Rhode Island.

I started to bite the fingernail on my thumb and soon, both my legs were bouncing up and down. The anxiety rapidly took over my body, I needed to stop reading, but I couldn't help myself.

The story heard around the world. In March 2005, the town of Shayla Harbor was turned upside down with the shocking revelations of two high school students, McKenzie Perry and

Gianna Edwards from Monte Academy. Mr. Nichols was transferred from Mitchell high school in Maine to take the position for the head of the English department at Monte Academy. The twenty-seven-year-old teacher was convicted of raping two of his female students.

The trial began on June 9, 2006. Outside the courtroom, Nichol's attorney Michael Wayne described his client, who has no criminal background, as "innocent." The trial lasted three months and the evidence against Nichols was extremely incriminating. The courtroom, families and press eagerly awaited the sentencing and celebrated when terms of Nichols' verdict was announced. He was sentenced to ten years in prison.

After seven years of good behavior, James Nichols is up for his second parole hearing. He was denied the first time, two years ago. He still pleads his innocence and it is causing the small community in Rhode Island to come together to keep him in prison. There has been an outpouring of letters and support on this behalf. No statements have been made at this time from the victims. More details as the story unfolds.

I stared at mine and Mack's names. You would think I would have gotten use to reading about us in the paper, but it never got old. My mother started to collect every article that was written on the trial, it was all over my house, and there was no way of ever getting away from it.

"Here you go, darlin," the waitress said, bringing my attention back to the present. "Such a shame that's happening."

"Huh?"

She nodded to the newspaper. "That man deserves to rot in prison for what he did to those girls. Just goes to show you that justice isn't always served." I chuckled and nodded.

I drank half of my coffee as I started to feel the effects of whatever I took. My eyes were glued to Mr. Nichols' photo in the paper and the memories slowly took over my thoughts.

"Hey, I'm taking off, I need to meet my dad," Mack said as we walked into the parking lot of our school.

"Oh okay, call me later," I responded, trying to remember where I parked my car. I clicked the keyless entry and followed the sound. I found it in the back of the parking lot and that was when I realized I left the back door ajar.

"Damn it!" I yelled.

I couldn't call my dad, he would just give me a lecture about being responsible and paying attention to my surroundings. It was the last thing I wanted to hear after a long day of school and cheerleading practice.

"Ugh."

I got in the car, knowing that it wouldn't turn on when I placed the key in the ignition. I banged on the steering wheel with my hands, frustrated at the situation I found myself in. I wanted to cry because I would have to call Triple A and my dad would find out either way. I could practically hear his lecture about how I never did anything right and how Mack was always better. I rolled my eyes at the thought. I popped the trunk open and walked around to grab the jumper cables.

"Problem?"

I jumped and banged my head on the top of the trunk. *"Ow!"* I whimpered and my eyes instantly watered.

"Oh shit!" I recognized the voice immediately and turned around to face him. *"I'm sorry. Are you all right?"* he sympathized.

"Yeah," I said, rubbing my hand back and forth on my head.

"No you aren't, you're crying," he addressed and stepped forward a few inches away from my face. His finger swept away a tear.

"I'm fine. I think it was just the initial shock," I clarified, trying to hide the color that crept on my face from embarrassment. I hated crying in front of people.

He smirked. *"Let me make sure you're all right."* He placed his hand on top of mine and lowered my head. *"You'll have a nasty bump for a few days, but you'll live. I'm sorry I scared you. I heard the alarm of a car and came over to make sure everything was okay,"* he explained as he rubbed the bump in a comforting and soothing way.

My stomach did that flip-flop thing that it did when I was in his presence, and I stepped back to avoid the inappropriate thoughts.

75

I cunningly smiled. "Now you need to make it up to me. You'll have to jump me." He laughed and shook his head. "Come on, I know you know how to jump a girl." He shook his head again but I could tell he was enjoying our banter.

"Let me go pull my car around. Can you stay out of trouble till I get back?" I nodded and smiled.

As soon as I couldn't see him anymore, I went into my gym bag and changed out of my sweaty tank top and sprayed body spray all over me. I closed the door as I heard his truck approach. He stepped out of his truck and I watched his eyes take in my appearance of a sports bra and cheer shorts.

I shrugged. "It's hot."

He groaned and gestured with his head to the front of my car. "Make yourself useful and pop the hood please." I giggled and did as I was told.

He folded the cuffs of his sleeves to avoid getting them dirty and I watched as he effortlessly brought the life back in my car. It didn't take him long to jump start my battery.

"Here," I said as I poured my water bottle out on his hands and he rubbed them together, cleaning off the oil. I handed him a towel next.

"You're all set, Miss Edwards."

"Thanks. Why are you working so late?" I asked, throwing the empty water bottle in the passenger side of my car.

"I was grading tests and coming up with material for next week."

I leaned my back on my car. "Oh. Are you always this much of a planner? Sometimes it's nice to live on the edge, you know? Not plan anything and just let things happen."

His eyes changed to a hint of curiousness in them, "Is that how you live your life?" he interrogated.

"Not really, just when the mood strikes. I'm actually quite a planner. Mack and I know exactly what we are going to do with our lives. It's all set out," I simply responded.

"Sometimes things don't work out the way you assume they will."

"Not with me and Mack, we're like sisters and have had these plans since we were kids."

He nodded in understanding. "I can see that."

I could feel the butterflies in my stomach. "You've been watching me?"

He cleared his throat and cocked his head to the side. "I observe all my students."

"Is that all I am? Just a student?" I rasped in a sexy voice.

His eyes narrowed like he was contemplating what to say. "Go home, G."

I stepped closer. "Is that what you want?"

He stepped back. "It's irrelevant what I want. Go home." He turned to leave.

"Mr. Nichols..." He paused and looked at me. "Thanks for jumping me, I hope it was as fulfilling for you as it was for me," I teased.

He chuckled and shook his head, placing his hands in his pockets. "Good night, Miss Edwards."

I wanted to remember those times, the happy ones, the ones where no one was around and it was just us.

But I couldn't...I mostly recalled the ones of hatred.

"We call Gianna Skyler Edwards to the stand."

I placed my hand on the Bible. "Do you swear to tell the truth, the whole truth, and nothing but the truth, so help you God?"

I nodded.

"Please answer yes or no to the question," I heard the judge announce.

"Yes."

The bailiff took the Bible and walked away. The District Attorney approached me and nodded at me, calming me down.

"Is your name Gianna Skyler Edwards?"

"Yes."

"Were you born on October 17, 1987?"

"Yes."

"Do you live at 155 Creswalt Drive?"

"Yes."

"Where were you the night of March 7, 2005?"

I looked straight across the room at the double doors. I never once looked at McKenzie or Mr. Nichols. I couldn't look at either of them. I had to stay strong.

"I was with McKenzie at the football game."

"What happened at the game?"

"We were drinking in the parking lot."

"What happened during that time in the parking lot? Did you see Mr. Nichols?"

"I object, Your Honor. He's leading the witness," his lawyer declared.

"Your Honor, I will rephrase."

"Motion denied Counsel," the judge stated.

"Gianna, what happened in the parking lot during the football game?"

"We were both upset over the fact that we got kicked off the squad and I had lost my scholarship. We weren't cheering at our last home game and we decided to get drunk instead."

"Did you recognize anyone in the parking lot? Anything happen?"

I knew the second I said his name everything would change. I was terrified.

"Miss Edwards please answer the question. Who did you see in the parking lot on March 7, 2005?" I didn't say anything.

"May I remind you that you are still under oath and are mandated to answer the question?" I stayed silent, not wanting to answer the question. I looked around the room at all the faces and what they expected of me; each one of them eagerly waiting for me to respond.

I looked down in my lap, hoping it would make it easier for me to answer. I wanted to be anywhere but there.

"He was in the parking lot. He was walking with his family to a car I didn't recognize, he looked like he was saying goodbye to them. We watched the car leave and then he walked to his truck."

"The 'he' that you speak of–" he paused *"–is he in the courtroom?"*

I nodded, remembering I had to answer. I whispered, "Yes…"

"Who is he, Gianna?"

I swallowed the lump in my throat and dug my nail into my skin. I felt nothing.

"Mr. Nichols. Mr. Nichols was in the parking lot that night."

I jolted when the waitress told me my cab was outside waiting for me. I placed a ten-dollar bill on the table before making my way to the taxi.

"Can you stop at the liquor store on the corner please?" I asked the driver.

I hurriedly walked down the halls of my apartment building; kicking my door closed and eagerly placed the bottles on the counter, I poured straight whiskey into a glass and took it down in one gulp; I repeated it three more times. I couldn't breathe, I felt like there was a hole in my chest that was allowing all the air to leave my lungs. I didn't know if I would ever be able to breathe again.

The red blinking button on my answering machine caught my attention. I pressed play. "Gianna, it's your mother–" Delete.

"Gianna, where are you–" Delete.

"Gianna, why aren't you–" Delete.

There were ten more just like that…

"Good morning, this is Christine Benson from The York Chronicle. I am looking for Gianna Edwards. We are doing a spread on James Nichols and would love to get a statement on how you feel about his early release–" Delete.

"Good evening, this is Chris Garrison from the Vegas times. I am looking for Gianna Edwards. We are very interested in interviewing you on the upcoming early release–" Delete.

There were seven more just like that…

"Gia…we…I…" Click, dial tone.

It was the first time I heard her voice, other than her answering machine, in six and a half years.

"Mother fucker," I yelled.

"Gianna, we have already established that Mr. Nichols was the one in the parking lot the night of March 7, 2005. What happened when you saw him?" the prosecution proceeded.

"Nothing; we watched him get into his truck and leave."

"What happened after that?"

"We followed him. All we wanted to do was get a chance to talk to him and see if there was anything he could do to help us. I lost my scholarship and we just wanted the opportunity to talk it out with him." It was the truth, I was telling the truth as the tears streamed down my face and I had to close my eyes to stop them.

"Proceed, Gianna."

I cried, "I can't..."

"Your Honor, permission for a recess to consult with my client?

"Granted. Court will recess for two hours." When I heard the gavel hit, I jumped.

He placed his hand on my shoulder and squeezed it in a comforting motion. He placed his hand on my lower back and escorted me to my parents. My mother immediately pulled me into a hug and told me she was proud of me. I excused myself to go to the bathroom. I splashed water on my face and heard the door close behind someone. I didn't have to wonder who it was.

"Are you okay?"

"What do you think, Mack?"

"I know, Gia."

"I can't do this. I don't think I can go back up there," I said, looking at our reflections in the mirror.

"Gia, we've come this far...you can do this. We can do this." I nodded.

"You look like shit." We laughed.

She helped me fix my makeup and we left the bathroom holding hands.

"Please rise. The court will now resume with Honorable Judge McMullen."

"I call Gianna Skyler Edwards back on the stand." The prosecution stated. *I looked over at McKenzie and she winked at me.*

"Gianna, what happened when you followed Mr. Nichols home? Please tell the jury."

"McKenzie and I got out of the car and knocked on his door."

"Did he answer?"

"Yes."

"What happened when you made it inside?"

"We tried to talk to him about our grades and he kept feeding us more alcohol."

"Liar!" Mr. Nichols yelled, jumping out of his chair. It was the first time that day that I finally looked at him. He looked straight into my eyes with hatred. I didn't recognize them anymore.

"One more outburst like that and I'll hold you in contempt, Mr. Nichols," The judge called, tapping the gavel twice.

"Were you drunk?" he continued.

"I was happy and buzzed, I guess."

"What happened next?"

"We pleaded with him to help us and he kept telling us he couldn't, that it was out of his hands. He got upset and started yelling at us, he threw things all around the house. He could tell that Mack and I were getting scared and he excused himself to go to the bathroom. It was then that Mack and I got out of there."

"Where did you go when you left his house?"

"I sobered up and I was driving us back to my house."

"What happened when you were driving home?" he grilled, wanting me to say it already.

"Someone ran us off the side of the road and I almost crashed my car."

"And..." he interrogated.

"Mack immediately got out of the car and so did the driver. It was a man wearing a black hoodie and a baseball cap and I couldn't recognize who it was. It was dark and the only lights on the road were

our headlights. It happened so fast, I blinked and a baseball bat was knocking out Mack. I tried to run to her but someone grabbed me by the back of my hair and told me that I was being a bad girl. I started to scream and asked him to please let go of me, but it just made him grab me harder." The tears once again streamed down my face, one right after the other.

"Keep going, Gianna. What happened next?"

"I kept screaming, hoping that someone could hear me, but he wrapped his hand around my mouth and dragged me by the side of the car. I bit his hand and punched him in the face. I scratched and fought with all the power I could muster, but it wasn't enough to get him to stop. He pushed me away, calling me a cunt and slapped me across the face. I fell to the ground and he got on top of me, beating me. It was then that I recognized who it was." I stopped, dreading the next question that would come.

"Who was it? Who was there that night?"

I closed my eyes, wanting to disappear. *"Mr. Nichols."* I kept my eyes closed, pretending that I wasn't there and that I wasn't really saying what came out of my mouth.

"He turned me onto my stomach and tied my hands behind my back with his belt. He left me there on the ground and I watched him walk over to McKenzie. He hit her a few times trying to get her to wake up. He said she had a pulse and that she was faking it. He called her a liar and a tease. That we were making him do this to us."

"Did you feel like you were making him do those things to you?"

"Objection, Your Honor. Leading the witness," his lawyer declared.

"Overruled. Answer the question, Miss Edwards."

"No. I don't think we were making him do those things to us. I don't know why he was."

"What happened next?"

"I watched as he ripped off all McKenzie's clothes. He hit her a few more times but she still didn't wake up." I looked over at Mack and she was looking down into her lap. My parents were sitting next to

her parents and our mothers' faces were tucked in the arms of our fathers. It was the first time I had ever seen my father cry.

"Gianna, please continue."

"He was saying obscenities to McKenzie over and over again."

"What was he saying? Tell the jury."

"He was saying that we deserved this. That she was a cunt, a fuck hole. That girls like us needed to be put in our places. That we started all this and he was finishing it. He took off all his clothes and pulled out a condom from his pants." I heard myself sob.

"He put the condom on before he stuck his penis in McKenzie's mouth, hoping to wake her. When she didn't, he got angry and he told me he was going to dump her body in the woods somewhere. I watched as he violated her mouth."

"What happened next?"

"He removed himself and pushed into her."

"Clarify, 'he pushed into her.'"

"He raped her. He pushed into her vagina and he raped her. I watched my best friend get brutally raped right in front of me and I couldn't do a damn thing about it." I broke down and sobbed.

"What happened when he was done with McKenzie?"

I sobbed uncontrollably to the point I was shaking and screamed, "I was next...he raped me next..."

I knew things were never going to be the same.

For anyone.

Chapter Nine

He was out.

He was free.

He had served seven out of ten years and was released on parole. It took two months for his parole hearing to conclude, and I didn't do one fucking thing to stop it–not one. I didn't think that he would be granted early parole, I thought it would be denied like the last time; never in my wildest dreams did I think it was possible that he would be released early. My phone hadn't stopped ringing since the minute he stepped foot out of the facility. It was everywhere; newspapers, TV, magazines. I couldn't get away from it. As much as I tried to keep myself occupied, it wasn't working. The alcohol wasn't having the same effect on me and drugs were something I did as recreational use; I tried to keep myself clean of that unless I was partying.

I'd been staring at my laptop for the last few hours and with every sip of wine I would take, my willpower reduced. I did not need to read about him, I did not need to know where he was, I did not need to know anything about him.

He couldn't hurt me again…

I was sitting on a barstool at my kitchen island while my mom cooked me breakfast; it was Friday morning. It had been three days since the closing arguments and everyone anxiously waited for the verdict. I swear I felt the phone ring before I actually heard it. My mom's eyes landed on mine from across the room but it was my dad who answered the phone.

"Hello?" he stated. "Yes. All right. We will be there. Thank you." He clicked end and looked at us. "The verdict is in. We're due back in the courtroom in two hours."

I ran to the sink and threw up. My mom was readily behind me, rubbing my back.

"It's okay, honey. Justice will be served. You will see. You have nothing to worry about. He is not going to go free," she reassured.

I turned on the sink and washed my mouth while watching the vile of vomit make its way down the drain. And just as fast as it appeared, it was gone, exactly like my life. My mom helped me dress and before I knew it, we were in the limo on our way to the courtroom. Mack and I sat beside each other and held hands the entire time. Our parents' eyes never left us. We parked by the front steps of the building and the nausea immediately returned. Mack squeezed my hand and I knew she was feeling the exact same thing. I squeezed it back, trying to be strong for her, for the both us. Our fathers took off their suit jackets; they quickly placed them on top of our heads to shield us from the press. Our mothers tried to create a bubble around us and as hard as they tried, it didn't matter. Microphones were shoved in our face and we had to push our way through the crowd.

I wanted to scream and tell everyone to get the fuck out of the way. I wanted to flick off the cameras and tell them to mind their own business. This didn't concern them. I couldn't do anything but bow my head and wait for the blast of air conditioning to hit my face when we arrived in the building. I know it's bizarre, but I looked forward to that cold breeze every time we got out of the limo, all I had to do was make it to the front doors. Our fathers put their jackets back on and I tried to catch my breath, but my heart wouldn't let me, it was pounding out of my chest.

"Are you okay?" Mack asked, mimicking my face I was sure. I shook my head no with panic written all over my demeanor.

"This is it, Gia. After this, it's over. We don't have to think about it anymore. We just need to make it through today," she vowed, grabbing my hand.

We walked behind our parents and took our regular seats in the front of the spectator gallery. My field of vision caught him instantly, he was dressed in a dark blue suit, his hands were folded in his lap and his head was down. He looked despondent, like he didn't know what to feel. I looked at him the entire time. Thirty minutes later and the judge walked in and we all rose. Everything proceeded in slow motion and I knew I would forever be haunted by this day. There was no going back.

The bailiff got the verdict from the foreman and handed it to the judge. I squeezed Mack's hand so hard I thought I was breaking her bones and she let me. He listed off each charge, repeating the same phrase over and over again.

"Guilty."

Everyone applauded when he was done listing each verdict. My parents pulled me into a tight embrace, putting me in the middle and squeezing the life out of me. I was numb to it all. I looked over at Mack as my head lay on my mom's shoulder. Her eyes said everything, and I knew nothing would be the same after that day. I lost everything.

I could feel him staring at me from across the room. My willpower was weak and I had to look at him. If looks could kill, I would have died that instant. Hatred spread across his beautiful face. I was wrong...

That's the moment I shattered. It happened right then and there for everyone to see.

He witnessed it, and for a brief second, I saw pleasure on his face.

He wasn't done hurting me.

I'd been staring at his picture for an hour. I was possessed as my hands took over and I Googled his name, there was image after image of him. Most of them were of him leaving the courtroom, dressed in a black suit and gray button down shirt, he looked older. He was still the most handsome man I had ever seen and I found myself touching the screen of my laptop just to feel close to him. I clicked picture after picture until I found a press video. I bit the corner of my lower lip as my hand once again took over as I pressed play.

"Mr. Nichols, can we get a statement please?" "How do you feel about your early release?" "What's going through your head?" "Are you going to be able to see your child?" "How is your family taking the news?" Please, Mr. Nichols, what do you plan to do now?" "What are feeling?" Reporters badgered.

"Please stand back, let him breathe," his lawyer informed. He whispered something in his ear and he nodded. "Mr. Nichols has agreed to release a statement."

Microphones clouded his face. "I would like to move on with my life. I need to move forward and forget about the past. I would greatly appreciate if you could respect my privacy during this time," he declared. His lawyer placed his hand on his back and tried to maneuver him away. The press was relentless and followed them all the way to their car. The video cut out as they were driving away.

I closed my laptop and it made a harsh sound. I threw it on the other couch like it was diseased infected. I paced around my living room trying to focus on something other than him. When that didn't work, I jumped in the shower. I washed and scrubbed my body roughly, wanting to get the imprint of him off my skin; the redder it turned, the harder I would scrub.

"Goddamn it!" I yelled.

"Ugh! I don't understand this. I hate this class. No! I don't hate this class. I hate this material. I mean who talks like this? Why do we need to learn something that was written centuries ago? I'm never going to use this; you know that, right? Its mindless, useless information teachers use to torture their students," I blabbed the word vomit.

He laughed. "You do understand it; you're just being stubborn."

My eyes widened. "I am not. I don't get this and it's stupid. Why are you trying to make me stupider."

"Don't talk about yourself like that. You're very intelligent, I've been helping you for the last two months and you understand the material, Gianna, you just don't care to apply yourself," he remarked.

"You sound exactly like my father. I do apply myself, I'm just not as capable as McKenzie is."

He folded his arms and leaned back on his desk. "What does McKenzie have anything to do with this?" he questioned.

I shook my head and grabbed my pencil. "Nothing. Never mind. Let's keep going. So Shakespeare—"

"G, that won't work with me," he asserted, making me look directly at him. He rarely called me G and when he did, it would send shivers down my spine. The look on his face was always the same, like he could see through me as opposed to at me.

I felt my guard coming down, the wall I created to keep people at bay lowering itself.

I shrugged. "Everyone expects something from me."

He nodded. "I know."

"What do you mean?"

"What do you expect? Huh? What would you like people to see?" he asked.

"I don't know anymore. I don't know if I ever know."

He chuckled. "You know, when you lie, you give yourself away. It's really interesting to witness; you're confident all the time, until you lie. It's your body's defense mechanism. I believe it's so someone calls you out on your bullshit. You're eagerly waiting for someone to call your bluff. Why is that?"

I was taken aback; no one had ever called me out before, not even Jake or Mack. I didn't know how to respond.

He grinned at my discomfort. "There's so much more to you than meets the eye. You should give people the opportunity to get to know the real you. I've had the pleasure of seeing her a few times."

I blushed and turned my face away; I wanted to crawl into an empty space.

"That shade of red looks amazing on you, brings out your eyes," he praised, taking me away from thoughts and back to his eyes. They were now dark and intense, his pupils had dilated. He pushed off his desk and locked eyes with me. He walked to the front of my desk and bent down, his hands grabbing at the ends for balance.

"Shall I compare thee to a summer's day? Thou art more lovely and more temperate: Rough winds do shake the darling buds of May, but thy eternal summer shall not fade, so long as men can breathe, or eyes can see, so long lives this, and this gives life to thee,"[5] he eloquently recited Shakespeare, never taking his eyes away from mine. I licked my dry lips and he followed suit. I wanted to be the one who licked at his lips and the feeling was mutual.

"Want me to tell you what I think it means?"

I fervently nodded.

"It means that love is eternal and it's in the eye of the beholder. A summer's day can transform however the climate may change, and then it will eventually move to another season. While summer may leave, it will always come back, as will the eternal love that they share. As long as both souls are breathing, they are one, because a force bigger than either of them can understand, has them connected for the rest of their lives. And this is the reason for their existence," *he explained and I found myself leaning in, trying to get closer to his lips that I so desperately wanted to taste. He started to lean in and that's when I closed my eyes. I heard the balls of his feet move and I opened them only to witness him getting up and moving away from me.*

Had I just imagined all that?

"Now do you understand Shakespeare?" *he inquired with the lust still evident in his eyes.*

I smiled knowing I didn't imagine it. *"Absolutely."*

Chapter Ten

The holidays came and went and several months had passed. My parents got a divorce two years ago and I blamed myself for it. The trial had doomed us all, and I think that's why my mom was set on keeping him behind bars. It helped her believe that it was all worth something. After the divorce, my mom stayed in North Carolina while my dad moved to Pittsburgh and bought a house on a lake. I didn't know what had become of their marriage, nor did I really care; I had my own demons to deal with. My mom bought me a Lexus IS 250 for Christmas, while my dad bought me a plane ticket to go see him. I took the scheduled flight and we spent Christmas together. I wanted to see my dad but I also wanted to see my baby sister Abby.

"How are you doing, baby?" he inquired, as we sat around the table with the normal festivities I cooked for us.

"I'm all right," I replied, spreading my mashed potatoes around my plate.

"You look tired."

I looked up at him. "Is that your nice way of saying I look like shit?"

His eyes narrowed. "Your sister's at the table, don't talk like that," he ordered. "And of course not. Gianna, I worry about you every single day. I can't tell you how happy I am that you came to spend Christmas with us."

I nodded. "You have a nice place, Dad. You look happy. I mean, I don't know what happened between you and mom, I can only assume." He sadly smiled and I downed my wine.

"You've been drinking a lot since you got here."

"It's the holidays, I'm celebrating," I said, raising my glass. "Here's to a better year for all of us and trying to put the past behind us."

He raised his glass. "I'll toast to that."

We ate dinner in comfortable silence and he helped me clear the table when we finished. I dried my hands on a dishtowel and folded it on the sink.

"Gianna," he said from behind me.

I turned, recognizing that tone immediately. "Yeah, Dad?"

"The drinking…how serious is it? Because from what I gather, it's pretty freaking serious."

"What are you talking about?"

He held up the white trash bag. "There's four wine bottles in here and you've been here for two days."

I shrugged.

"I didn't realize you were like this, Gianna. This stops now. Do you understand me?" he chastised making me feel like a teenager all over again. That was why I stayed away from my parents, especially my dad, he didn't understand me and he never had.

"What are you doing out there in Vegas? Why don't you come and stay here with me for a few months? I could use the help."

I wanted to say yes, but I wanted to drink more, in the end that won out.

"I'm okay. It's the holidays; they make me think too much. That's all."

He tightened his jaw like he did when he was thinking about what I was saying.

"I'm going be checking up on you. This ends now."

I nodded and looked toward the bedrooms, wanting to finish this conversation at all costs. As if reading my mind Abby walked in on her chubby little legs making me laugh. "GG, will you play wif me?" she asked, holding up her baby dolls.

"Of course I'll play with you," I responded, grabbing her hand and making our way to her bedroom.

I felt his eyes and judgment on me the entire time.

I had cleaned up my act some, and by that, I mean I was still doing the same shit, only I became more careful about it. My outside appearance reflected nothing of what I was on the inside. I looked picture perfect and my parents couldn't have been more proud; they finally thought I was getting my life in order. I needed the financial stability that they provided, so I played my part.

I looked like the girl I used to be, carefree. The reflection that portrayed itself back at me was one that I was extremely familiar with, and as much as I wanted to pretend she was back, she wasn't. There was no point in lying to myself like I did to the world. There was no turning back for me and I wouldn't even know where to start, even if I wanted to.

Which I didn't...

I couldn't...

The phone calls and letters for my statement regarding Mr. Nichols' early release started to dwindle down and it wasn't front-page news anymore. It made things a little easier for me. I started answering my phone and actually checking my mail. The press that still followed his case didn't report much. He wasn't doing interviews or taking advantage of his fifteen minutes of fame, which surprised me. I thought the complete opposite would have happened. I wasn't following the case by any means, but the articles that did make it into my view didn't describe any detail on what he was doing with his life.

I knew he would never be able to teach again, but I was still curious about how strict his parole would be. If he had to wear an ankle bracelet and not be closer than several hundred yards from a school or children. I often wondered how fucked up his life was, and if it was better or worse than being in prison.

After Christmas, I started to write in a journal. The headaches and insomnia returned and I decided to write about my feelings. My therapist had suggested it years ago. I'd been writing for the last several months; not regularly, but enough to where there was a crease in the binding and the pages looked worn. Sometimes my writing was deep, and then sometimes I would scribble. It all depended on what mood I was in, what I was willing to share on blank pages, and of course, how intoxicated I was. It was raining outside and I sat on the seat below my bay window. I watched the dark clouds appear as the rain drizzled down on the concrete pavement. I closed my eyes and let my thoughts take over.

"Damn it! It's pouring!" Mack yelled.

"I'm going to shower before heading out, Mack. I feel gross."

"Oh ok, well I'm going to head out. I'm meeting my mom." I nodded at her.

I showered and changed into my white sports bra and black cheer shorts. It was still pouring when I jogged out to my car. I threw my bags in the trunk and started to walk to the driver's seat when I realized Mr. Nichols' truck was still in the parking lot. I smiled and ran up to the building, making my way to his classroom. The door was closed and when I knocked, he gestured for me to come in without looking up from the papers I assumed he was grading. I came in and closed the door behind me.

His face was a mixture of shock and surprise when he looked up at me, and his mouth opened slightly as his eyes roamed my entire body; he wasn't subtle about it.

"Umm...do you have a towel?" I announced, taking him out of his daze of looking me over. I pulled the hair out of my face. "I mean, I'm all wet."

"I see that," he stated, trying to look professional, like he wasn't just ogling my disheveled appearance.

He swallowed hard before getting up to walk to the closet on the other side of the classroom. He grabbed a towel and threw it a few feet away from me. I caught it in midair, with a sly smile on my face. He didn't want to get close to me and I softly giggled.

I placed all my hair on the side of my face and rung it out, and then lightly grazed my body. He sat in his desk chair, trying to keep busy from watching me. He nervously moved around random things on his desk, scattering them everywhere. My wet shoes squeaked on the tile floor as I walked to his desk, and his head rose with caution displayed all over his face. I stopped on the opposite side of his desk and threw the soaked towel in his lap and he laughed.

93

"Thanks," I said.

He nodded. "Can I help you?"

I chuckled. "Yes."

"Miss Edwards, I don't have time to play games. What are you doing here?" he asserted, using his teacher tone, the same tone he used in the classroom and when we were in front of students.

I shrugged and played with the tips of his pencils that were together in a holder. "I came to talk to you about tutoring next week," I explained, peeking up at him through my wet lashes.

"With that attire?" He gestured with his finger. "You're violating dress code I could write you up."

I stopped moving the pencils around. "Right. I'm sorry. I completely forgot. I came right from practice, I wasn't even thinking. I saw your truck still in the parking lot and took a chance that I could let you know about next week. I don't want to get in trouble." He nodded toward the chair behind me.

"I don't need to sit down."

"What about next week?" he prompted.

"Oh! I don't think I'm going to be able to make tutoring."

"Why is that?"

"Well...Jake's in town and..."

"Jake?"

"My boyfriend."

He nodded. "I see."

"Yeah...he's in town and I kinda need to spend time with him."

"So Jake is more important than your studies. I can see where your priorities lie," he reprimanded. There was something in his voice that was new and I didn't recognize it. Jealousy maybe?

"Are you mad?"

"Now why would I be mad, Miss Edwards? I don't have to worry about my grade." He snickered.

"G," I reminded without thinking.

Our eyes locked and I bit my lower lip. We stared at each other for a few minutes, not saying anything. I wanted to know what he was thinking. There were times when I knew with just a look, and then times like this when I had no idea where his head was. He referred to me as "Miss Edwards" when he was trying to show authority over me or make me feel like his student. I hated when he referred to me as that, it was like he was sticking a knife in my heart, and it made me feel like I had imagined all the nice things that happened between us. Those were the times I looked forward to, when all our walls were down.

"There must be something I can do; something we could work out together," I suggested, breaking the silence.

He raised an eyebrow and stopped playing with the red pen in his lap. "Are you asking for special privileges?" he taunted.

His demeanor changed and I recognized it immediately. I got down on my knees in front of his lap and he didn't move an inch, nor did he push me away. If there was any apprehension on his part, then he hid it well. I put my hands on his thighs and watched for any refusal in his eyes. There was none.

"I'm sure there is something I could do."

The knock on my door took me away from my thoughts.

"I'm coming!" I yelled out.

I opened the door to find the UPS man standing there with a package. I signed for it, smiled, and brought it inside with me. I placed it on the table and realized that there was no return label on. I ripped it open and pulled out the contents. There was a 5x7 picture of me and Mack cheering at one of the last games before we got kicked off the team. I hadn't realized I was crying until a tear landed on the picture.

We looked happy.

We landed in New York to do a campus tour at Julliard. The school we both anxiously awaited our acceptance letter for. We planned to go to this school since we started cheerleading and there were no other options for either of us. It was Julliard or nothing.

"What the fuck did you pack? I can't grab it," Mack yelled.

"Oh my God! I can't grab it either," I replied, watching my bag move around the baggage claim.

"Fuck...we suck," she said, laughing.

95

"We totally do. Okay, this time when it comes back around, you grab the back and I'll grab the front," I proposed and she nodded, trying not to laugh.

"There! It's right there!" she shouted.

We both ran for it simultaneously before it got away from us again.

"Hell yeah it worked." I celebrated and we high fived.

"Now what?"

"Ummm...I don't know...get a taxi?"

"We suck at this. We shouldn't travel on our own. It's not going to end well."

"Let me call Jake, he will know." I grabbed my phone and dialed the number.

"Hey, baby," he answered.

"Hey! So we just landed; where do we find a cab?"

"Outside."

"Right...but do we just go up to one or do we have to wait in line somewhere?" I questioned and I could hear him laughing on the other end.

"Dude, you guys cannot travel alone."

"Shut up!"

"Yes, go outside and there should be a cab service somewhere, you're in New York, babe, there are cabs everywhere."

"Okay." I gestured with my hand for her follow me. *"We want to find some weed."* I could hear her laughing behind me.

"Where are you going to find that?" he questioned.

"I don't know; we're just going to ask someone."

"That's pretty illegal."

"No, we have a plan. Mack is going to ask them if they're a cop first." She looked at me and we both started laughing.

"And that's supposed to do what?"

"By law they have to answer." She nodded, agreeing with what I was saying.

"I'm pretty sure that's a myth."

We stood in line for a few minutes but it was fairly easy to find a cab. The driver said it would be thirty minutes to our hotel. I talked to him for a while, trying to break the awkward silence, while Mack just stared out the window.

Why the hell was she being so quiet?

"Are you a cop?" she announced out of nowhere and my eyes widened. I knew we had talked about it, but I never thought she would actually go through with it.

"Ummm...no." He laughed. "Why?"

"Where can we get some green? You know, weed?" I shook my head and tried not to laugh while Mack was so nonchalant about it.

"Oh wow! You guys are in New York; this is land of the plenty. Welcome to the city. How much you guys looking for? I'll hook it up."

We all started laughing. That was me and Mack, completely random and highly amusing. Only we understood each other and that's what made our bond so strong. We definitely knew each other in a past life.

I grabbed the tape from my drawer and taped the picture to my fridge. It made me smile and I missed Mack terribly. It was easy to pick up the phone and dial her number; the hard part was not hanging up before it rang. There was so much I wanted to tell her, so much I wanted to explain. There wasn't a day that went by when something would happen to me that I didn't want to call and tell her about, knowing she would be the only one to understand. I often wondered if she thought about me...she had to miss me. Our friendship and love for each other wasn't something I imagined, everyone saw it. I looked in the envelope making sure nothing else remained. There was another picture but this one was of us at homecoming. We were dancing with each other.

My feet were throbbing from my shoes. I knew the heels were too high, but Mack insisted that these were the perfect shoes to wear with my dress to Homecoming. We had been drinking since the limo picked us up and I was slightly intoxicated. Jake and I were all over each other, kissing, groping, and dancing our asses off on the dance floor. I mingled with everyone just as I was expected to do. Mack and I kept sneaking off into the bathroom to take the shooters we had in our purses. She was as drunk as I was but she was able to hide it better. I think I thrived with alcohol; it made it easier to be who I was.

Jake went off to go score some liquor for the after party at Logan's house. Mack had been dancing with Brandon and that's when I took the opportunity to get some air. I wanted to get away from all the fake people I called my friends, the social circle everyone wanted to be a part of. I took off my shoes and picked up my dress, wanting to go to the only place I ever felt successful at. I sat in the football stands, taking in the atmosphere of the lavish green grass and the smell of fresh cut grass. The overhead lights causing us to be the center of attention, which I loathed but no one would believe me. The stands that held the uproar of proud parents were now quiet and peaceful. Nothing in this world compared to being on the sidelines, cheering for my team while my school watched and praised.

I sat on the fifth bleacher and rubbed my feet. "You look beautiful."

I recognized the voice and looked down and smiled. "You don't look so bad yourself, Mr. Nichols." I narrowed my eyes and cocked my head. "Did you follow me out here?"

"What do you think?" he replied with a hint of teasing in his voice.

"Yes."

"Would that be appropriate?" he confessed, trying to keep the smile at bay.

"Are you ever appropriate?" I simply asked.

He finally laughed, breaking the façade. "Is there room for me to sit next to you?"

I looked back at the empty bleachers. "Hmmm…I don't know," I teased.

He sat next to me and we looked up at the sky. "I'm going to miss this school. Is it weird that I'm sort of scared to go to college? Mack is so confident about everything that sometimes it's hard for me to relate. I try to keep her enthusiasm but I'm nervous about the real world. I don't want to disappoint anyone, especially my dad," I revealed.

That was the beauty of being around him, I was able to open up to him and tell him things I would never or could ever say to anyone else. He never made me feel vulnerable and always understood where I was coming from.

"That's an understandable fear."

"Yeah. My dad has been especially hard on me these last few years, more so than my mom. He is always comparing me to Mack, and sometimes I feel like I can't keep up. I mean, I've always felt like that. But it's gotten worse." I placed the hair that was in my face behind my ear, I wanted him to see me.

The real me.

"Sometimes I feel like he wishes that Mack was his daughter. Is that horrible to think? I mean, I know he loves me, but I don't see pride in his face like I do when he looks at Mack. Even when he talks about her it's different. His voice changes and his smile is wide the entire time. When he talks about me, it's as if he has to, not because he wants to."

He nodded in understanding.

"I mean, I love Mack, she's my sister. We have all these plans; I just don't want to mess them up. And the last thing I want is to let anyone down."

"What do you want, G?"

I smiled and breathed out a puff of air. "I want to travel the world." I nervously laughed, sharing something with him that I had never told anyone.

"I want to see everything I read about in books. And taste all sorts of different food and not worry what it will do to my figure. I want to wake up every morning and not look in the mirror and wonder who is looking back at me." I whimpered, trying to hold back the tears. I felt my eyes start to water.

I raised my eyebrow. "I want to fall in love. Not "I love you, I love you too," love. I mean mind consuming, can't live without you, soul devouring love."

He positioned his hand on top of mine that was in my lap in a comforting way. "There is so much more to you than meets the eye. What's so wrong with this person?"

"I've lied to everyone since I can remember. I can't go back now. It's too late."

He shook his head. "No, it's most definitely not. The drinking isn't you, G." I pulled in my lips. "You don't think I can tell? I mean, do you honestly want your boyfriend to touch you like that in front of people? What do you think people are thinking when you put on a show like that?"

I shrugged my shoulders.

"You aren't this perfect persona that you try to make everyone see, and the fact that I'm the first person to call you out on it worries me." I shrugged again.

"I want to be free. I want to feel like I do when I'm with you all the time," I confessed, making my eyes widen in surprise of what I just shared with him.

"Oh my God, I'm sorry–I mean–I–" He put his thumb on my lip, shushing me.

"I want to feel like that, too," he revealed, catching me completely off guard.

"Saying things like this, G, could get both of us, especially me, in a lot of trouble," he disclosed, never taking his eyes from my lips.

"The way you're looking at me could also get us in a lot of trouble. Especially me, because I have no will power when it comes to you."

He breathed in my words that obviously caught him off guard. "Miss Edwards..." he warned in a conflicting tone.

"G."

He licked his lips and groaned. "I better go," he said, standing up.

I quickly grabbed his hand and pulled him back toward me. We both looked down on our interlocked fingers.

"I–" he said.

"Gianna." I heard a shout from afar. It was Jake.

"Shit," I shouted.

"Go," he ordered. I looked down at our hands one last time before I let go.

I ran as quickly as I could.
Not toward Jake.
But…away from Mr. Nichols.

Chapter Eleven

I tried to open my eyes.

At first I thought I was dreaming; my head felt heavy and my body even heavier, the room felt like it was spinning. I was lightheaded, and even though I had just woken up, I was tired, exhausted even. I slowly moved my head side-to-side, trying to wake up. It was then that I realized there was something on my eyes keeping me from being able to see or open them. I tried to say something but nothing came out. My mouth was bonded by what I could only assume was tape. I wanted to scream, I should've felt fear, but I was drained of any emotion. I allowed it to take over and passed out.

I awoke again, but this time I was less hazed and I recognized immediately that my displacement had not changed. I was in the exact same place I was before. There were binds that had my hands tied and held together above my head, and my feet and thighs were tied as well. I wanted to scream, but it came out as a muffled shriek. I didn't care and I tried it again and again until my throat burned from the vibrations. My fight instinct kicked in and I moved rapidly, trying to break free from the binds. I did that until my body couldn't anymore and I was sweating profusely. I lay there and tried to recall how I could've found myself in that situation, breathing heavily. I couldn't remember anything and my last memory was of being home.

I should have been crying, and I couldn't tell if I was in shock because I didn't feel anything. I was numb. It was then that I felt the back of a hand touch the side of my face and I froze, not moving one muscle. My mind went into overload; someone had been with me the entire time. They watched the turmoil I just exhibited and didn't make a sound.

Who does that?

His hand was still on the side of my face and hadn't moved. It was comforting and creepy all at the same time. My breathing was labored and my heart was racing. Questions started to arise in my mind, one right after the other.

Who are you? What do you want with me? Are you going to hurt me?

I knew it had to have been a male; the hand on my face was large and rough. Other than that, I didn't have a clue as to who would've wanted to take me. If it was just for sex, I would've probably given it to him; I would've also let him tie me up if that's what he was in to.

Before I could continue with my mindless thoughts, the tape was roughly pulled from my mouth and I screamed out in pain. All the illusions of this possibly being a dream became a nightmare within seconds.

"What do you want?" I blurted out, trying to seem fearless. People can only hurt you if you let them and I learned that a long time ago.

The next thing I knew, the back of a hand was hitting me across the face like he knew what I was thinking.

I groaned in pain, and without thinking, I reacted. "What the fuck? What do you want?" Again, I was hit across the face before the words even left my mouth.

That time, tears streamed down my face. "Please stop…just tell me what you want…" Once again, I was hit in the same spot, and even though I knew it was impossible, I swear I saw stars through the blindfold. My stomach felt sick and my body recoiled. I wanted to avoid passing out, terrified he would do something to me. My head hung low; I didn't have the strength or ability to hold it up anymore.

I shuddered when I felt his hand caress the cheekbone that he hit repeatedly; it was gentle and tender as he smoothly ran it up and down. My breathing was elevated and I couldn't control the tears and confusion that were pouring out of my shaken body.

"Shhh…" he whispered.

At first, I thought I imagined it, but then I heard it again. "Shhh…" It was low and vibrant.

"Shhh…"

That sound would forever be embedded in my mind. I didn't dare say another word. The simple, yet, powerful sound of what he was implying burrowed deep among my bones and made itself at home. His hand hadn't moved from my cheek, as he continued to caress it in a back and forth motion. I wanted to scream or say something, but I was not ready for the repercussions.

His hand moved away and I instantly missed it. It was replaced with what felt like a cold washcloth. He ran it over my face and neck, and it was soothing. It provided me with a false sense of reassurance, even if it was only for a few minutes. I let myself think that everything was going to be okay. He left the washcloth on my injured cheek and water began to drip to my lips. I promptly closed my mouth shut, not wanting to swallow anything he was giving me. Not even a moment later, my nose was pinched closed and I instinctively opened my mouth for air. The thought of him wanting to suffocate me presented itself and I was shaken. Water dripped into my mouth and it was then that I understood he was asking me to drink. As soon as I attempted to swallow, he let go of my nose and I took as much water into my mouth as possible.

I was starving for it, and at that point, I realized that I had no say in what would happen and I needed to follow instructions. The dehydration was apparent and I didn't care that it was getting all over my upper body and the mattress behind me. I took in every ounce of what he was giving, completely greedy for it. When the water stopped, I closed my mouth to enjoy the moisture that replaced the dryness. I didn't have time to revel in it before I heard the sound of duct tape being ripped. I was pushed into the mattress with a knee on my chest and sternly grabbed by my chin to keep me in place. The duct tape was placed on my mouth and the sensitive skin was evident when it was pressed into place.

I waited for his next move as my heart raced and hysteria threatened. The bed dipped and I stiffened when I felt air brushing my face, no, that wasn't air, it was breathing. It was labored and relaxed, satisfied even.

"Shhh…" he murmured in my ear, causing goose bumps to cover my entire body.

"Those lips that Love's own hand did make breathed forth the sound that said 'I hate', to me that languished for her sake: 'I hate' she altered with an end, that followed it as gentle day, doth follow night, who like a fiend from heaven to hell is flown away. 'I hate', from hate away she threw, and saved my life, saying 'not you,'"[6] he whispered.

The bed dipped again and I heard footsteps, and then a door closed and locked. I took a deep breath expecting it relieve some nervousness and anxiety. It didn't work.

He had finally found me…

I sat on a dock outside that overlooked the lake. My parents had dragged me to this wedding and it had just started. I'd stolen a bottle of wine from the bartender when he wasn't looking. I didn't have a glass so I had to drink it straight out of the bottle. I turned when I heard footsteps behind me, terrified it was my dad.

I smiled. "What are you doing here?"

"I thought that was you," he acknowledged, taking a seat next to me.

"You should take your shoes off, the water feels great."

He nodded and proceeded to take off his shoes and socks. "It does feel great," he affirmed, swishing his feet along the water, knocking them into mine so I would do the same.

"I know the groom from college. I actually grew up in this town and I couldn't wait to get out." He must've seen the confused look on my face, wondering why he was there.

"Oh," I said, not knowing how to answer. He had never shared anything with me before and I wanted to take in every word.

"Your parents know you're out here?"

I shook my head no.

"I bet they don't know you're drinking either?"

I smiled and shook my head no again.

"Miss Edwards, you're just trouble with a capital T, aren't you?"

I laughed. "Not entirely. What are you doing out here?"

"I'm not big on weddings. It's for everyone else. You end up spending all this money on a day you hardly remember because you're

the guest of honor and everyone wants to talk to you or take pictures. I barely even remember my wedding, I hate being the center of attention, but Sarah insisted on a big wedding and our parents expected it from us.

I sighed; I didn't want to talk about his wife or marriage.

"Want to drink?" I asked, taking a huge gulp, wanting to erase what I had just heard.

"I think I should take the bottle away from you."

"Oh! Come on. We aren't on school property so technically you're not my teacher right now. You should live a little Mr. Nichols, it keeps you young."

He laughed. "Oh...is that what does?" He shoved my shoulder with his. "Give me the bottle."

"Ugh! Party pooper." I took a few quick swigs before he pulled it away from my mouth, making me laugh and spray half of it out onto his hands and face, which only made me laugh harder. He started to laugh at my silliness and wipe away the wine from his face and I did the same to mine.

"You missed a spot," he said as he swiped at my cheek. He let his hand linger for a second, then made a noise in the back of his throat and quickly moved it away.

"You know I'm breaking all sorts of rules and regulations right now," he observed.

"Eh. I won't tell if you don't. Secrets are fun."

He chuckled. "What are you doing out here?"

"I don't know. I can't stand to be around my parents right now. My dad is just...I don't know and these kinds of weddings are so lavish and cliché. I would do a destination wedding in some please exotic like Tahiti where only he and I share our vows."

He nodded and grinned. "That's exactly how I would have done it."

"Where's your wife?" I blurted, catching him off guard.

"We're separated. We've actually been separated since a few weeks after school started."

"Oh." I looked at him with wide eyes. "Why?"

"We've been together since we were kids. We actually grew up together, our families expected us to get married and so we did. Things have been rough the last few years. We had Cara thinking that it would help, and now three years later it's still the same."

"Do you love her?" Jesus...I had word vomit.

He nervously chuckled, swishing his feet around again in the water.

"I do–" he paused "–but–"

"I understand," I interrupted. I knew exactly what he was going to say, he didn't have to say the words. It was how I felt about Jake.

"It's weird to think you're a dad. You don't act like an adult," I teased, trying to change the subject.

"Is that a good thing or bad?" he inquired, looking relieved.

"It's good. I know that's why all the students at school like you so much. You're easy to talk to."

"I remember what it was like being your age. It's tough," he simply replied with a charismatic smile.

"You're not that much older than me. And...I'm eighteen; I'm an adult, too."

"Nah, a decade isn't that much older," he retorted and we laughed.

Smartass.

"Your dad just wants what's best for you, you know? It's what any father wants for their little girl."

"I'm not a little girl," I stated, looking directly into his eyes.

"Oh yeah?" He placed a piece of hair behind my ear and his knuckles grazed my cheek.

"What am I going to do with you, G?" he whispered.

"Anything you want," I instinctively replied.

My chest heaved up and down and my breathing became erratic. I closed my eyes waiting for him to kiss me. He had to kiss me...I knew he felt it, too. There was no denying it.

Instead, I felt his forehead lean against mine and I opened my eyes to find that his were closed. He looked lost–in thought, in life, in everything. I recognized the look on his face because it matched the look on mine. The face that I only shared with the mirror when I stared at my reflection and I knew no one else could see it but me.

We were exactly the same. I knew in that moment that he was as lost as I was and our lives crashed together for a reason.

Everything happens for a reason, and he was my reason.

I woke up screaming from the duct tape being ripped off my face again. It sounded muffled and strangled from the dryness in my mouth. I had no recollection of how much time had passed, and the blindfold made it harder to distinguish if it was night or day. I wanted to keep screaming, but my face was sore and stung and there was no doubt a bruise on my cheek. He didn't make a sound as I tried to twist and turn to remove some of the discomfort I felt from being tied up. I couldn't see anything, not his face, not where I was, not one thing. I thrashed when I felt his hands on my ties, not wanting him to touch me. He slapped my face, not hard this time, just enough to get me to stop.

I was frozen, immobile again. He was close to me, closer than he had been before, and I could smell his scent. It was intoxicating to me; consumed every part of me, including my arousal. I was covered in sweat, and the heat coursing its way through my body made it apparent how badly I wanted him to touch me. I could feel my nipples harden and my skin tingle. Although I couldn't see, I knew he was staring at me, I could feel his eyes wander around every part of me, and he knew what I felt and what he was doing to me. I didn't want any part of it, but my body's reaction to his touch proved that he still had power over me.

He could control me.

He still owned me.

Body, heart and soul.

His grip tightened around my wrist, and my first thought was that he was going to hurt me. He was going to tie them tighter and cut off more of my circulation. But he didn't, he massaged them, trying to relieve my discomfort. I turned my head to the side, away from him as hot tears made their way down my face. He was being kind to me, although I would much rather prefer his hatred than his kindness.

His forefinger and thumb rubbed at the most sensitive part of where the bindings were cutting and I moaned. Even though I couldn't see his face, I knew he was smiling. He was enjoying what he was doing to me and I hated him for it.

"Please..." I whispered, "Please..."

He immediately stopped. I knew he was fighting some internal battle with himself, his demons, and I was one of them. He sneered and moved away, and I could finally breathe, my body returned to me, to its rightful owner. The same process as before was repeated. However, this time he fed me warm oatmeal. My stomach was sensitive with every swallow I took. In the back of my mind, I was well aware that if I didn't get alcohol in my body soon, I was going to start to go through withdrawal.

The last time I went through withdrawal I thought I was dying. I felt like I was dying. I didn't last more than a few hours before I was taking my next drink. I could hear the tape being ripped and before I could stop myself, I pleaded, "Please..."

I wouldn't scream; he knew I wouldn't. He didn't make a sound, contemplating what I was asking I'm sure. I took a chance and repeated it again. There was eeriness in the room everywhere; it was thick and cold. There was a power struggle happening and I nervously awaited the results. When the bed dipped, I knew I had won, and I silently smiled to myself.

Once I heard the door being locked, I welcomed the darkness with open arms, allowing myself to slip back into dreams of the man I once knew.

Chapter Twelve

Jake opened the car door for me. "Thanks, babe."

"Of course," he replied as we walked inside the restaurant.

He still took me to those expensive dinners that I didn't care anything about, but I didn't tell him otherwise.

"Reservation for Jake Henderson," he told the hostess and she nodded, grabbing menus and telling us to follow her.

We were led through a corridor of booths and seated right by the window that overlooked the entire city.

"Wow, it's beautiful," I stated.

"Not as beautiful as you," he praised, making me smile.

We ordered our appetizers and I ordered a club soda while Jake indulged in a vodka tonic. I listened to him tell me about his classes and all the new and exciting things he had coming up and pretended to absorb every word. That was until I saw him.

He walked in with an adorable little girl in his arms and a woman not far behind him. She was beautiful; her blond, curly hair cascaded down her back and she was wearing a tight fitted, black dress. They were seated a few booths away from us and I was directly in his field of vision. I looked back at Jake who was still lost in his story about one of his fraternity brothers getting arrested; I nodded and pretended I was still listening.

But I wasn't listening at all; my eyes and thoughts were to the table a few feet away from me. The little girl was sitting on his lap coloring, completely entertained as he talked to the woman. They were exchanging laughs and when I saw her hand raise to caress his cheek, it took everything in me to not go over there and rip her hand off. I witnessed all the subtle glances that they gave each other and I just knew that his hand was on her thigh. When he whispered something in her ear, she blushed and teasingly flipped her hair to the side.

A thousand emotions made their way through my body.

He was a liar.

Just like me.

I didn't know how long I sat there and watched their performance of a happily married couple enjoying a night out, but it was long enough that I felt sick to my stomach. I reached over to grab Jake's drink and took it down in one gulp. He was shocked and I provocatively smiled, scooting closer to him.

"Sorry, I was thirsty," I stated, trying to brush off his confusion.

"I see that."

I placed my hand on his thigh and kissed his neck like I knew he loved. "I miss you. I don't like it when you're away from me," I lied, trying to erase the images of him and his family from my brain.

"I miss you too, baby."

I grabbed his chin, turning his face to me and kissed him. I kissed him with everything I had, I kissed him like I hadn't seen him in forever, I kissed him like I hadn't just spent the last two days with him, I kissed him like he was everything and anything, I kissed him like he owned me.

I kissed him like he was Mr. Nichols.

He groaned and grabbed the back of my neck like he couldn't get me close enough to him, and that's when I opened my eyes. They immediately locked with Mr. Nichols'. The look on his face said everything I wanted to see. The hurt, anger, and jealously seethed from him. Which only made me kiss Jake with more passion and luster.

"Baby, Jesus, Gianna, what's gotten into you?" he huskily grumbled, pulling away from me.

We ordered our main courses and the entire time we were waiting for them, I flirted, enticed, and seduced Jake, knowing that Mr. Nichols was watching it all. After dinner, I excused myself to the restroom and kissed Jake lovingly before leaving. I walked right past his table, never looking at him or paying him any mind. It was like he wasn't there and didn't exist. I closed the door behind me and right before I was about to lock it, it was roughly pushed opened. I stepped back and watched as he locked the door, leaning his forehead on it before turning to face me. It was like he needed those first few seconds to contemplate what he was about to do.

"What the fuck?" I yelled, boiling with anger.

"Watch your mouth," he retorted, making me even more pissed.

"Fuck you."

It took him three strides before he was in front of me, grabbing me by the throat and pushing me up against the wall. I didn't cower down and held my head high, matching his intense, fuming gaze the entire time.

"What was that?" he questioned with clenched teeth.

"I'm out with my boyfriend while you're out with your wife."

"It's not what it looks like."

"You expect me to believe that? You're a liar! You lied to me. I have never lied to you! You're the only person I have never lied to. How could you do this to me?" I shouted, trying to hold back the tears that I could feel in my throat.

"G–"

"Don't fucking call me that! You're never allowed to call me that again!" I threatened, forcing myself not to react to his hand around my neck that was making my knees weak and my pussy throb.

"Calm down and let me explain. You're acting like a child."

"I am a child! Isn't that what you like to tell me?! Isn't that how you think of me, just some child that you can lie to and play with! That's all I am to you, someone you can fuck with!" I roared and he gripped my throat tighter.

"That's not what this is, G. It's fucked up, I am your teacher and you're my student. Do you have any idea how much trouble I could get in?"

"I'm eighteen," I reminded.

"It doesn't matter."

"What do you want?" I interjected, not having the patience to keep playing these games.

He loosened his hold as he struggled with his response before placing his forehead on mine. "Stop asking questions you already know the answers to." I stilled, not expecting that to be his answer.

We stood there, both of us breathing heavily, completely consumed with one another, with our eye contact strong, with the chemistry screaming at us.

"Do you want this?" he asked after a long silence. "Because once we cross this line there is no going back. Do you understand me? You're mine," he demanded, once again gripping my throat.

"Please..."

His mouth collided with mine with such force that my head hit the wall. I was dizzy with the heat rising in my core. That was what I've wanted and needed for so long, and when I felt his tongue make contact with mine, I shamelessly moaned. His hold around my neck tightened while he pushed his cock firmer against my pussy like he could read my mind.

"God, you taste and feel exactly how I've dreamed," he admitted as an involuntary sound escaped his lips.

"If I profane with my unworthiest hand. This holy shrine, the gentle fine is this: My lips, two blushing pilgrims, ready stand, to smooth that rough touch with a tender kiss,"[7] he recited, with love and longing.

Being that close to him wasn't nearly enough for me, I wanted him inside me, and not just sexual. I was mad for him, desperate and feverish. I wanted the good with the bad; I was losing myself to him and this ecstasy we created. I knew I would never be the same after this kiss. He owned me, he always had. I quivered at the thought of being his, only his.

His movements grew more demanding and urgent. We were both running on pure lust, impulse, instinct, and abandonment; everything felt right. It didn't matter what surrounded itself around us because we were one and the same. That night, in that bathroom, we lost ourselves to something neither one of us understood or could control. The universe had decided it for us.

I loved him.

He was my person.

My soul mate, my one and only.

He was the first to break our kiss, our connection, and I whimpered at the loss. I didn't want to go back to pretending. I didn't want to be that person anymore. I wanted to ask him so many questions, there were a million thoughts carousing in my mind. I stayed silent, not wanting to ruin the moment, and I silently prayed that this wouldn't be our last time together. He wouldn't be that cruel to give me a taste of him and then take it away. Would he?

I had to trust him.

We composed ourselves and went back to our lives. I wanted to kick and scream and drag my feet. If he had asked me to leave with him, to run away with him, I would have done it in a heartbeat, no questions asked. He had to know that right? He understood me and could see me for who I really was? That was the beauty about him. I was in a place between heaven and hell, a devil and angel on each shoulder. The only choice I had was to sit back and enjoy the ride of this emotional roller coaster.

I sat back at the table with Jake and I should have told him, I should have ended things with him right then and there, but I couldn't. I was scared of disappointing everyone and that made me a coward. I continued to be what everyone wanted me to be because that's all I knew.

But when you play with fire, you're bound to get burned.

"Baby, you all right?" Jake questioned, taking me away from the ramblings in my mind.

"Uh, yeah...I'm fine."

"Here take a bite of this chocolate cake," he offered, bringing the spoon to my mouth.

The chocolaty goodness melted upon contact with my tongue. But I couldn't swallow, why couldn't I swallow? My breathing had stopped, I couldn't breathe! I was choking...how was I choking? That's not what happened. I don't remember that happening! What's going on?

I'm dying...

My eyes opened and I was choking. I couldn't breathe! Fuck, I was going to die from my own vomit. I turned my head to the side, trying to get it out of the back of my throat, but there was no use. Tears streamed down the sides of my face at the realization that I was going to die from alcohol withdrawal, and then I heard the locked door open and being slammed shut. I couldn't see anything and it caused more paranoia. I heard shuffling and then rope being cut. My arms immediately fell by the top of my head and then there was more rope being cut. I couldn't move; my limbs were asleep from lack of my movement. Strong arms picked me up and I was turned onto my stomach. My back was hit repeatedly and chunks of vomit made their way out of my mouth.

After what felt like hours, I gasped for the first time and I had hope that I wasn't going to die tied to a bed with a blindfold over my eyes, while my *captor* decides what to do with me. I threw up everything I had in my stomach and my body finally gave out on me, making me fall face first, right next to my vomit. I felt relieved, but that didn't stop the shame from creeping in. I was literally lying next to a pool of my own puke; the blindfold intensified my senses and the smell of it made me want to throw up all over again.

I just lay there in a state of shock, trying to not think about the fact that he was sitting right next to me, and I knew I had to be a pathetic sight. The sensations in my legs returned first and then my arms quickly followed, they tingled all over, almost like the feeling of when you're trying to keep your foot from falling asleep. I could shake them and bring back the movement quicker, but I was mortified and praying that he thought I had passed out or something. I didn't want him to see me like this. I didn't want to remove the blindfold because then it would make it real. He really kidnapped me, and I really almost died, and now I was pitifully lying next to my puke. I knew he was staring at me, contemplating what to do next. I'm positive I had ruined his plans.

In the forefront of my mind, I kept thinking that I needed alcohol, I was going to start shaking soon, and a seizure wouldn't be far away. How the fuck would I explain that to him?

"I know you're not sleeping," he stated, taking away my false security.

Asshole.

"You've been sleeping for the last two days and I can tell the difference in your breathing."

Several minutes went by and I didn't move or say one damn word.

"This is a surprise. You don't have anything to say? Not going to try to manipulate your way out of this? I mean, that's what you're good at. Where's Gianna, huh? Where's Queen B?" he patronized.

"Get up! You fucking smell and you've puked all over yourself."

I didn't move and he kicked the bed with his foot.

"Get the fuck up or I will make you get up, and trust me, you do not want that to happen," he roared, making me swallow the awful taste in my mouth from anxiety.

I didn't recognize his voice.

I didn't know the man before me.

And for the first time since this whole ordeal...

I was terrified.

Chapter Thirteen

I laid there and tried to shake off the nervousness. I was hoping he'd get angrier and just give up and leave the room. But the G part of me, the part that I tried to ignore, the part of me that still belonged to him, that he still owned, wanted him to touch me; to make me do it because then at least he would have been touching me, and I wanted so badly to have his hands on me. How fucked up was that?

I waited for his next command, trying to internalize everything I was feeling, but I knew he could smell it on me. My desire for him, even after all those years, was still just as strong, if not stronger. I heard his footsteps and then felt the tips of his fingers drag from my ankles up to my calves and thighs; he stopped right at the edge of my panty line. His two fingers lightly tapped back and forth, and I shuddered.

"Isn't this what you want, Miss Edwards?" he asked, reading my mind, exactly like I knew he would.

I didn't answer. I didn't know what I was supposed to say and God help me, I wanted him to keep going.

"Hmmm…" he hummed, and then harshly slapped my pussy. "When I ask you a question, I expect a goddamn answer," he clarified, and then slapped it again. "Isn't this what you want? What you've always wanted…MY FUCKING ATTENTION!" he yelled, slapping my pussy over and over again, awakening an ache that had me withering beneath his touch.

I couldn't take it anymore as my body continued to betray me. "Yes! I wanted your fucking attention! That's all I ever wanted!" I screamed.

"Watch your fucking mouth, Miss Edwards!"

I heard the sound of the belt before I felt it crudely hit the backs of my thighs. I bit the inside of my cheek, trying to suppress the scream, not wanting to give him more satisfaction to what he was doing to me. The belt hit my calves next and I scratched at the mattress, next it was my feet that got hit repeatedly, and I bit my cheek so hard I tasted blood. It wasn't until he hit my back over and over that had me screaming and begging for him to stop.

"Awe...come on, don't you want to play? Ten lashes per year that I spent in prison, that seems fair to start off, don't you think?" he threatened, striking me a few more times.

"FUCK YOU!" I yelled, making him hit me harder.

I knew he was starting to draw blood because I felt it coming down my sides and that's when he stopped. All I could hear was our erratic breathing.

"Is that any way to talk to your teacher? Where is your respect?" he jested, breaking the silence. "Who am I, Miss Edwards? Don't make me ask you twice."

I hesitated for a second. "Mr. Nichols."

"No...not Mr. Nichols. Who am I? I know you want to say it. Here is your chance...call me by my name, just like you love to do."

I whimpered. "I don't want to play these games. Just do what you want." My stomach churned and I could practically taste the bile at the bottom of my throat, not from what had just occurred, but from my body wanting its nourishment.

The only thing that ever kept me going.

I felt cold metal on my back and I froze. I heard fabric being cut and realized that he was cutting off the only clothing I had on. The solitary comfort he allowed me was now being stripped away. Once he was done, there was no movement or sound for several minutes and I wondered if he was admiring my body.

"Get up," he demanded out of nowhere. I moved slowly, not wanting to upset my stomach, and the second I stood, I fell to the floor. With my ass in the air and my forehead resting on the concrete floor, I rubbed the clamminess and sweat from my forehead with the back of my arm.

"Get up!" he shouted, making me jump.

I braced myself on the side of the bed and used all the energy I could muster to pick myself up off the floor, and immediately grabbed my stomach once I was standing.

"Are you hungry?" he asked and I chuckled at his reasoning of what was wrong. I shook my head no.

"Walk," he ordered.

I stumbled on my feet the first few steps. "I can't see."

"Just fucking walk straight until I tell you otherwise," he ordered and I nodded.

We made our way out of the room and walked through what seemed like a long hallway. I couldn't see a damn thing in front of me, but the stench in the air made my nauseous state even worse. I heard him open a door and then I instantly smelled the outside. Fresh air!

"Where are we going?" I asked, nervous that he was going to kill me and dump me in the woods somewhere.

He grabbed my hair, pulling my neck back. "Did I say you could talk?" he chastised in my ear.

He let go with a hard shove and I almost fell to my knees. "Walk."

I tried to keep the pace that made him stop shoving me, but I only made it a few more steps before I fell to the ground. I couldn't control it and heaved bile and liquid that smelled horrid.

"What the fuck is going on? I thought you were throwing up before from shock. What's wrong?" he asked me.

"Alcohol...I need a drink. Please..." I breathed out between my dry heaves.

"What the fuck? Why?"

"I'm an alcoholic..." I confessed. It was the first time I had ever shared that with anyone, it may have been the first time I had admitted it to myself out loud. "My body is going through withdrawal and if I don't get a drink soon, I could have a seizure and go into shock. So unless you feel like killing me today, I could die," I explained, spitting out the ruminants from my mouth.

"Why the fuck are you an alcoholic?"

I followed his voice and looked up at him through the blindfold. "Why the fuck do you think?"

"Get up," he commanded. His tone changed, it was much darker. Angrier.

"I can't…it hurts to move…please…" I begged and started to cry. I couldn't help it. My body was physically giving up on me.

"Get the fuck up!" he yelled, not caring or sympathizing.

"Ahhh!!" I screamed, trying to compose myself enough to stand. I stood, grabbed my stomach, and leaned over.

"Walk. We're almost there."

We walked for what felt like miles. My bones were stiff from not moving them for days; the withdrawal made it worse and more intense.

"Stop," he said from behind me.

That's all it took, I stopped for a second and fell to the ground in pain, going straight into a fetal position.

"Miss Edwards," he belittled from above me.

I hated it when he called me that and he knew it.

He slowly removed the blindfold from my eyes but I kept them closed. I didn't want to look at him; if I did, then this whole ordeal was real. I wasn't ready to come to that realization. I couldn't look into the eyes of someone I thought I knew; he wasn't there anymore, and looking at him would crush me.

"Ugh…" I let out and rolled onto my back, gasping for air as my chest heaved up and down. I'm sure I was quite a naked site. I could feel the blinding sun on my eyelids and it instantly caused my head to pound.

"Gianna," he whispered, trying to get my attention. "Look at me."

I shook my head no.

"Open. Your. Eyes." I continued to shake my head no.

The unexpected, freezing cold water on my breasts bolted my body to a sitting position and my eyes immediately opened. I had to block the sun from my eyes with my arm; I thought my irises were on fire. It took a few seconds for my vision to finally adjust to the sunlight and I looked around, noticing I was in an empty field with a creek a few feet in front of me. *I guess that's where I will be bathing.*

I took a deep breath and looked in the direction of my *captor*. I stared at his feet and saw his work boots first, and then I slowly worked my way up his body. He was wearing jeans and a white V-neck shirt, his muscles tightly fit around the sleeves and his torso. He was much bigger than he had been before, he must have spent most of his time in prison working out.

He looked older, there were soft wrinkles around his eyes but it only added to his appeal. His hair was longer and more pieces fell around his face, framing it. He was as handsome as ever, even more so. I quickly wondered how his appearance worked out for him in prison. And that's when it clicked...he was going to punish me for what I did.

For what we did.

Is Mack here, too? Has he taken both of us?

"I'm sorry," I confessed. The words left my mouth before I even realized I had said them.

He narrowed his dark blue eyes at me, they were blank, lifeless, and empty, there was no emotion behind them. However, I did see some remnant of the man I used to know, his eyes flashed with forgiveness and just as fast as it appeared, it disappeared.

I hated him.

For everything.

"Get up," he commanded, never taking his eyes off mine.

"I can't," I replied with sincerity.

He threw a bar of soap on the ground next to me and gestured toward the creek. He was going to allow me to bathe myself, and despite my repulsive appearance and smell, it was the last thing I wanted to do. I grabbed the bar of soap and crawled toward the water. I couldn't stand up and I knew damn well he wasn't going to help me. My hands were the first thing that touched the freezing cold water and the farther I crawled, the more dirt came off my body. I attempted to wash myself as best as I could.

He must have sensed I was ready to get out. "Your hair, too. You hurled all over it."

I shot him a look of hatred and he laughed at me. "I can't...please..." I shamelessly begged for mercy. He wasn't going to show me any, but it didn't stop me from trying.

He stepped forward, closer to me to where his boots were getting wet. "Please? Are you asking me to take pity on you because you're a fucking drunk? Whose fault is that, Miss Edwards?!" he sneered, screaming at me even though I was only a few feet away.

No one could have prepared me for what happened next. He ran over to me, grabbed my hair at the top of my head, and dunked me head first into the water. He left me under there for several seconds and I thought this was where he was going to kill me. He was going to drown me. Before the last breath escaped my lungs, he brought my head back up. I gasped for air and spit out the water from my mouth, trying not to choke.

"You think just because you apologize it makes everything okay?!" he shouted into the side of my face, and dunked me back under the water before I even realized he let me up.

"Ahhh!" I breathed out when he allowed me to resurface.

"You stupid fucking slut! You stupid cunt! You are nothing but a conniving, dirty, fucking liar! You manipulate everything around you, and the fact that you are trying to do it with me right now–" he yelled and got close to my face "–makes me want to fucking kill you."

He shoved me back under, but this time, he held me there until I lost the ability to hold my breath. Bubbles of air resurfaced as I fought him with every ounce of willpower and strength I could muster to get him to let me back up, he did, only to dunk me repeatedly.

"Please! I'm so fucking sorry! Please!" I pleaded, trying to catch my breath and voice. He roughly pushed me away with disgust and I fell backward into the water. My foot caught on something and I felt a sharp pain run through my ankle.

"Shut the fuck up and wash your fucking hair, Gianna! Don't make me come back over there," he warned.

I found the bar of soap and washed every inch of my body and then my hair, until he told me to stop and get out. It was frigid when I got out of the water. I was still hysterically crying at that point from the confrontation. He threw me a towel and it was barely enough to cover my breasts.

"Walk," he once again ordered.

It was as if I was having an out of body experience. I watched myself limp through the field, and then through an old, abandoned asylum. I never once stopped crying. We walked into a new room; I knew it because it didn't have the same stench. There were bars on every window, but at least there was light. A dirty mattress lay in the middle of the room next to a few bottles of water. In the far right corner, there was a bucket and the dreadful realization that it would be my bathroom.

"Get on the bed." He sensed my apprehension. "Miss Edwards..." he cautioned. I slowly walked toward the mattress and sat on the edge.

"Remove the towel." I peeked up at him through my lashes to find his eyes still remained dark and callous. I threw the towel at his feet and he smirked at my attempt of being rebellious.

"You still look exactly the same," he revealed.

"I find that hard to believe," I knowingly replied.

I saw his Adam's apple move as he walked over to me, each footstep deliberately calculated and precise. He kneeled down to my level, sitting on the soles of his shoes. He crudely grabbed my chin and he reared my face, settling it to look directly at him.

He smiled. "Spread your legs, Gianna."

"What?" I asked in confusion.

"You heard me. Don't act all coy, Miss Edwards. You fuck anything that has a cock. Now. Spread. Your. Fucking. Legs. For. Me," he drawled, accenting every word. "Be a good a girl," he mocked in a tone that had me wanting to smack the smug look off his face.

I pulled my lips into my mouth and slowly opened my legs, inch by inch. He still hadn't looked down when they were fully opened and all of me was exposed.

"Isn't this what you always wanted, me to look at you? Huh?" He let go of my chin and slapped the side of my face, not hard but enough to let me know he was in charge.

"Huh? Gianna?" He slapped the other side, and he did it over and over again until I finally screamed out yes.

"That's what I fucking thought." He pushed me back onto the bed and my head turned to the side. I knew where he was looking now and I didn't want to witness it.

"Your pussy is still pretty, Gianna. Nice to know that all the men you've fucked haven't ruined it. You always were a little cock slut," he humiliated, taking away the last of my dignity.

"It's very pretty, actually. It's just the right shade of pink." I sucked in air from the tears falling down the side of my face.

"Gianna..." he said in a singing tone. "When someone pays you a complement you should say thank you. Where the fuck are your manners? I let you bathe, I gave you water, and now I told you that your cunt is pretty. What do you say?" he taunted. "Huh?" He slapped my pussy and I whimpered.

He did it again and again. "Thank you, thank you, thank you!" I screamed.

"Much better. We are going to have to work on those manners and respect, Miss Edwards," he scolded. "Now. I have another guest waiting for me."

I sat straight up. "No!"

"Yes...what kind of host would I be to not include my guests of honor? I'll tell you something though, I never thought Mack would be the strong one in this scenario. Which is all the more reason to make her scream, don't you think?"

"Fuck you!" I shouted.

The back of his hand hit me across the face and I fell straight into the mattress. "Don't be needy, Gianna. You know how much I hate that." The door closed and the room locked.

I screamed at the top of my lungs, just so that she would know I was there and prayed that she could hear me.

Chapter Fourteen

I had no sense of time. I didn't even know how long he left me in that room alone. It could have been a few hours or a few days, everything was blending together. I wasn't tied to the bed anymore and I had the liberty to move around, although I couldn't. Lying in fetal position was the only thing that stopped me from wanting to throw up. The shakes were getting worse and my body felt like it was crumbling from the inside out. My bones hurt, and I would go from sweating to freezing cold. My body couldn't decide what state it wanted to be in other than miserable. I heard the door unlock, followed by footsteps. I didn't have to turn to know who it was.

"You haven't moved at all," he announced.

"No shit," I grumbled. The shakiness in my voice was apparent.

He threw something on the bed and I glanced at it from the corner of my eye. I knew that bottle. I quickly tried to turn around to grab it.

"You're pathetic. I would rather have you drunk than unconscious."

I nodded, agreeing with him. He was right, there was no use denying it. I sat up and reached for the bottle. My hands were shaking so bad that it made it difficult for me to get the top off. Once I finally managed to get it open, I brought it up to my nose and inhaled the intoxicating smell of cheap ass vodka. I placed it on my lips and gulped as much as I could.

"Ugh…" I yelled, wiping at my mouth with the back of my arm. I took a few more swigs until I had the nerve to look up at him. He looked at me with revulsion and remorse all at the same time.

125

"Thank you," I whispered.

"What the fuck happened to you? Who are you?" he questioned, never taking his gaze away from my eyes.

"I don't know anymore. I haven't known in a really long time."

He groaned something under his breath, shook his head, and left the room.

I went back to drinking my bottle and before I knew it, half of it was gone. The shakiness and nausea also left. I took my newfound drunken state for a walk around the room. I stumbled a little when I first got off the bed, I couldn't remember the last time I actually felt drunk. Drinking had become my regimen to not feel like shit, not because I wanted to get inebriated. I laughed at myself when I realized I was naked.

It was entertaining now.

"What have you gotten yourself into now, G?" I sighed and half giggled to myself.

I made my way over to the window, and at first, I thought I was imagining it. Alcohol can do that to you, right? There, before my very own eyes, was McKenzie. I hadn't seen her in years. Mr. Nichols was walking behind her and I could see her turning around every few seconds to say something. I couldn't tell if they were having a conversation or if they were arguing. My question was answered when I saw him shove her. I lost my shit. I started banging on the window, screaming at the top of my lungs. She didn't deserve any of this, although part of me wanted her to suffer. The part that still loved her, the part of me that missed her like crazy, the part of me that was still tied to her by memories and emotions wanted her to be safe.

"Mack! Mack! Mack! Stop it! Mack!" I yelled repeatedly.

It didn't matter they couldn't hear me or see me. I was just exhausting myself trying to get their attention. It dawned on me that it had always been like that. Nothing had fucking changed in all this time. The realization was a rude awakening in my drunken state. I went from being concerned to being angry. I hadn't allowed myself to feel angry in such a long time, I avoided it with liquor, and there I was, drunk as shit and feeling everything. It made my vision blur and I seethed with rage. I should have moved away from the window. I should have gone back and just kept drinking until it all went away; it had always worked before and it would probably work again. I couldn't get my goddamn legs to move. It was like I was permanently glued to that position. I waited until I saw her again. When she returned, I took in her appearance; her face was the same but older, she was still beautiful.

I was sad when I couldn't see her anymore. My emotions were all over the place…my brain was hyperaware of everything I was feeling, like it had been deprived for so long that it was now returning full force.

The door slammed, taking me away from my reflections.

"Well, look who decided to get up. You seem like you're feeling better."

I turned around, leaning on the windowsill. His eyes wandered from my face all the way down my body. I would be lying if I said I hadn't felt satisfaction from the look in his eyes.

"Where's Mack?"

The question caught him off guard and he cocked his head to the side, moving closer to me. He stopped when we were about a foot apart. "What is up with you guys? Do you not talk anymore?"

I laughed. "I haven't spoken to Mack in a really long time. Why are you hurting her? She didn't do anything. It was all me. She did it for me."

It was his turn to laugh. "I find it amusing that she plays the same card that you do. You both are manipulative bitches."

"We never meant for any of that to happen. It got so out of hand so fast. It took on a life of its own," I explained, the alcohol making it easy for me to do so.

"And that makes it all right? All is forgiven now? We're even," he interrogated with caution in his tone.

"We're far from even, Mr. Nichols. We're maybe closer though, an eye for an eye. Is that what this is all about?"

"You're drunk," he stated, finally taking in my disheveled appearance.

"And you know what they say about drunks and kids, right? They always tell the truth," I snapped.

127

He backhanded me across the face before I even saw it coming, and then grabbed me by my hair and dragged me to the bed face first. I closed my eyes, trying to pretend I was somewhere else. He flipped me over so I was on my back and held me in place by my hair.

"Look at me, you little cunt," he barked, and tried to open my eyes with his fingers. I rolled my eyes to the back of my head.

"Look at me!"

I didn't move or make one sound. I knew exactly what he wanted from me and I wouldn't give him the gratification of ever controlling me again. He aggressively grabbed my wrists and locked them together with his grip above my head. He growled as he positioned himself on top of me, spreading my legs. I felt the roughness of his jeans against my pussy. He started to smack the sides of my breasts and I could feel them reddening with every slap. When that didn't work, he attacked my nipples, pinching and kneading them.

"Goddamn it!" he shouted.

He unbuckled his pants and made another growling sound. I closed my eyes harder and waited for him to fuck me.

"What the fuck!" he screamed in my face. "Fight back, Gianna. Scream at me, push me, do fucking something."

"I can't!" I yelled, opening my eyes to stare at him.

He violently slapped my pussy a few times; I still hadn't moved or made a sound. I looked into his eyes, waiting for him to do whatever he wanted to me. When his fingers spread my lips, he swiped his finger back and forth a few times and that's when he realized I was wet.

"What the fuck!" he screamed, slamming his fist in the mattress by the side of my face. He abruptly got off me and started pacing. I lay there, staring at the ceiling and waited for his next move.

"Nothing is going the way I thought it would. This situation is more fucked up than I had anticipated. What the fuck is wrong with you guys? What happened?" he questioned, to no one in particular, I'm pretty sure he was talking to himself.

"We fucked up. We fucked up everything," I answered.

He slid down the wall and sat on his ass with his knees close to his chest. He rested his forearms on his knees and bent his head down.

I rolled over sideways and laid my head on my arm. He looked up and we stared at each other.

"You look the same, Mr. Nichols…a little older, but still the same."

He didn't say anything; he seemed dumbfounded and in shock or something.

"Can I see Mack?"

"Why do you think you're here, Gianna? Do you think this is a fucking party?"

"You can hurt me. I know you want to," I simply stated.

He groaned and pulled the hair away from his face like he wanted to tear it out.

"I want you to hurt me," I said, barely above a whisper.

He shook his head in disappointment, it was the first time I saw real sympathy on his handsome face. "You're killing yourself. The drinking."

I shrugged. "I'm already dead, I have been for a very long time."

He shook his head again, only this time, the anger had returned. "You think I'm fucking stupid, don't you? You think I don't know what you're doing. What you've always done. You should have been an actress, Gianna. You missed your calling."

"What happened that night–"

"Which night?" he interrupted.

"You remember?"

"Of course. I remember everything, especially that night. I think about it all the time. I have spent the last eight years of my life thinking about us. That's the reason all of this happened, isn't it? You didn't get your way," he spoke with conviction.

"No!" I sat straight up. "That's not why! You did this!"

He scoffed in disbelief, "You're full of shit. You were fine with it."

I narrowed my eyes. "That's not what happened! I was never fine with it! You're a fucking liar!" I yelled.

He viscously laughed, "Does Mack know? Did you ever tell her?"

I shook my head no.

"It's interesting to see how much you guys truly hid from each other. I mean, for two girls who used to call themselves sisters. You need to learn something about secrets, little girl, they always come out. One way or another, the truth has a way of coming out and making itself known when you least expect it."

"Does that make you the judge or juror?"

He smiled. "There she is. There's Miss Edwards…I've been waiting for her to make an appearance." He slowly got up and walked over to me.

He kneeled down and leaned forward. "See…here's the thing, I want you to hate me," he spoke into my ear. "I want to hurt you. I want to make you bleed," he grabbed my hair and yanked back my head, I yelped from the intrusion on my scalp.

He looked directly into my eyes. "I want to hear you scream and beg me to stop. Not from pleasure, Miss Edwards, but from fucking pain." He wrapped his other hand around my throat and I immediately heard my heartbeat through my ears.

"I could choke you to death right now and you would let me. What a sad, pathetic person you have turned into, Miss Edwards. At least the girl in high school had balls and went after what she wanted. This girl is nothing but a fucking drunk. You're everything that you never wanted to become. What a disappointment you must be for everyone, especially your father." I spit in his face and it landed on the corner of his mouth. He grinned, brought out his tongue, and licked it off. He roughly pushed me into the mattress and then pulled me up by my hair. I reached to place my hands over his to relieve some of the pressure, but he grabbed my hands and held them at my back.

He let go of my hair for just a second to open the door, and shoved me forward to walk. It was hard to walk with my hands held behind me and my head pulled back, but he didn't care. He moved at a quicker pace; I tried to keep up but stumbled on my footing a couple of times.

"Where are we going?" I shrieked, trying to control the fear I felt.

"Shut the fuck up, Gianna. Don't say one more goddamn word. We're going where I want you to be."

"But–" He pushed my arms higher and I shut right up.

We walked up the stairs until we made it to solid iron double doors and he kicked the left side open. I was met with a breeze and sunlight.

"Walk," he ordered.

We were on the sundeck of the building and all the railings were gone. My heart dropped to my stomach and my eyes widened in fear. I used all the power I could to push him back and try to get away; I didn't even nudge him. He applied more pressure on my scalp and arms and moved effortlessly where he wanted me.

We went right to the edge; I sucked in a breath and closed my eyes.

"Open your eyes, Miss Edwards," he said in a singing tone.

I vigorously shook my head no. He spread my legs open with his knee and pulled my arms higher, making me scream until I finally opened my eyes. All I could see before me was a vast open field. He lowered my head by my hair and it became clear that we were at least two stories high. I trembled and gasped in air, trying to bend my knees to sit on the ground.

"Stop," he ordered. "You see this, Miss Edwards? I can do whatever the fuck I want with you. Just like I always have been. You are nothing to me. You never were. A poor little rich girl, who wanted my attention, you were always so needy for it. And guess what? I fucking used you. I used you because I could. I used you because your pussy is poison. I used you because I'm a man and that's all you've ever been good for, I could smell it on you just like everyone else could," he deviously stated. "Do you have any idea the shit people said about you? You thought people loved you and wanted to be you, but you couldn't be more wrong! They fucking hated you. Everyone pitied you and they loved Mack best. They just wanted to get to her and they knew they could do it through you. She's better than you, always has been and always will be." He got close to the side of my face. "And

131

your father knew it," he whispered. "He knew you were broken and pathetic. If I push you and let go, you're done. And not so much as one person will know it. They will just think you're hiding. All you've ever done in your life is hide. Look ahead of you...do you see the clarity? Do you see who's in control?"

"Yes..." I sobbed.

"Should I let you go? Do you want to die?" he bellowed.

When I didn't answer, he pushed me forward and let go. "NO!" I screamed as he wrapped his arms around my waist and pulled me back in, making us both fall to the ground with me in his arms. My body shook and I started to cry hysterically.

"Shhh..." he repeated my ear. "That's what I thought."

I clung to his arms like a baby. I clung to him, wanting him to hold me and love me and tell me he was lying. I clung to him like he was my everything.

He rocked me back and forth. "Shhh..."

It was more emotion than I had felt in a long time. I often thought I wanted to die, and he just proved to me that I didn't. I knew he was far from done with me.

And for the first time in eight years...

I felt alive.

Chapter Fifteen

We made our way back from the creek where I bathed again. Neither one of us had spoken much. He had been bringing me a bottle of vodka every other day or so. I had lost track of time in a cloud of thoughts, emotions, and endless memories. I was on the bed facing him while he took his regular spot against the wall. He had started coming in my room at night and we would causally talk about nothing.

It was comforting.

"Where is Mack?"

"She's downstairs in one of the rooms. She's losing her shit," he pulled the hair away from his face; I noticed he did that when he was confused.

I took a swig of my bottle and extended my hand for him to have some. I saw a glimmer of a smile appear on his face. He covered it quickly, but I saw it. He reached for the bottle, took a few swigs, and handed it back to me. We went back and forth a few rounds before he placed it in between his legs.

"What do you mean?" I asked him, breaking the silence.

"I mean she's losing it. I had no idea what I was getting myself into with you guys. I wasn't expecting this, not even close," he rationalized, like that made it okay that he was holding us hostage.

"What were you expecting?" I questioned, never taking my gaze away from his.

"You guys were inseparable and I thought your dreams had come true."

I nodded. "So the plan was to take us away from our happily ever after?"

"Something like that," he replied, taking the bottle up to his lips.

"Now what? What happens now?" I eagerly awaited his response.

"You were always such a poor little rich girl, weren't you, Gianna?"

I shook my head no.

He laughed. "Oh come on, let's not lie anymore. Aren't you tired of all the secrets you keep so dear to your heart? Nothing ever happened to you. You wanted attention and the only way you could get it is if you played the woe is me card. No one understands me. I'm so broken," he mocked.

I kept shaking my head no. "That's not it. I can't help the way I feel, the way I've always felt. You're right, nothing happened to me but it didn't stop me from feeling like I didn't belong," I clarified.

He rolled his eyes. "You had everything at your disposal and it was never enough. Just own up to it for once in your fucking life."

"No! I'm not taking responsibility for something that's not true. Do you think I wanted to feel like that? I tried to be what everyone wanted me to be. I didn't know how to be honest with anyone and some people are just born broken. I'm one of them. You can believe whatever the fuck you want to believe, but I was always honest with you. I don't have many childhood memories because I tuned most of it out. I went through my life as a spectator. I'm still going through my life like that. So fuck you!"

His eyes shifted when he placed the bottle to the side. They actually glazed over.

"Mr. Nichols...it got out of hand. I swear we never thought it would turn into what it did," I carelessly spoke.

"Oh yeah? What the fuck did you think was going to happen when you falsely accuse someone of rape? It's not like it was just one person crying rape, it was two!" he declared; his tone changed. He was back to being the man I didn't know, the one I tried to avoid.

"I don't know. We were so drunk. I was so upset. It just seemed like a good idea at the time. We were young and stupid. You played your part, too. I don't know what you want me to say to you," I explained, trying to reason with him.

He stood with an eerie demeanor. *Fuck, I had lost him.*

"Stand up," he demanded.

"Mr. Nichols," I whispered, sitting up.

"Stand the fuck up!" he shouted, making me jump.

I moved backward on the bed, putting my hands in the air in a surrendering motion. "Mr. Nichols..." I repeated, hoping he would snap out of it.

He lunged at me, grabbing me by the hair. My body rapidly following the pace he set as he placed me on the ground. My knees hit the floor with a crack that made me want to throw up from the pain.

He pulled my hair upward. "Stand up." I slowly moved, placing one foot before the other.

"Turn around, put your hands on the bed, and spread your legs." He said to the side of my face.

"Do you think we're friends, Miss Edwards?"

"What?" I asked, confused. What the hell just happened?

He moved to stand in front of me, never letting up on his hold. "Do you think we're friends? Did you think we were?"

I tried to understand his ramblings. "I don't know what you mean."

He laughed. "That whole year, all you ever wanted was for me to pay attention to you. With the way you spoke to me, the way you dressed, your demeanor and presence. You may as well have had a sign that said, 'slut.'"

"That's not what happ—"

"Shut up!" he shouted. "I know everything. You don't think teachers talk? You don't think we all knew what a lost little girl you were? Still are. Always letting Mack pick up the broken pieces, Miss Edwards. You always came in second best when it came to her, and you still do," he deviously spewed, and I took in every word.

"Isn't that why you did it? Why you lied? I know the truth and so do you, and that's why you drink. You drink to stop thinking about me. The fantasy and the reality are all fucked up in your delusional head. Isn't that right?"

"You! You played your part, too. You can't think that you can put me through what you did and expect me to not fucking drink. You loved me, too! You told me!" I shouted trying to get him to admit it.

He grinned, "Did I?"

His fingers walked from my lower back to my ass cheek. "You know what they do to you right before they take you to prison?" I turned to look at the side of his face.

"They make you stand in a similar position you are standing in now. They make you watch as they put on latex gloves and then they have you bend over. Once they have you in this uncomfortable, awkward position, they push two fingers into your asshole and move them around. It's called a search, and they do it to make sure you aren't carrying any drugs." His fingers never stopped walking back and forth on my ass cheeks.

"Gianna, call me by my name...I know you want to. I know you've always wanted to. Here's your chance. Say it."

"Mr. Nichols," I rebelliously replied.

He flipped me over, threw me on the bed and climbed on top of me, holding my hands over my head.

"Not that one," he warned.

"Mr. Nichols," I said again, just to piss him off.

He once again grabbed me by my hair at the top of my head and swung me from the bed to the floor. I hit it with a bang.

"Ahhh!" I screamed in agony.

"Crawl."

"Please."

"CRAWL!"

I got on my hands and knees. "WHERE? Where the fuck do you want me to go?" I yelled as he pushed me with his foot, making me fall to my side.

"This is what you want, isn't it, Gianna? You want me to fucking hurt you. Why? Why do you want me to hurt you?"

"BECAUSE I FUCKING DESERVE IT!" I screamed at the top of my lungs.

"Why do you deserve it, Gianna? Huh? Fucking say it."

I grabbed my side and sat straight up, looking right into his eyes. "I'm a liar. I lied. I sent you to prison because you sent me away. You lied to me so I lied to everyone," I stated through gritted teeth. I could feel my face turning red from anger.

He cracked his knuckles and opened the door. "Crawl until I tell you to stop."

I crawled on the filthy, uneven floor that hurt the fuck out of my hands and knees.

"You know how many times I crawled on my hands and knees, Miss Edwards? How many bathrooms and floors I had to clean with a goddamn toothbrush?"

He shoved my ass with his foot and I almost fell over again. "I'm sorry," I whimpered through my tears. "I'm sorry." I didn't want to play this game anymore.

"Not yet…but you will be," he stated with conviction.

He didn't allow me to get up the entire time, and we had to go down a flight of stairs. I had to crawl backward the entire time and missed the last step, falling over. We made it to the first floor and it was dark and creepy and we were only in the hallway.

"Stop," he demanded in front of a room as he opened the door. "Go," he ordered.

I shook my head back and forth. "No, I don't want to go in there. Please don't do this! Please," I begged.

"Gianna…" he threatened.

I sighed, knowing he would make me do it, and crawled into the dark, tiny room that had padded walls. I knew once he shut the door it would be pitch black. He walked in after me and smiled.

"Have you ever heard of solitary confinement?" As soon as the question left his mouth, my heart dropped. I looked down at the ground and closed my eyes.

"It's punishment when you're bad in prison. Anything can get you in to solitary confinement. Have you been a bad girl, Gianna? Do I need to punish you?" he integrated, making me cry.

"How many times do you think I was put into solitary confinement in seven years, huh? Just think about it. Give me a number, any fucking number."

I shrugged. "I don't know," I whispered.

"You don't know? Oh come on, Miss Edwards. It's not fun if you don't play along. There is a code in prison, a certain food chain. You want to know the order? Well…let me begin by saying that child rapists aren't taken to kindly. I was placed in solitary confinement a lot, not because I was bad, but more for my own safety."

"I'm–"

"Shut the fuck up. I'm telling a story," he reprimanded.

I looked up at his face. I didn't recognize the man before me. He wasn't Mr. Nichols anymore; I had no idea who he was. This person was new and he scared the fuck out of me.

He put his finger up to his mouth. "Where was I?" he paused. "Oh yes…child rapists aren't wanted or welcomed lightly. They are the bottom of the food chain. See, Miss Edwards, everyone has a mother or a child and you don't fuck with either of them. Do you want to know why I was placed in solitary confinement the first time?" I shook my head no. I didn't want to know. I wanted to go back into the other room.

"You don't? That's not nice. I'm trying to open up to you. Isn't that what you always wanted, for me to confide in you? Tell you all my deepest, darkest secrets…"

He bent down behind me and started caressing my back with the tips of his fingers. I openly sobbed.

"I think it's better if I show you," he murmured in my ear.

I heard him unbuckle his belt then pull down his zipper and I knew what was next. He placed his hand by my mouth. "Spit." My eyes widened. "Spit into my fucking hand, Gianna." I opened my mouth and spit into his hand. "More." I spit again.

I looked straight ahead at the padded wall and heard as he stroked himself.

"I wouldn't even know how this was done if it wasn't for you. You ruined me and I'm going to ruin you. You've always wanted to be someone else, Gianna; now, how does it feel to be me?" He rammed

138

his cock into my anus and I wanted to scream in pain. My lower body fell to the ground and I scratched at the concrete floor, praying that it would replace the stinging that I felt in my asshole. He pulled out and shoved back in; he did it a few more times until he stopped when he was in balls deep.

I wept in agony, not just from the discomfort but also from the meaning behind it. There was no foreplay, there was no throb, and there was no ache; there was nothing. He wanted me to feel like I was being raped, like he was using me, like I was his toy he could play with. It didn't matter how many times I had meaningless, empty sex, this was so much worse.

I love this man.

He was supposed to be different...

He didn't let up on fucking me, using me like I was nothing but some slut on the street, like we hadn't shared something deep and meaningful. His words hurt me, but his actions killed me. He fucked me with determination and hate. With each thrust, he took away one more piece of me; it was exactly what he wanted, and since I didn't give it away voluntarily, he took it himself.

"Is this what you have been thinking about for the last eight years?" he accused, with no empathy or sympathy behind his words.

I started to dry up and he pulled out his cock and spit on it and on me, and smeared it into my anus before he thrust back in. I hated him. In that moment, I wanted him to die.

"Fuck me..." he groaned in pleasure, and it made me sick to my stomach. It took everything for me not to vomit right there before him as he fucked me raw and with no remorse.

"Your asshole is so tight. That's what he said to me over and over again." He paused and shook off the memories. I couldn't tell if he was with me or if he was back in that cell. Is it sick that it gave me hope that he wasn't thinking of me but of the person who did that to him? I took comfort in that as he violated my mind, body, and soul.

But most of all, my heart.

"You wanted my attention all the fucking time, Gianna. Always spreading your legs in class to show me you weren't wearing panties. Showing me your pink pussy any chance you got." He jerked back my head, making me yelp as he fucked me harder. My ass was sore and the tears just flowed, I had no control over them.

"You have nothing to say? Why is that?" he grunted and stopped when he was balls deep again, and then slowly moved himself in and out.

"Jesus you feel good," he growled and smacked my ass. I jerked forward.

He was stripping everything away from me. I would have nothing left after this, and I would be broken beyond repair. I wanted to pretend I wasn't there, that this wasn't happening. He smacked my ass harder, bringing me back to the awareness of what he was doing to me. He wouldn't allow me the solitude to hide in. He was sweating, panting, and getting off on it all.

"How's it feel to have my attention now? Is it everything you always wanted and thought it would be?" he mocked as he started to thrust roughly and urgently again.

I looked down to see a puddle of tears gathering on the concrete floor. He pounded into me a few more times. I heard his breathing pick up and I knew he was close to coming.

"This is all you were ever good for and it's why you give it away so easily, because you fucking know it."

I sobbed, he had officially broken me.

He immediately stopped. He stayed still, not moving as my hand wiped away my tears. The feel of his skin touching mine revolted me and I felt the vomit in the back of my throat.

"Look at me," he ordered. I didn't move or say anything.

He pulled my head back by my hair. "Look at me. Fucking look at me!" he roared.

I opened my eyes and immediately found his, they were dark and soulless. He quickly pulled out and jolted back as if I had hit him across the face.

"G…" he said in a tone that was almost painful to hear.

I looked up at him as a single tear fell down the side of my face. "James…"

He backed away from me with caution. I didn't know if it was for my protection or his. I watched as his eyes changed and he had returned to me. He was James again, my James. It was the first time I had seen him in eight years. I wanted to run to him and seek refuge in his arms. I wanted him to take me away from here and take care of me. To show me how much he loved me. I was sure he was going to reach for me. I knew I saw the love flash across his eyes. And just as quickly as it showed up, it left. He blinked and it was gone. He backed away from me, turned, and left the room, slamming the door and making me shudder as he locked it. I looked around the pitch-black room. I was use to darkness–I had lived in it and I created it. But nothing could have prepared me for this type of darkness. I laid down in the puddle of my own tears and thought about everything.

My whole life was one big secret and lie. I couldn't regulate them anymore and I couldn't keep them apart. I couldn't convey what the truth was or what the lie was.

It all blended together.

Making me who I was.

The person that I hated.

Chapter Sixteen

I didn't once think he was taking advantage of me; it never even crossed my mind. He would leave these letters in my locker that were sonnets from Shakespeare, mainly Romeo and Juliet. My heart fluttered every time I would open my locker.

"What's up with you?" Mack questioned, making me slam my locker shut.

"Holy shit, Mack! You scared me," I said, placing my hand on my heart.

"We always meet at our lockers before cheerleading practice. What's wrong with you? You've been really weird this last month."

"Oh!" I retorted, opening my locker to avoid looking at her eyes.

"Oh? That's your answer?" she mimicked.

"Yeah...there's nothing to talk about. I'm just stressing over school and stuff. My dad's on my ass, Mack," I stated, leaning over the door to look at her.

"Your dad's not that bad, Gia."

"What the fuck is that supposed to mean? Are you siding with him?" I accused.

Her eyes widened. "No! Not at all, I'm just saying."

"Since when do you just say?"

"What? Why are we fighting? And why are you getting mad at me? I didn't mean anything by it."

Why was I getting mad at her? Were the lies getting too much and I was taking them out on her?

I laid my hand on my forehead. "I'm sorry, Mack, I didn't mean to jump on you like that. I'm just stressed out."

"I get it. No worries. I'll see you at practice," she reasoned, walking away.

I grabbed her by the arm. "We cool?"

She smiled. "Of course."

Once she turned the corner and I knew she was gone, I eagerly grabbed the note and made sure no one was looking or around before opening it.

Tis torture, and not mercy. Heaven is here Where Juliet lives, and every cat and dog and little mouse, every unworthy thing, live here in heaven and may look on her, but Romeo may not.[8]

Meet me at Alderson Park, midnight.

I placed the note in my pocket and took a deep breath. Cheerleading practice ran exceptionally slow and I tried to keep my mind on the routines, but I couldn't. I wanted the minutes to go fast and not stop till it was twelve o'clock. The rest of the night went just as slow, if not slower. I ate dinner with my parents, took a shower, and said goodnight to them just as I always had. I dressed in a spaghetti strapped, yellow dress and white sandals. I rigged my bed with pillows that resembled my body, but I knew my parents wouldn't come into my room. They never did after we exchanged goodnights, and they were heavy sleepers with the same routine. My dad passed out around ten and my mom would watch TV until 10:30-11.

I quietly made my way out of the house and grabbed my mom's bike that I left on the side of the house a few hours earlier. The entire time I pedaled, my heart was in my throat; I was nervous and excited and couldn't get there fast enough.

I got there at exactly midnight but didn't see his car anywhere. My heart sank thinking he didn't show up and changed his mind. I climbed the closed gate and jumped once I was over to avoid slipping and getting scratched. The park was a few yards from the gate and was hidden with trees. I was thankful I brought a flashlight because I could barely see a few feet in front of me. I think I held my breath the entire time, even though I knew that wasn't possible. The soft candle lighting was the first thing that caught my eye and I swear my heart stopped. He had shown up and was sitting on a blanket with a few candles surrounding him.

Our own little paradise and oasis, away from everyone.

Where it was just the two of us.

I made my way over to him...my happily ever after.

"Hi," I greeted, trying not to sound shy or insecure, which is exactly the way I felt.

"You're nervous," he acknowledged.

Of course he knew, he was the only person I couldn't hide from and he wouldn't let me.

I nodded, not being able to find the words to express what I felt and what he meant to me.

He smiled. "Come here, sit down," he ordered, extending out his hand for me to take it.

I grabbed it and he immediately pulled me to him in a playful manor. I fell right on top of him and we laughed.

"There she is," he observed, grinning.

I beamed and tried to sit up. "Nope! I like having you on top of me, and now that I'm finally holding you, I'm not letting you go."

"Can we at least sit up?"

"Oh, you don't like laying on top of me?" he accused, before flipping me over onto my back with him on top. "How about now?"

"This is good." My skin felt hot all over.

"Good to know, girl who likes to be on the bottom," he joked, kissing me on the tip of my nose. "You're beautiful, and not just on the outside, you're beautiful everywhere."

"You're beautiful, too."

He scooted over to lay on his side with his head on his hand, but kept his other hand entwined with mine over my heart, and his right leg laid overtop mine.

"I parked my truck down the street, I didn't want anyone to think someone was hanging out here. I wanted us to have some privacy where I could touch you. I've been thinking and dreaming about nothing but touching you, G. I've never felt like this. All I do is think about you," he declared. "You're an enigma to me; I love that you only share yourself with me. And as much as I want you to open up

and let people see the real you, a huge part of me wants to be completely selfish and not share you with anyone."

I chuckled. "I can't lie to you. I've been able to lie to everyone in my life since the day I was born, but I can't do it with you. And not only that...I don't want to," I explained.

"You don't ever hide from me because I'll always find you," he spoke with conviction. I knew right then and there I would forever be his. I belonged to him and no one else could take that away from me because I no longer had control over it. It was just the way it was.

I wanted to ask him about the future and what was going to happen with us. All of this...the hiding, the secrets, and the lies were for a reason, right?

It all had to mean something?

"Stop thinking...stop thinking and just feel. Can you do that for me?" he pleaded.

I took in his words and let myself do just that. I let myself live in the moment with him because right then and there, nothing else mattered.

"I use to love swings when I was a kid. I remember our parents use to yell at Mack and I to get off those freaking swings." I said, trying to change the subject.

"Do you trust me?" he asked.

The word trust had such a fickle meaning to me. Did I ever trust anyone? If I did, wouldn't I be able to tell them the truth? Wouldn't I be able to be who I was? Trust that no one would judge me, trust that no one would hate me, trust that everyone would understand me?

That's what trust is, to know I would be accepted for who I was, and that they would love me unconditionally and without reservation.

Trust.

I trust no one.

But...I trusted him.

"Yes," I easily admitted.

His eyes lit up and it was only for me. I had never seen that look in his eyes, it was like he had just won the lottery, as if he knew everything I was thinking without me having to say a word or explain it. He knew me more than anyone, including myself.

"Come on," he urged, standing up and pulling me with him.

He dragged me over to the swing-set a few feet away. He placed me on the swing and kneeled before me.

"Why are we thus divided having kissed? Why are we yet two bodies and not one? Why have our separate spirits leave to run. Two sundered paths of thought? Love, incomplete, seems ever but begun, and yearns to consummation never won, that moaning kiss the same sands night by night. So I, who famish at possession's goal, must kiss and kiss, yet kisses ne'er console, Love's over-burdened heart that is not eased,"⁹ he recited, with a tone that I had never heard.

He licked from the inside of my thigh and worked his way up, taking my dress with him, and then leaned back to sit on his heels as his eyes devoured my body. I had gone completely commando, and by the look in his eyes, he very much appreciated what he saw. Everywhere he caressed, he left an awakening behind. My skin felt like it was on fire, and heat spread straight to my core, making my pussy throb in anticipation.

He took a deep breath and clenched his jaw. "Your body is sinful. I want to sit at your alter and just admire you. Fuck..." he groaned. "How did I get so lucky?"

Laying his hands on my thighs, he squeezed them like he wanted to crawl into my skin and make us one person. He spread my legs wider apart, moved forward, and inhaled my scent. My chest heaved as I stared at him, not knowing what to expect next.

"Want to play a game?" he teased.

"Yes," I answered with hooded eyes.

"Put your hands on the chains and hold on," he demanded, coming close to my face. "I want to taste your pussy." He kissed my left cheek. "I want to lick your pussy." He kissed my right cheek. "I want to suck on your clit." He kissed the tip of my nose. "And I want to push my tongue so far into your cunt–" he taunted a few centimeters from my mouth "–and make you come, until every ounce of you is

146

dripping down my face," he groaned, licking my top lip. "And then I want to kiss you and have you lick it off," he urged. "But you can't take your hands off the chains, or else you don't get to come. And trust me, I want to make you come."

I never had anyone talk to me like that, and fuck if it didn't have me melting in the seat. He eased his way down, placing my feet on his shoulders and stared at my pussy for a few seconds before doing this growling, snarling thing, then he went in for the kill. Seeing his head nestled in between my thighs was a sight that would stay with me forever. It was intoxicating and suffocating; he lapped at me like he couldn't get enough of me. I was lost in ecstasy of feeling his mouth on my most sacred area. He ravished me slowly at first, but it became more intense and urgent as time passed.

My head thrashed back and forth and I kept my eyes solely devoted to what he was doing to me. When he buried his tongue in my opening, I almost came right then and there, but I held back, not wanting the moment to end. His eyes had a playful hue to them, as if he read my mind, and nipped at my sensitive flesh, making me yelp. When he started making loud noises of pleasure, my legs started to tremble and close on their own, but he held them open with a firm grip. He enjoyed manipulating my body how he wanted; he pushed two fingers into my sex and simultaneously moved them with his mouth. I knew I would never be the same. There was no coming back from him.

I was falling apart, not because of what he was doing, but because it was him that was doing it to me. I gasped and started to squirm, and he sucked harder and pushed in deeper. When he grazed my nub with his teeth, my back arched and my head fell back, I came hard. He growled deep within the back of his throat and lunged forward with his entire body and I almost fell back off the swing, but he caught me with one arm around my back and the other placed behind my neck. His tongue spread my moisture all around my mouth, and the mixture of him and myself had me coming apart all over again.

"Jesus, baby, you come with everything you have," he whispered. "You don't hold back anything from me, not ever." I kept the same pace he was giving me, trying to show him that he was the object of my affection as much as I was his. We kissed for what felt like hours, not being able to get enough of each other.

147

I walked away with his heart that night and he walked away with mine.

I had absolutely no idea how much time had passed. It felt like days. I crawled around the room a few hours after he left me and I found a bottle of vodka tucked in a corner. I wanted nothing from him, but that didn't stop me from drinking it. It's pretty crazy to think about what the body and human mind can get accustomed to if given the opportunity. I got use to the darkness. I lived in it my entire life. It gave me a false comfort to sleep in the front of the room, by the door. When I was awake, I was drinking, and the more I drank, the more I reflected. It was almost therapeutic. How fucked up was that? I waited for the door to open and it never did. I was almost done with my bottle and I was more worried about what would happen when I was done, than I was about leaving the room.

I didn't want to think about Mr. Nichols, so I thought about Mack. I should have seen the cracks begin to surface but I didn't. Maybe if I had, things wouldn't have changed, maybe we could have saved our friendship and not let it turn into something unrecognizable. But it didn't matter because my thoughts of Mack always led back to him.

"Where do you keeping running off to, Mack? I feel like I never see you anymore."

"Huh? What do you mean?"

"What do you mean, what do I mean? You're never around."

"Oh, I don't know what you're talking about. We are hanging out right now." I watched her eyes shift from me to the door behind me. I turned to see my dad standing there.

"Hey, Dad, did you need something?"

"Your mom wants to know if you're going to be here for dinner."

"I don't think so."

"What are you guys doing tonight?" he asked, looking at Mack.

"I don't know, Kyle," she responded.

"All right. Gianna, have you been studying?"

"Mmm hmm. Haven't I, Mack?" She nodded and I smiled back at my father, hoping that would be enough to get him to leave. It was.

"That was weird," I stated and she shrugged.

"What do you want to do tonight?" I asked and then my cell phone buzzed with a call from Jake.

"Hey, doll," I answered.

"Hey, baby. Guess what?"

"Huh?"

"I'll be in town in about an hour. How about I pick up my favorite girl and take her out for some ice cream and then maybe we can go back to my parents and watch a movie in my old bedroom," he said in a suggestive tone.

"Ummm...why are you coming home?"

"That's your response?"

"No! I'm sorry. I'm just confused is all," I explained.

"I can't come home to see my girlfriend?" he accused.

"Of course you can. I miss you, too," I expressed, trying to make him feel at ease.

He chuckled. "Great! Get that sexy, beautiful ass in something for me and I will see you soon," he ordered and hung up.

I hung up and threw my phone on the bed. "Jake's coming home."

She smiled. "Oh yay!" She cocked her head to the side. "Why aren't you more excited?"

I smiled. "I am! I'm just surprised, I haven't seen him since dinner a few months ago."

"Is everything okay, Gia? You've been really strange?"

I bit my nail; I couldn't take it anymore. "Actually, Mack, I gotta tell—"

Her phone buzzed and she grabbed it to look at it. "Shit! I got to go. I forgot I promised my mom I would help her with something." She placed her phone in her back pocket and got off the bed. "Can we talk about this later?"

I nodded and she left.

I was going to tell her everything, but I took it as a sign from God that she wasn't meant to know. Mr. Nichols, James, which I began to call him, we were spending a lot of time together; I'd hang out at his house mostly, just because we couldn't be seen in public together. Every time I was with him, I wanted more, I was greedy for it. I told him everything and never held back one damn thing; he was so easy to talk to and always understood where I was coming from. He knew it all, from my dad, to Mack, to school–I hid nothing. We usually just talked, and even though we would rent movies and made plans, we never did them. I enjoyed hearing the stories about his life and how he grew up similar to me.

His parents had the same expectations. He told me it gets to a point where you have to let it go and let things be. I prayed that it would happen for me, for us. We even talked about his wife, he said they were going to get a divorce and share custody of Cara, and that it was amicable. He was going to keep the house and she was going to move back in with her parents for a little while, unsure of what she wanted to do with her future. We never talked about Jake, and I was grateful for that because I didn't know how to respond. And the fact that he was away and I barely saw or spoke to him, made it easier. The less we talked, the more I was convinced he had secrets and was doing his own thing, but he probably felt the same way I did and didn't know how to break it off with me. I was his safe spot.

It had been a few months since the park night and we still weren't intimate. We continued to mess around, but as soon as it would get too much, he would immediately stop, much to my disapproval. In all honesty, we barely even did the messing around stuff, we didn't have to. Our connection was strong and powerful and we didn't need the sexual things to be happy and content. Being around each other was enough for us. He told me about his favorite dinners and I tried to cook them for him, and he would chase me around the house when I wouldn't let him touch me. He told me about his dreams and aspirations and I told him mine. I was happy, I mean really happy for the first time in my life. But every time I left his house, I left myself there, and I was back to being Gianna. The real me stayed with him though, right in his soul, where no one could take me away.

Jake and I went to eat ice cream. We shared a large chocolate ice cream with rainbow sprinkles and fed each other. He accidentally missed my mouth and got it on my nose and he started to lick it off me, which proceeded to us kissing, and then me pulling away.

"Hey..." he said, grabbing my chin to look at him. "What happened?"

I didn't want to look at him, it all was becoming too much. I didn't know what to do and he hadn't promised me anything, but he didn't need to, right? We were kismet and we would be together after I graduated.

I shook away the thoughts. "Nothing. We're in public," I addressed.

He grinned. "Is that your subtle way of saying you want to go so we can be alone?"

I panicked. "I'm on my period," I lied.

"Oh...I thought you just had your period two weeks ago. You said you had bad cramps when we talked on the phone."

I licked my lips. "Right. I missed a pill and it's thrown off my entire cycle now. I think that's why my cramps were so bad."

He nodded. "It doesn't matter. I came here to see you, not make love," he vowed, making me feel like an even bigger piece of shit.

He kissed me and I kissed him back. "Miss Edwards." I knew that voice. We both turned to see Mr. Nichols standing there. He was livid, his hands were closed fisted by his sides and I was almost certain he wanted to knock Jake the fuck out.

"Do you think it's appropriate to be sucking face in a family establishment?"

"We weren't," I replied, trying to remain in a neutral tone when I really wanted to apologize and put him at ease.

"Tell that to everyone that was watching the show. Why don't you have some more respect for yourself." I blushed from embarrassment.

"Mr. Nichols, right?" Jake intercepted, making him look directly at Jake. His face said it all; he wasn't even trying to hide his reaction.

"Yeah, Jake, he's my teacher. Maybe we should go."

"I don't think your parents would approve if I called to tell them what I, and half the town, just witnessed," he threatened, stopping me dead in my tracks. He knew my dad would freak out on me. I couldn't tell if he was being serious or not.

Jake grabbed my hand and lifted me off the seat. *"Let's go, baby, back to my place where we can be inappropriate in private."*

I looked back at him as we walked out and he never took his eyes away from our interlocked hands.

Chapter Seventeen

It was around midnight when I pulled into my driveway. Flashing headlights caught my attention and I looked back to see a white truck down the road. I smiled. I reversed and followed him; I knew where we were going. Twenty minutes later, we pulled into his suburban community. He opened the garage and signaled for me to park in there; as soon as I did, he shut it.

I made my way into his house and he walked through the front door and placed his keys on the coffee table. He went straight toward the kitchen and grabbed a beer from the fridge. I didn't move from the spot by the garage door. I had no idea what was going to happen and I was terrified that he would end us, whatever us was.

He chugged almost the entire beer before we locked eyes. "Are you mad at me?" I inquired before I lost the nerve.

"I have no fucking idea," he breathed out, catching me off guard. He hardly ever cussed.

"G, you can sit where you want. Stop hiding by the door." I nodded and moved to the couch. I sat in the smaller love seat all the way toward the right side, and he sat on the coffee table in front of me.

"I'm sorry," I apologized.

"I'm not," he said without hesitation. "What the fuck was that?"

"Nothing. I haven't seen him since that night at dinner." I shrugged. "We barely even talk to each other on the phone."

"Why were you with him?"

"Because he surprised me and came into town," I informed.

He cocked his head to the side and narrowed his eyes. "That's not what I meant. Try again."

"He's my boyfriend," I stated.

His eyes widened. "Did you fuck him?" he countered, catching me completely off guard.

I nervously laughed, "What?"

"Did. You. Fuck. Him?" he hissed, using emphasis on every word.

"Ever?"

"Today," he questioned impatiently. "Have his hands been on you? Has he been inside you?"

"No!" I screamed, not meaning to.

"When was the last time he DID fuck you?" he accused. "Answer the fucking question, Miss Edwards." I hated it when he called me that and he knew it. He was trying to hurt me.

"Not since...not since the last time he was here when school started, I didn't fuck him that night after the restaurant. I couldn't." His eyes glazed over as if he expected me to say something different. They were calm again; they were the eyes of the man that I loved.

He hunched over and put his face in his hands in a frustrated and confused gesture. My hands found his hair and I scratched his head, trying to relieve some of the tension. But mostly, I just wanted to touch him.

I sighed. "What are we doing?" I questioned, unable to not know anymore.

His eyes peeked up at me like he was contemplating what he was going to say next. He took a deep breath and sat up, looking right at me.

"I love you. I fucking love you, G. I've loved you since the moment you walked into my classroom. I tried...no I'm lying. I can't even pretend to sit here and tell you that I tried to not love you because I didn't. I couldn't. I don't know what the future holds for us, or if we even stand a chance at making this work, but I can't walk away from you. The thought of not seeing you or being with you kills me. There is no me without you," he vowed.

I smiled and attacked him, and by that, I mean, my body completely toppled over his. He fell flat on his back and I kissed every inch of his face over and over again. "I love you! I love you! I love *you!" I repeated endlessly, and not nearly enough. He laughed and swiftly removed my shirt and bra. My pants and panties quickly followed. I was completely naked and he was still clothed. My breathing was jagged, as was his, and I lay there as his eyes took in every inch of my naked form.*

"You're breathtaking," he praised. I wrapped my legs around his waist and he carried me into his bedroom where he laid me down.

"I want to see you, too," I said.

He grinned, and I admired his physique when he removed his shirt and then his shorts. His erect cock sprang loose immediately, and I couldn't help but gawk at it.

I blushed. "Wow."

He kissed me. "Stop being so adorable."

We kissed, just enjoying the new sensation of having skin on skin contact. He tasted like beer and something musky, manly; I couldn't get enough of it.

"Tell me, baby. Have you ever been with a man?"

"Yes," I responded, confused.

"You've been with a boy, G, a boy. I'm a man and I'm about to show you the difference," he growled and urgently kissed me again.

His resistance against us not being intimate shattered. Our bodies tangled together under white sheets that smelled exactly like him. I was surrounded in a euphoric state of him everywhere around me, and I wanted to take residence in it and never leave. If we stayed in his bedroom like this for the rest of our lives, I would have died happy and content. That is where I belonged and no one could tell me differently. I rejoiced in knowing that I would be taking a part of him home with me. Being in his bedroom, his married bedroom, further proved to me that I was his everything.

I placed his hand over my heart and he placed mine on his, and I swear they were beating in unison.

"I want to feel you all over," he groaned. "I want to get lost inside of you."

No one had ever spoken to me like that before. I took in every word and sound that he made.

155

"Of all my loves this is the first and last. I could give all and more, my life, my world, my thoughts, my arms, my breath, my future, my love eternal, endless, infinite, yet brief, as all loves are and hopes, though they endure. You are my sun and stars, my night, my day, my seasons, summer, winter, my sweet spring, my autumn song, the church in which I pray, my land and ocean, all that the earth can bring. Of glory and of sustenance, all that might be divine, my alpha and my omega, and all that was ever mine,"[10] he quoted, making me almost die right there in his arms.

He pulled me closer to him and entwined our entire bodies together, like he couldn't get me close enough to him. His fingers found my folds, and he groaned when he felt the wetness that waited for him and only him. He rubbed the slick moisture that increased my arousal and need for him. He brought it up to my mouth and spread it all around my lips before placing it back on my nub, making slow, torturous circles. His tongue bit my bottom lip before he sucked it into his mouth and lapped at me, tasting all my juices like I was his favorite cocktail. His fingers made their way into my opening and I panted, withering beneath him. I felt my inner muscles twitching and convulsing around his fingers, and the tighter I got, the faster he would pump.

"I want you to come, baby. I want you to come so hard. You're mine and I want to own your body, mind and soul, and I don't even know if that's enough," he urged in a tone of abandonment.

His hand moved from my heart to my hair, to my shoulders, and then to the curve my neck, pulling me closer to him.

"Open your eyes, I want to see those beautiful green eyes come apart."

My body burned everywhere for him, and I couldn't get enough of him or his movements. It was like he knew every contour of my body, exactly how to touch me to send me in a frenzy. It didn't take long for me to feel the effects of his touch and for my climax to emerge. He pulled my neck forward and placed his forehead on mine, we looked into each other's eyes, mouths gaping open, getting lost in one another.

"I love you," he whispered, and that was my undoing.

I moaned and shook with release. He didn't stop until I was begging him to be inside me. He slowly moved on top of me, and to feel the weight of him was a feeling like none other. There was nothing in this world that I could compare to the way I felt in that moment, being there with him, surrounded by nothing but our love and devotion to each other. I let down my guard and every wall with this man; he knew me for who I really was. I felt like this was the first time I was truly giving myself to someone and we were about to make love.

My arms went around his neck as he slowly thrust inside me, making me feel whole and complete. It was the first time in my life that I felt like I belonged somewhere, my place was right beside him. When he was inside me fully, he stopped and looked at me with emotions I couldn't begin to describe. I saw everything in his eyes; they always spoke the truth to me.

"God, I don't want this to end. I want to make love to you forever," he doted.

I moved my hips forward as he thrust in, and our bodies moved in sync with one another as we made slow and passionate love. It was everything I have always wanted and didn't know I could ever have.

We were just James and G.

He smiled a sincere, loving smile down at me as he kissed my lips with fury, and I tried to respond but I couldn't. My mind was on the sensation of him being inside me and in the moment of us finally being together. My only responses were the instant satisfying moans that escaped, which only deepened the emotional feel of him pushing inside of me.

Moving a little faster, he panted, "Does that feel good? You feel fucking amazing? Will I ever be able to get enough of you?"

"Yes...yes...God yes..." I screamed.

I could feel the intense pressure building up from my pussy to my abdomen. Our eyes consumed each other just as much as our bodies did. Our hearts were pounding, we were covered in sweat, and completely out of breath. I took in every caress and movement and matched it as best as I could, wanting him to know that I belonged to him. Just like he wanted me, too. My breathing labored and my pussy clamped down, I stared directly into his eyes as I came with nothing but love and utter devotion for him. He thrust in a few mores times, but exploded deep within my core, right where he belonged.

We laid there for several minutes, completely oblivious to everything around us. I didn't want him to pull out and he must have thought the same thing, because we lay there wrapped up in each other.

Where we were one.

Chapter Eighteen

I had run out of alcohol. I felt like shit and I'm sure I looked like it, too. I was starting to go stir crazy from being locked in a dark room for I didn't know how long. And as more time passed, so did the feelings that resonated from what he did to me. It all came tumbling down like a force field and I was right at the bottom of it. I didn't stand a chance. He wasn't the man I knew anymore, the man I loved; or maybe it was all an act. Maybe I just imagined it all…

Hate.

It's such a strong word, and even though it only has four letters, it carries a mean punch. I never thought I could hate anyone more than I hated myself, but I was wrong.

I hated him.

There was nothing left.

I lost the fighting battle.

The door opened and the light that followed made me crouch into a corner and shield my eyes. They burned. Something landed at my side that felt like cloth against my skin. My eyes fluttered open, and little by little, they became accustomed to the brightness. It was a shirt that was thrown in my direction. I followed the path from where it came from, and there he was, sitting with his back leaned against the opposite wall, slouched over.

He looked up when he felt my eyes on him. "Put it on," he ordered.

The man before me was remorseful, the man before me was sad, the man before me had love in his eyes.

The man before me was James.

I was never one for praying; I didn't even know if I believed in a higher power, but I found myself closing my eyes and praying for the lord above to give me strength for what I was about to do. I grabbed the white, collared shirt he threw and put it on, making sure to button it all the way down. I wanted nothing exposed to him anymore. Not my body, not my mind, and especially not my heart.

"Are you okay?" he asked.

I looked right at him and busted out laughing. I was laughing so hard it made my head fall back and my stomach hurt.

"Oh my God!" I said in between laughing. "Are you really asking me that? What the fuck do you think? I've been sitting in a pitch black fucking room for how many days?" I stood up, not being able to control my emotions. "Take a look around you," I stated, gesturing with my arms around the empty space. "Does it look like I'm at a five star resort? I mean, you're sitting close to my piss, Mr. Nichols." I shook my head disgusted. "You're unbelievable."

He stared at me with inquisitive eyes. "I know. Listen I'm so–"

"Don't you even fucking dare!" I yelled.

"You need to calm down," he barked, trying to control his temper that was looming.

"And you need to go to hell," I remarked.

He chuckled. "I've been there, fuck...I'm still there. I have no excuse for what happened the other night."

"How many nights has it been? How long have I fucking been in here?"

He pulled his hair away from his face and raised his knees to have his elbows sit on them.

"You've been here around four weeks and you've been in this room for four days."

I scoffed, "So it took you four days to come in here...I see how devastated you've been about the fact that you sodomized me, but at least you actually raped me this time."

"That wasn't rape," he argued through gritted teeth.

"Oh yeah? Tell that to my asshole, Mr. Nichols, because it begs to fucking differ!" I screamed, making him wince at my words.

"But I guess you got your payback, right? And that is what this was all about. You wanted to get back at McKenzie and me...well con-grat-u-fucking-lations, teacher of the year, you succeeded," I taunted.

"I never meant–"

"Bullshit. You wanted to hurt us. You've wanted to hurt me, but guess what, asshole, you can't hurt me as much I have hurt myself." He turned his face to the side, trying to avoid my words, as if they caused him pain hearing my reality.

"Look at me!" I seethed. "Look at me!" I repeated. "Fucking looking at me, James!" He instantly turned his face and it was first time in this whole ordeal that he saw me...he saw G, he saw what G turned into.

I was done hiding.

"I'm a drunk. I'm a whore," I divulged with conviction. "I wish I could tell you that what happened the other night was the first time that's happened to me. It's not. I have woken up in beds that I don't even remember lying in." I closed my hands in a praying motion, bringing them up to my mouth. "All the men's faces blend together; I don't see any of them. I just see someone that will make me feel anything other than wanting to take a knife to my wrist," I chuckled.

I pointed at the air. "I already did that though." His eyes widened. "I didn't mean to, at least that's what I like to tell myself. You wouldn't leave my mind, James." I grabbed my head, wanting to pull out my hair and started to pace the room.

"I couldn't get rid of you. I know I fucked you over, but you fucked me over first. I was pissed and hurt. Why? Why lie to me with sonnets, Shakespeare, and love if all you wanted to do was fuck me?" I agonized, trying to hold back the tears.

"That's not what happened," he said, barely above a whisper.

"Really?" I stopped and turned to him. "Why do you keep lying? The jigs up! Just tell me the truth, please..."

He took a deep breath and bowed his head in defeat. I slowly walked over to him and sat right in front of him with my knees to my chest and my arms wrapped around them. His head leaned to the side on his arms to look at me. We stared at each other for a while, not knowing what to say or how to say it. I was exhausted. His hand reached out for mine and I knew what he was going to do. He grabbed my left arm and flipped it over. He closed his eyes and made a pained noise from the back of his throat.

I could see his internal struggle with wanting to look at them, but that didn't stop his fingers from touching the scar tissue. They rubbed back and forth on the rigid skin that I didn't even notice anymore.

Just like my lies, my scars became part of me, too.

He opened his eyes and immediately found mine. "That thou hast her it is not all my grief, and yet it may be said I loved her dearly; that she hath thee is of my wailing chief, a loss in love that touches me more nearly. Loving offenders thus I will excuse ye: thou dost love her, because thou know'st I love her; and for my sake even so doth she abuse me, suffering my friend for my sake to approve her. If I lose thee, my loss is my love's gain, and losing her, my friend hath found that loss; both find each other, and I lose both twain, and both for my sake lay on me this cross: then she loves but me alone,"[11] he recited. "We are one and the same," he stated, and then flipped his arm over to show me his truths.

Right before my very own eyes were matching scars, our battle wounds identical to one another.

"When did you do that?" I choked out, not being able to tear my gaze away from his slashes.

"Which time?"

I closed my eyes from the impact of his words. This was all too much. I wouldn't make it out of there alive. He was slowly killing me. A single tear fell from my face, and when I felt his finger wipe it away, I subconsciously grabbed his hand and brought it up to my mouth, tenderly kissing each scar. He let me. When I opened my eyes, I saw that his were red and glossy.

"I was pregnant with your child," I finally declared, liberating myself from the lie I've never shared with anyone.

I wanted to be free.

Forgiven.

I closed my eyes again. I couldn't look at him. The pain from it all was eating me alive.

"What the fuck are you talking about?" he spewed, drastically changing his tone as I knew he would.

"You remember the cabin that you rented for Valentine's Day," I chuckled from nervousness. "You remember how we made love everywhere for two days straight? We couldn't get enough of each other, getting lost in our bodies, orgasm after orgasm…"

"Yes. That's all I thought about in prison when I would stroke my cock," he informed, catching me off guard with his crudeness.

"We left there with more than just fulfillment and satisfaction. We left with our creation."

There was a long pause. "G, look at me."

I shook my head no. Not missing the fact that he had called me G.

"Please…" he groaned.

I took a deep breath and braced myself for what was to come, words can really damage you more than anything in this world. They have the power to change one's emotions and feelings toward anything. Without words, we wouldn't be able to cause war. That's why thoughts are guarded so closely, because they have the impact to produce words that can cause our strengths or weaknesses to prevail.

Like they say; words can be forgiven, but never forgotten.

It was now or never.

I opened my venomous eyes and narrowed them at him. "What's wrong, Mr. Nichols?" I mocked. "You don't want to play anymore? I thought you were having a good time. Is it not fun to play with broken toys?" I expressed with glossy eyes.

He shook his head in dismay. "I didn't know. If I would have known, things would have been much different. You never gave me a chance."

"That's bullshit. I knew the truth. I've always known the truth. I was at your house. I heard you and your wife make up. I heard everything. You used me! The entire fucking time! You used me. After everything I shared with you. It was all a lie. I was something to get your dick wet."

"Gianna, Jesus Christ you were there? Where? How did you even get in?"

"I used the key you kept under your rug by the front door," I chuckled.

"Gianna, my wife- my ex-wife..." he exhaled. "I was captivated by you the second you walked into my classroom. I knew you were my student, I knew it was wrong, but it didn't stop the thoughts I had of you. It was sick and it was twisted. I was disgusted with myself. That didn't stop our paths from colliding. We were a fucking train wreck, G, right from the start. We were doomed." He shook his head trying to reason with me.

"I was the adult, I was the one in charge, and I couldn't help but feel like I manipulated the situation."

"I came on to you."

"And I never turned it down. I let it go on. It continued because I allowed it. The more I was with you; the harder it got to stay away. I started to think about the future...I thought about the future every time we were together. The fact that I had unprotected sex with you was just icing on the cake," he added.

He braced himself for what he was about to say. "Sarah called me out of the blue one day, wanting to work things out. I didn't understand because we both had decided to go our separate ways, but she told me she was pregnant...and I'm sorry, but I took it as a sign from God. What would you have done in my situation?"

I sat there, shocked from his revelations. My mind couldn't process what he was disclosing fast enough.

"Pregnant? You told me you were going to get a divorce! You told me you weren't together since the beginning of the school year!" I yelled and tried to get up and away from him, but he caught my arm, making me stay to listen.

"We hadn't. But I fucked up and she came to me and was upset and crying. And we didn't make sense, G! We never made sense. It plagued me and I had a moment of weakness. I thought–I don't know what the fuck I thought...one thing led to another and it just happened. Oh my God! I thought about you the entire time. And I felt awful when it was over and so did she. We agreed it was over. When she

164

came to me eight weeks later and told me she was pregnant, then I knew. I knew that was it for us. We weren't meant to be, and as much as I wanted it to be different, it wasn't in the cards. I didn't think that you would turn on me because I let you go. I did the right thing. I may have done it too late but I tried to do the right thing."

I stood right up and hovered over him. "That makes no fucking sense! You didn't think about that before you decided to stick your dick inside me and get me knocked up–"

He stood up and closed his fists to his sides. "You said you were on birth control."

"Yes. I was. I wasn't lying."

He laughed. "How the fuck am I supposed to tell the difference, *Gianna*? All you have done is manipulate everything to your advantage. How do I know you're telling me the truth? How do I know you aren't lying? You want my sympathy, right? You want me to forgive you!" he yelled, pacing the room back and forth.

"Well...I can't fucking forgive you! I went through hell and back because of you. I'm still living in hell and I have no idea when I'm going to be free of it. And now you tell me you were pregnant...come on...do I look that fucking stupid to you? What do you take me for?"

I sat down, I had to. Between the lack of alcohol, new knowledge, and confrontation, I was done. I placed my hand on my forehead, clammy, just what I thought.

"I don't know what you want me to say. I'm not lying."

"Are you all right?" His tone seemed sincere.

"No. I'm not all right. I need a fucking drink."

"You really are an alcoholic, aren't you?"

I chuckled. "No. I'm not. I'm actually lying. I'm manipulative, remember?" I wanted him to go away, to have the liberty to wallow in my own misery. The misery I created.

He sat down next to me, leaned forward, and pulled my hand away from my face. "Why, G? Why all the lies?" he questioned with a confused face.

"Because I was angry. I was eighteen and I just wanted you to hurt. As much as I was. I'm not saying what I did was right, but it seemed right at the time. I never thought it would turn in to what it did. I didn't think you'd go to prison. I just thought you'd get fired." I sighed and held my stomach, trying to relieve the cramps.

"You're a fucking mess; I mean, look at you..." he tried to rationalize, but all I kept thinking about was when he would bring me another bottle.

"You want a drink, don't you?"

"Unless you want me to go into a seizure and start throwing up everywhere, I suggest you bring me something to drink."

He shook his head in a disappointed manor. "And then what? Huh? What happens after this?"

"I don't fucking know! Are you going to kill us? Because if you are, just fucking leave me here. I'll die without any alcohol...isn't that what you want?" I shouted, trying not to slur my words.

"Look at me, James! Do I look like someone who is fucking happy? Do you think I haven't regretted what I did to you? What I caused myself...I ruined my life...for what? For some man who was going through a mid-life crisis and fucking paid attention to me. That's it. I was a broken little girl and I now I'm fucking shattered. I'm so shattered I can't even begin to put myself back together. The pieces are all fucked up! There's nothing left."

I didn't care anymore; if he left me there, I would have welcomed the darkness with open arms. I lost the will to fight for anything long ago. He stood and placed one foot before the other and left the room.

This unbearable weight was on my chest and heart from the lies, the secrets, and the betrayal. The tightening in my throat and chest was almost unbearable, I was asphyxiated in it. I couldn't tell the lies from the truth anymore. How could I let it get so bad that my perception was altered and disoriented? Was this from alcohol withdrawal? I groaned in pain, leaning forward to catch myself on the floor.

I heard his footsteps down the hall; I knew what he was bringing back with him. He wasn't done with me; he hadn't hurt or punished me enough. All it would take is for me to not drink it, to not take the sip that leads to more. I could turn it down and let this be the end of it all.

Who was I kidding? The second he would hand it to me, I would chug it like it was the last thing I would do. There was no going back for me, only a standstill.

I watched through hooded eyes as he sat in front of me, placing the bottle at his side. He was going to make me beg for it.

"Where is it?" he questioned.

My eyes went from the bottle back to him. "What?" I retorted.

"Where's the baby? If you're not lying, then where's our child?"

I had to let him go, and the only way to do that was to kill him, too.

I looked right at him and spoke with conviction, "I killed it. I killed your baby, James. I killed our child."

His mouth gaped open and his eyes changed from...

Love, hurt, pain.

Hate.

And then he lunged at me.

Chapter Nineteen

My back hit the concrete, knocking the wind out of me, and I gasped as he grabbed the lapels of my shirt. He roughly grabbed the sides of my face with one hand and the other grabbed the bottle.

"Drink," he demanded, with execution behind his tone.

I kept my mouth shut as hard as I could and thrashed my face and body back and forth, trying to get him off of me. His hold tightened, making my cheeks dig in and my mouth open. "Drink!" he yelled, aiming it closer to my lips.

I didn't want to be treated like a child, a prisoner; I would drink when I fucking wanted to.

"Drink."

"Fuck you!" I spit out, jerking my face from side to side.

He squeezed my cheeks harder and my mouth opened. He poured vodka in and just kept going; it spilled down the sides of my face, down my neck, and toward my back. I chugged until I started choking. It burned when it made its way down my nostrils. I tried to move from his grasp, but he never let up. I wheezed, choking in air as he drained the entire bottle in my mouth. He was going to drown me. When it was empty, he threw it across the room and screamed. I heard it shatter against the wall and that's when I used his momentum to push him away. He fell backward onto his ass and caught himself with his arms. I quickly backed away and went toward the shards of glass. I clutched one in my grasp and held it in front of me, winded and trying to catch my breath.

He cocked his head to the side. "What are you going to do with that?"

I hyperventilated, placing my hand on my chest to try to calm myself down.

"Isn't that what you wanted, little girl? Do you feel better now? Did I make it good for you?" he scorned.

I used the back of my arm to wipe away the liquor as I continued to find my bearings, "Not as good as it was for you," I violently replied. "You're enjoying every fucking part of this! Who's the monster now?!" I screamed.

His pupils enlarged and he sprang forward, smacking my wrist before I even saw it coming. The shard of glass flung out of my hand.

He grabbed my hair and pulled back has far as it could go.

"Ahh!" I screamed, trying to claw at him.

"Not as much as you enjoyed it, Miss Edwards." His hand grazed my breasts and I tried to push it away, but he was stronger than me. He shoved me backward and up against the wall; I hit it with a thud. If it hadn't been for the adrenaline, it would have knocked me out. He removed his hand from my hair and it went right to my throat. He shoved me higher up the wall, making it impossible for me to move. Our chests heaved up and down, almost in sync with one another, and then we locked eyes.

And that's when I saw it.

Lust.

His mouth met mine with abandonment and desire. His tongue went to the back of my throat, claiming me. He wanted to brand me and I took in every marking. His tongue tasted the inside of my mouth and all over like he couldn't get enough of me. I took his lead and kissed him back with the same enthusiasm; it was messy, sloppy and passionate as hell. He tasted better than I remembered, and when his fingers reached for my pussy, I moaned.

It was as if a bucket of cold water had been poured on him. He immediately moved away from me and held my throat tighter, pushing me further into the wall. His face was shocked and appalled, and I could tell he was angry with himself. Our breathing was still elevated, and he wiped away any residue of me that was left on his face, trying to get clean of me.

He squeezed around my neck, not letting go. I was losing air and he wanted me to. He had his lips pursed and the look in his eyes told me he wanted to hurt me and fuck me…he kept squeezing until I could barely breathe. The temporary loss of blood to my brain made me start seeing stars and the pressure made it blinding. My head fell to the side and I was sure my face was turning blue. He let go right before my eyes started to close, and I fell sideways coughing for air. I coughed, gasping, trying to breathe in as much as I could.

He just got up and left me, without so much as one word.

He let down his guard.

And it infuriated him that I knew it, too.

It gave me comfort in a situation that I knew was about to turn ugly. Mr. Nichols wasn't fucking around when he told me he wanted to make us pay. He was going to rip away every last bit of us, if it was the last thing he did. I wanted to live in the bubble that I had created for myself, where no one could hurt me, unless it was me. I was my own worst enemy. My past had finally caught up with me and he was placing it directly in front of me.

As soon as she walked in, I found her gaze; it was like a magnet pulling me toward her. The vitality of ours sins immersing in the air and suffocating us with nothing but the truths that we held onto so tightly.

"Hmmm…no love? No friendly exchanges? Not even a hello? I don't understand, Mack and Gia are back together again." He clapped his hands. "It's time to celebrate and rejoice! Let's have a fucking party girls! Come on, Mack, you've been whining about seeing your Gia, well here she is. Let's kiss and make up, huh?" he taunted, shoving her toward me.

"You ladies aren't making me happy. I've gone through a lot of unnecessary bullshit for the last month between you two cunts and now I want you to fucking embrace each other and make me feel like it was all worth it," he warned.

Neither one of us looked at each other, and I watched him slide down the wall with nothing more than a sinister look on his face. He looked at me and his eyes were perplexed and concerned, for whom I didn't know. He looked almost crazed.

He shook his head, taking his stare away from me, "Now...let's try this again...Gia, say hello to your *best friend* Mack."

McKenzie was sitting down with her back against the wall and her hands were covering her ears, she looked terrified.

"What's your problem?" I asked.

She scuffed, removing her hands and pointing right at me. "You! You're my problem. You're nothing but a liar! You were fucking him the entire time. My life has been in shambles because of you! And now I come to find out that you were lovers...why the hell did you even involve in your fucked up affair? I had nothing to do with it."

Mack came in here with guns blazing; if she wanted a war, then I was going to give her one.

I laughed, "Oh Mackity Mack is not playing fair. People who live in glass houses, shouldn't throw stones. Huh?

She looked surprised and then looked over at Mr. Nichols like he was supposed to save her or something.

"Keep your pretty eyes over to her, I didn't say shit," he retorted, surrendering with both hands in the air. "Gia, baby, why don't you tell Mack here what you know," he taunted, standing up and walking over to me, letting his hand slide around my waist. He lifted my shirt, humiliating me in front of her. I didn't want her to see me like this...it only added fuel to the fire.

I tried to ignore his hands on me and focused my anger toward the person who deserved it. "You want to know the truth, oh *best friend* of mine. I know all about your little indiscretions. I've known since we were eighteen." I cocked my head to the side, "I'd like to think it started then but that's more then likely a lie. Another secret. Am I right? How long did it go on, Mack? How long were you fucking him behind my back? How long were you betraying my mother and I? Huh?" I accused, making her eyes widen in surprise with a mixture of fear.

"What are you talking about?"

"Are you kidding me? You're really going to sit there and pretend like it didn't happen. I needed you. I have never needed you more then I needed you that day. I was coming to tell you everything.

There was going to be no more secrets or lies. I was coming to tell you the truth about it all. Then I find out Mack isn't so perfect, right? She had secrets too! Secrets that would not only destroy me! But also my fucking FAMILY! Did you think about that? Did you ever even consider what you were doing?" I yelled.

"Gia, you're not perfect either. You kept secrets, too," she accused.

"Shhh…" I said with my finger. "You're a liar too!"

"God! I fucking love this. Keep going, I'm highly entertained," Mr. Nichols coaxed, walking away from me. "Go ahead, Gia, tell your *best friend* what you've wanted to say for the last nine years. Tell her what you know," he enticed.

"You think you're the only one that's hurting, Mack? You want to pretend you didn't play a role in how everything turned out. Poor, little, innocent McKenzie, always getting the pity. Everyone always loved you best and you fucking knew it, you played into it."

"Pity?" she asked. "I don't understand. You were coming to tell me about Mr. Nichols? About your relationship with him?"

"I was coming to tell you much more then that, Mack. I was pregnant with his baby," I announced. "I was so scared and I needed my best friend. I needed my sister. But you weren't there…and when I didn't find you in your room, I heard you down the hall in your dad's office. Want to guess who I heard you with?

I had been sitting in the same place for several hours as I stared at not one, but five positive pregnancy sticks. One even had a smiley face on it. The moment the first stick turned positive, my maternal emotional instincts kicked in and I started to think about the future, not only with James, but also with our child.

At first, they were vain and it was all about what it would look like? Would it be a boy or a girl? Would it be a daddy's baby or mommy's? Would the delivery hurt? Would I be an attractive pregnant person? How much weight did I have to gain? Would I have to change my diet?

What kind of mom would I be? What kind of dad would he be? Would he want the baby? Would he be excited or mad at me?

The fears, hopes, and dreams were much more evident now. But it was no longer about me anymore...it became about us.

I was an us now.

I was excited but extremely nervous. I was only eighteen and I had no idea what I would do with a child, sometimes I felt like I was still one but that's pretty normal, right? My hormones were all over the place; one minute I wanted to jump up and down and shout from the rooftops that I was pregnant with the love of my life. And then the next minute, I had tears in my eyes from the anxiety of the future.

We never really talked about the future. Our tumultuous love affair was extremely complicated to say the least, and now adding a baby into the mix would make or break us and I wasn't naïve enough to not know that. The part that truly bothered me was that I thought we shared everything, the good and the bad. I realized that day that we never talked about the future; we discussed the past and the present. About the fact that we loved each other and we were soul mates, but instead of that providing me with a sense of reassurance, it didn't. It ate at my insecurities of why we never talked about the future. Was it because there wouldn't be one?

That didn't make sense... what was the point of it all?

I was overthinking everything, he would be ecstatic and feel the same way I did. We would find a way to make it work. I had faith that everything would work itself out and at the end of the day, as long as we were together, that's all that mattered.

The rest would fall into place.

After I stressed about all that, my mind wandered over to Mack. How would I explain all this to her and make her understand that we were the real thing? That this wasn't some high school crush and he wasn't taking advantage of me. I knew that was going to be the first thing she would think, and it would probably be the first thing anyone would think, especially my parents. My mom would have to understand, she was a woman. She carried me in her womb; she felt the same connection that I had to my baby. It had to be maternal. My dad would want his only daughter to be happy, and I knew he would be upset at first–I mean, what father wouldn't–however, he would accept it.

My parents would come to terms with it. Plus, it's a baby! Who doesn't want a baby around?!

I would tell James, and then I would tell Mack everything. I would beg for her forgiveness if she felt betrayed. I couldn't lose her; I wouldn't survive it. I needed Mack, I needed my best friend, I needed my sister. Then James and I would tell my parents together.

I had it all planned out. The truth would set us free and we would have our fresh start with no more secrets or lies. I wanted to keep this baby; I wanted to have it with him. We had so much love that it created a little person, a piece of him and a piece of me.

Us.

To know that I was carrying our child inside of me was an unexplainable feeling of contentment, harmony, anxiety, nervousness, and excitement. It was all rolled into one, each sentiment playing off the other. Our baby was made for a reason and that reason was for us to be together.

Forever.

After I analyzed and picked at every possible scenario until I felt like I was going to combust, I decided to just get in my car and surprise him.

I drove to his house with a heavy heart about the anticipation of the future possibilities. I parked my car by the clubhouse and walked the remaining hundred feet or so to his house. When I turned the corner, what I saw nearly knocked me on my ass. He was playing with Cara, he would pick her up, tickle her, and then throw her in the air. She wiggled and squirmed until he placed her back on the ground, and then they repeated the process all over again.

Her giggles were contagious. I hid behind the trees, watching the intimate interaction, trying not to laugh at the silliness. I hadn't seen him with his little girl, but he talked about her often with love and pride in his eyes. All the fears of him not being happy about our little miracle slowly escaped my mind. He was a good father and it wouldn't be any different with ours.

My foot was midair when I watched her come out.

Sarah.

She had a robe on and her hair was pulled up out of her face, looking like she had just woken up from sleep. James placed Cara on the ground and she ran inside the house, screaming and giggling the entire way, expecting him to chase her. Sarah had the most content and loving expression on her face as she watched James walk over to her. He pulled her into the nook of his arm and she wrapped her arms around his chest, he kissed her forehead and they walked inside together like that.

I didn't move from the place I was standing for what felt like hours. I was in shock, numb. Did that really happen? Did I watch them play the picture perfect family? Was he lying to me? I couldn't wrap my head around it and I clenched my stomach in a comforting gesture. How could he do this to me? Was I just a game? A cruel joke?

I walked back to my car in a daze and I honestly don't even know how I made it back to my house in one piece. I barely recalled driving.

He lied.

I was wrapped up in a fairy tale that had no happy ending.

Logic, delusions, lies, secrets, and betrayal were all important pieces of the puzzle. All misplaced and scattered. I drove home and parked my car in the garage. I walked to Mack's house in an autopilot state of mind.

Put one foot in front of the other, Gia.

Tell Mack everything.

She will understand.

She will help you.

She will always be there for you, she always has.

Everything will be all right...

Her car was in the driveway but I didn't find her in her room. I looked in the bathroom next and I was about to call out her name when I heard whispering coming from her dad's office. I could have sworn I heard my father.

What was my father doing there?

The closer I got to the cracked door, the clearer the voices were heard, and it sounded like they were arguing. My heart began beating heavily and hard. I could feel the pulse in my neck pounding and my palms grew sweaty.

Why was I so nervous?

I placed my hand on the door, and what I saw changed my life forever.

It changed all our lives.

Chapter Twenty

"Oh my God, Gia! You knew?" She shook her head back and forth, "I swear, I swear to you I tried to stop it. I promise!" she pleaded, taking a step toward me.

"Liar! You didn't do anything! Not one thing. I heard you! I heard both of you!" I angrily replied.

"It got so out of hand, I swear I tried," she confessed.

"I can't believe you. You fucked my dad all the way through high school! What kind of sick person does that? What the hell did my mom ever do to you, Mack? She treated you like you were her own daughter, her own flesh and blood! How could you do that to her? How could you do that to me?" I yelled, trying to control my temper.

"You're not innocent either, Gia! You kept secrets, too," she reasoned.

How could she even try to compare the two? James wasn't anyone to her, and I didn't break up my best friend's family. She had some fucking nerve trying to make excuses for her actions by blaming me. Like the fact that I had secrets made it all right that she was fucking my dad.

"This is fucking epic! Let's keep this going," Mr. Nichols boasted, clapping his hands, causing the loud echo to vibrate the close walls.

I wanted to scream, run away, and hide, but that wouldn't change anything. This was some fucked up version of therapy, a game that he was playing with both of us. Adding fuel to the fire, making it burn vivaciously before brutally shoving us in, like some witches at the stake being punished for their sins. It's exceedingly easy to hate someone, but to see it through someone else's eyes is like watching a train wreck, you want to turn away but you're glued to the fucking catastrophe in front of you. You can't help but watch and hope everyone comes out alive, but knowing they won't doesn't stop you from staring.

I wanted to punish her and that's why it all happened, she had no idea how much she drove me toward the anger and resentment that I had against everyone. She was supposed to be my best friend, the one person I could trust, and to learn that it was just another lie, another illusion, ruined me.

It made me become this woman I hated.

"Go on," he snickered, making me turn my hate toward him. "It's story time! You're up, Mack, tell us about fucking Mr. Edwards."

I could feel the vein on the side of my head start to throb, producing a piercing headache. I wanted to put my hands on my ears and block out the noise, the chaos, but I knew better than to think he would let me. He would tie me to the bed and make me listen to it; the sick fuck would probably record it and play it in my sleep to generate nightmares. He had no idea that I didn't need to sleep to experience them. They happened every day with my eyes opened, it was much more prevailing when I was awake, much more real.

I dug my nails into my skin, trying to take away the pain he was creating, anything to take away the hurt that I felt having to relive that day. The day that everything came tumbling down and set forth a domino effect that was still happening at that moment, right in front of us.

He deviously looked at Mack and I knew the worst had yet to come. I could see it in his eyes; they never lied to me like he did.

"Tell Princess Gia how much you loved her daddy's cock in your pussy," he sneered.

And that's when Mack snapped and lunged for him like a crazy person. He quickly caught her around the neck and slammed her face first onto the floor without a bit of distress. She was no match for him. I would know. His shoe dug into her face as he held her there.

"Oh…you stupid fucking cunt. Don't forget for one second who's in charge of the show. Now be a good girl and follow the rules and no one gets hurt. You know how angry it makes me when you don't listen. Gia…" he sang. "Tell her! Tell her that she needs to listen to avoid getting punished. Do you understand? Mack? Answer me!" he yelled.

"Yes," she mumbled.

"Good girl," he ordered, removing himself from her.

She stood and looked at me. I should have helped her. But I would be lying if I said I didn't feel some satisfaction from her distress. She fucking deserved it.

"I don't know about you but I think it's time we have a pow wow. Both of you sit," he demanded.

We sat down as far away from each other as possible, but he didn't allow it and made us move to sit Indian style directly in front of each other. I saw the worry written all across Mack's beautiful face, even after all these years she's still one of the most beautiful girls I have ever seen. The years have been kind to her, although she doesn't deserve one damn bit of it.

"Mack, I think you should go first. Tell Gia here a bedtime story," he insisted, circling around us like he was conjuring how to hurt us next. I knew what he wanted and I could tell that she was clueless.

What had he been doing to her this entire time?

"Hmmm," he thought, tapping his chin with his finger. "How about we begin with how many times? I think that's a good place to start. How about you, Mack?" I swallowed the lump in my throat, not wanting to know the answer. It was one thing to assume but entirely different to have facts.

"ANSWER THE GODDAMN QUESTION!" he yelled, ripping her hair back, screaming in her face.

He was losing control, becoming the man that I didn't recognize, the one that terrified me. If I couldn't get him to have mercy on me, there was no fucking way it was happening with her.

"I guess it was a lot," she replied, trying to sound nonchalant about it.

How could she be so cruel?

"Hmmm…that's not a good enough answer. Let's clarify so there's no confusion, shall we?" He nodded. "I think so…I believe it was for two years? Right, Mack? You know what? Better yet…let's

start with how many boys got inside your pussy in high school?"
Again, she looked at me.

What the fuck was he talking about?

"None," she answered.

I narrowed my eyes. "What the hell are you talking about, Mack? We lost our virginity together. You dated a whole bunch of guys in high school," I reminded.

"Oh…I'm sorry to break it to you, Gia, baby," he patronized. "Mackity Mack didn't have sex with anyone in high school, she was actually harder to get inside then your cunt of a mom, which is probably why your daddy fucked her. She only fucked Mr. Edwards in high school. Aren't I right? Tell her!"

I cocked my head to the said. "Mack?"

"It's time for the truth…tell her who popped your cherry."

Oh my God…there were more lies? Did we ever really know each other? Did I imagine it all? That wouldn't make sense because we wouldn't be here if I had? Right?

He knelt before her and ran the backs of his knuckles down her cheek. "Poor Mackenzie doesn't want to play anymore. She doesn't want to hurt Gia's precious feelings. Did you ever once think about my feelings? Did it ever occur to you what would happen to me when you lied to a courtroom full of people that I raped you! Let's all play nice now and tell the truth. Tell Gia whose cock stole your virtue? Be the good girl I know you can be."

She closed her eyes, like looking at me caused her pain, and for a second, I saw my best friend. "Your dad." And just like that it was gone.

"My dad? My dad took your virginity?" I questioned with a scowl.

"Yes. I swear I tried stop. I promise."

I shook my head. Liar! "Bullshit! Jesus Christ, Mack. How the hell would you feel if your dad did those things to me? How would you feel if I fucked your father right under your goddamn nose for two years." I retorted, trying not to let my eyes give me away. I didn't want to cry.

"Ohhh...I know." Mr. Nichols clapped. "This is the perfect opportunity for story time again," he goaded, in a singing tone. He sat against the wall off to the side of us and crossed his arms and ankles. "And go..." he provoked.

"Yes. I was trying to break it off with him that night," she recalled.

"Okay...that sounds pretty believable. Where were your parents?" he interrogated.

"They were attending a house warming party for something my mother had just closed on."

I remembered that party. That's how I was able to take the pregnancy tests without worrying that they would be around. I had the liberty to have some privacy.

"I get it. While the cats away, the mice will play. You called and he came." He raised his eyebrows, "Literally."

As much as I didn't want to hear it I needed to know the truth. I needed answers for the questions that plagued me for years.

"That's not what happened!" she seethed, looking at him. "I was doing good ignoring him and staying away from him. He came over looking for Gia. I was looking forward to having some alone time. To actually have the house to myself." she explained.

I found it interesting that she, too, wanted privacy. Did she feel like I did? Smothered by our supposedly close friendship?

"Perfect! I understand. Then what happened?" Mr. Nichols asked.

"I need to stand up," she requested, looking to him for permission.

She always was so weak.

"Fuck! I totally forgot to include Gia on the fun. You see...your friend Mack here has gone a little crazy. She has to pace the room as she tells you about riding your dads cock."

I relived everything that happened that day, even though it was the last thing I wanted to do.

The door was slightly ajar and I placed my palm on it. "Mack, you're acting like a child," my dad scolded.

Why was he treating Mack like that? He never spoke to her like that.

"That's an interesting choice of words, Kyle. We can't keep doing this, Gia is getting suspicious. I can barely look at her anymore. It's too many lies piling on each other, I feel like I'm suffocating. I can't do this anymore," she pleaded.

Can't do what? What the fuck was going on?

"Shhh...you don't know what you're saying," he stated, grazing his finger on her bottom lip.

My mouth went dry.

"I do, Kyle. This whole affair is fucked up. Gianna and I are best friends and you're making me lie to my best friend. Do you have any idea how hard that is for me? Do you even care? I have been fucking my best friend's dad for two years now," she revealed

Have you ever felt winded, like you couldn't breathe? I felt like I had just taken a shot directly to the heart. I couldn't move, inhale, or exhale. I stayed planted where my feet were firmly grounded and listened to my father seduce my best friend, the person I grew up with, the girl that was a sister to me. Another sibling that my parents treated better than me sometimes. I heard him say nasty and vile things to her that no daughter should ever have to hear a father say.

He spoke to her like a boyfriend, like a husband, like a lover. I watched him bend her over and fuck her on her dad's desk. The very desk that we used to sit on while we bothered her dad to come throw us around in the pool, the same office we use to play Barbie dolls in, waiting for our dads to pay attention to us as they discussed business. I thought back to every memory, every recollection, reminiscing it all while he thrust in and out of her with the same enthusiasm that James fucked me with.

The timeline of our lives were in sync and webbed together. There was no Gianna without McKenzie. I tried to tune out the noise all around me, trying to concentrate on the fact that I had no idea who McKenzie really was. She was supposed to be my sister, my partner in crime, my best friend...how could this have been happening and I'm just figuring it out. Had I been so blind? How could I have missed this? He had put Mack on a pedestal for as long as I could remember, and it wasn't because she was better than me. It was because he was fucking her, the little girl he watched grow up as if she was his own.

How fucking sick was that? I wanted to throw up and I could feel the disgusting bile make its way up my throat and into my mouth. How had I found myself in a fucked up limbo, an alternate universe, I stepped into the gates of hell where Mack was the devil and my dad her demon. They were lovers behind mine and my mother's backs. It happened right under my own nose, under everyone's noses. At least I took my discretions outside of our homes. They didn't even care that someone could catch them. Where was their decency and moral compass? Where the fuck was their compassion?

Who had Mack been all along? She never knew me, and I sure as hell never knew her.

I wanted to scream and make a scene and cause havoc all around me. All the walls were tumbling down and they were bleeding.

Bright red, filled with lies, deceit, and sadness.

I rubbed off the mascara that was dripping down my chin. Tears I hadn't noticed were streaming.

I knew then that nothing would ever be the same again. I went from loving Mack to hating her. It happened in a blink of an eye as I heard my father bring her to orgasm.

The very last words that left his mouth shook me to my core.

"I love you."

Chapter Twenty-one

"Shut the fuck up!" I screamed, as I stood up. I felt like I was a string and was being pulled, manipulated to the max.

He laughed. "Why? I was enjoying the story. It's all in good fun, Gia. Look at me when I talk to you." I narrowed my eyes at him.

"Much better. Mack's having a good time," he ridiculed, moving close to her to pull her hair as she tried to get away. He didn't let up and grabbed her with one hand on the back of her neck, placing her where he wanted.

My fingers were twitching. I stared both of them down and witnessed as he placed her directly in front of him, slowly moving his hand to her lower abdomen.

"You want to know how I know? I bet her pussy is wet," he taunted, with his fingers moving closer to her core.

I didn't answer, I watched in slow motion as my past and present collided with each other.

His fingers moved with ease to the center of her legs. "I win! She's fucking soaked," he growled in her ear and tightened his hold around her neck.

The fact that she was getting off on the day that my youth and innocence were heartlessly taken away from me made me want to hurt her. And to watch as James touched her so intimately like he knew her sweet spots, crazed me. My blood was boiling. Had he fucked her while we were there?

I closed my eyes, trying to take away the image of them being together, but it was just replaced with my father's hands caressing her nub.

"Mackenzie's pussy feels amazing…maybe I should fuck her right in front of you, Gia? Do you want me to bring your friend to orgasm just like your daddy did? Hmmm," he groaned.

I opened my eyes and they immediately locked with his, they were primal. I watched as he kissed down the side of her neck and he never broke eye contact with me. I looked down and caught him circling her clit with the same enthusiasm he had done to me and the string snapped. I heard it snap clear as day as I witnessed her body convulsing from her orgasm, the orgasm that he delivered.

I couldn't take it anymore and I charged at her with the years of hate I had built up. I did not see Mack. I did not see my best friend. I did not see my sister. I only saw the hate, lies and secrets. The betrayal. I saw a friendship built on nothing but secrets. Secrets that destroyed us. Lies that ate us up.

I saw what I hated to admit.

I saw G.

He saw me coming and smiled cunningly, stepping away before I pounced on top of her like she was my prey. I had been waiting for this moment for as long as I could remember and it didn't disappoint. Mack's body fell to the ground with a thud with my body right on top of hers. She let out a whoosh sound and I was on my knees with a closed fist hitting her directly in the face. The impact immediately shifted her face to the right and my hand throbbed. I ignored it.

I hit her again and it landed on her cheek, she screamed that time and it only egged on my need to physically hurt her. My hands latched on to the top of her head and I pulled her hair to slam her head into the concrete floor over and over again. Both of us screamed at the top of our lungs. Her hands moved on top of mine and she dug her nails into my skin until I bled and had to let go. Once I did, she flipped us over with ease and I guarded my face, knowing it was her turn to come at me.

"Fuck! I'm sorry, Gia! I'm so fucking sorry!" She attempted to move my arms from hovering over my face and I fought with all the strength I had to not look into her eyes.

"Fucking look at me, Gia. LOOK AT ME!" she yelled, making me try even harder to shield myself.

"Fuck you!" I replied in a hoarse tone.

The scene erupted into more screaming and thrashing around until Mr. Nichols got involved and held my hands above my head. I tried to wiggle and move away from both of them to no avail.

"Time to stop hiding, Gianna. Listen to your best friend as she grovels and begs for your forgiveness," he whispered close to my face gripping onto my wrists and holding them tighter.

"Shut the fuck up!" she yelled, trying to hold my legs down.

I kicked and flayed around, trying to loosen their holds on me.

"I'm not done playing! The shows not fucking over, Mack. Tell your best friend how much you loved fucking her dad. Tell her how he was always hard around you and would often take you to a secluded corner to fuck you silly. How you would only dance for him when he was in the stands, his obvious erection peering through his lust filled eyes," he revealed, making me scream in pure agony and torture.

"Don't think people didn't see you. It's not like you guys did a very good job at hiding it. I saw the day he fucked you on school grounds without a care in the world that his wife would catch him, or better yet, his daughter! 'Kyle,' you moaned over and over again," he groaned, enjoying the turmoil he was causing.

"I always wondered if your mom knew, Gia. She went on a fucking crusade to crucify me, getting all the community and reporters involved. Why? I know why…it wasn't because her precious "daughters" were raped. It was because it made your daddy finally pay attention to her. She was able to have good ole daddy's attention. Your parents watched you like a hawk after what you guys claimed. It brought them closer. The truth is, you guys getting 'raped' was the best thing that ever happened to their marriage. Gia's mother knew it. She took her frustrations out on me in court and then let daddy fuck her later. Women know shit like that and I'm sure she knew something was going on. She may have not known it was Mack, but she had to know he was fucking around on her."

She had tears streaming down her face and I knew she was imaging my father with someone else and it caused her pain. Her cheek was bruising and there was blood on the corner of her lip. Her tongue grazed the cut and she hissed in pain.

She loved him.

She loved him as much as I loved James.

"This is bullshit! You act like I'm the only one to blame, Gia? Look around you! We're in a padded room because of you and what we did! For what? For nothing!" she spewed. "Not one fucking reason! For what, Gia! Why? What were we thinking when we decided to do what we did?"

"Get off me," I shouted through gritted teeth.

"What?" she answered, confused.

"GET OFF ME!" I yelled. "It was my idea! It was NEVER your idea! It was all part of the plan. I hated you! I wanted to hurt you just as much as you hurt me! You were part of the plan just as much as he was," I vindictively divulged.

He laughed, "Ooohhh…secrets, secrets…Gia's up now! Tell Mack about how you planned it all. Tell her how you were pissed that she was fucking your daddy that you set out to punish her. It's your turn, now," he ordered, egging it on more.

"Gia?" she questioned, getting up and backing away.

"Yes! You were part of the plan, Mack," I taunted, spitting blood to the dirty floor. "That day you wrote your name on my paper was all part of it. The day you agreed to write my name on top of your page was the day I smiled. I would have the last word."

"What the fuck are you talking about?" she asked, pulling her swollen lip into her mouth.

"Your little friend here, made sure you got caught," Mr. Nichols chimed in. He was enjoying this. The fucker was enjoying every second of it.

"What do you mean?" she asked, glaring from him to me.

"You see, Mack," Mr. Nichols chanted, getting up and letting me go. "Gia didn't write her name on the other test, she wrote yours and that's how you got caught. Gia made you go down with her, she wanted you to lose everything, just like she had. Isn't that right? Am I missing a piece of the puzzle, Gia, baby?" Mr. Nichols beamed with self-satisfaction while my mind thought about that day.

I left the office and walked home. I made it into my shower before I crouched to the floor in agony. I cried and cried and then cried some more. The devastation was overwhelming; it was an emotionally shattering sense of loss that I experienced on all accounts. The illusion of security or false sense of safety was shattered. I started to listen to the destructive thoughts, where there were only feelings of humiliation followed by real sadness over my losses. Everything was taken away from me.

My best friend.

My father.

My family.

My soul mate.

I bawled and let go of all the illusions and fantasies I had. And after what felt like hours I turned off the shower and grabbed the towel from the counter. I wrapped myself up and went straight to my bed. I lay there and stared at my pruned skin for hours. Not knowing whether to cry, scream, or laugh. I woke up the next morning the exact same way. I felt like I had aged years in one night. I dressed and went to school. I avoided Mack all day, feigning a headache. She let me have my desired privacy.

I dreaded going to sixth period and I almost skipped, not being able to face him.

"Miss Edwards," he addressed as the class walked out. "I need to discuss this paper with you. Please stay after class." I didn't move from my seat and when everyone had exited the room, Mr. Nichols shut the door. He didn't even walk back to where I was sitting in the back of the class. He leaned on his desk and sighed.

"We can't do this anymore, Gianna."

He called me Gianna. No longer G.

I never moved my gaze from his. "And why is that?"

He crossed his arms, "Where do you want me to start...you know why we can't."

"I thought you loved me," I stated.

His eyes glazed over, James was back. "I do. You know I do. But I'm your teacher and you're my student. We can't keep doing this. It's wrong."

I cocked my head to the side. "Was it wrong when I had your dick in my mouth a few days ago? Because you never stated it was wrong when you came in my mouth and ordered me to swallow."

He put his hand on his forehead in a frustrated gesture. "Jesus, Gia."

"What's wrong, Mr. Nichols? I'm just repeating what you said. I'm sort of confused. You know, since I am your student and all."

He finally walked over to me and got down on his knees in front of me. "I'm sorry," he whispered, placing his hand behind my neck and his forehead on mine. "We can't do this anymore. We shouldn't have ever gotten started in the first place. It's my fault. Not yours. You are a beautiful girl and you have so much ahead of you."

"What if I want you?"

His other hand grazed my cheek. "It's not possible."

"Why?"

"I just told you, Gianna."

"Stop calling me that...why do you keep calling me that? It's me. You know who I am," I agonized.

He sighed, "We can't. I can't anymore."

I looked him right in the eyes. "Are you sure it has nothing to do with your wife?"

He hesitated. "No. It has nothing to do with her." I nodded.

He lied. As if he was telling me a bedtime story

His eyes never lied to me.

Liar, liar, liar, I wanted to scream.

"I'll always cherish our time together, and if things were different- ugh, I mean...if I weren't- if you were just a little bit older. It would be so much different," he explained.

I jumped out of my desk and jumped on him, I threw my arms and legs around him, holding him close and not wanting to let him go. He wrapped his arms around me and I turned my head to breathe in his smell.

"Please don't leave me. Please. We can work this out, and we won't have to be intimate until I gradate from school. Please, just give me a chance. Give us a chance. Please. Please don't do this..." I

shamelessly begged. I felt every bit the little girl I knew I was portraying.

He kissed my neck and nuzzled my shoulder. I reveled in the feel of him. "I can't, Gianna. I hope you understand. One day when you're older, you will understand that we don't always get what we want, it doesn't matter how much we want it."

"Please," I openly sobbed. "I love you. I love you. I love you." I repeated, praying it would make a difference.

He moved his face to look at me and kissed my forehead, it had a fatherly feel to it and it made me sick to my stomach.

"No, Miss Edwards."

He placed the nail in the coffin. My head fell forward and I cried and wallowed in my own tears. I held him as close as I could. I was suffocating in him. I wanted to etch him into my skin where I knew he would never leave me.

"You need to go," he dismissed, removing my limbs off of him so easily. Like I was nothing. He got up and walked away.

Away from me.

Away from us…

I cried by myself for a few more minutes. Never moving from the same spot on the floor he had left me, where he turned his back on me, on us.

I peeled myself off the floor, not even looking his way, and exited the room.

I walked out of the classroom in a stupor and went to the ladies room. I locked the door behind me and went to the mirror. I washed my face and finally looked up at my reflection. I looked exhausted.

I looked broken.

A much more broken person than I was when it all began. No person could complete me. No one wanted to. I lost my entire identity. But I discovered who I really was and what I really wanted.

It needed to start with Mack.

If I couldn't be happy, then neither could she…

Chapter Twenty-two

Mr. Nichols escorted Mack back to her room. I had never seen her so disoriented and distraught before, not even the night everything went down. McKenzie was always the one to hold everything together. Her strong persona and mentality was what helped her survive, it was contagious and I often found myself hoping some of it would rub off on me. The self-destruction I just witnessed was not the Mack I knew and loved. Had everything finally caught up with her? Was she breaking as much as I was? Was it worse for her because she was so strong?

I didn't know why I felt bad for her, I hated her, but that's not entirely true. I loved her, too...how can you love and hate someone at the same time? They are on two opposite ends of the spectrum, two completely different definitions, but how can they be entwined in my heart. Being right doesn't change the way things are, how things are portrayed. It also doesn't make it any less real.

I heard his footsteps down the hall before I saw him. He came in and sat on the opposite wall, directly in front of me. His eyes were still dark, distant, and cold.

He crossed his arms. "So you had an abortion after you came and saw me with my family? Or after you saw Mack fucking your dad? Or after I broke it off with you?" he degraded. "I'm just trying to keep all the lies in order."

I narrowed my eyes. "Yes. I found out I was pregnant and I was coming to tell you, I saw you with your *family* and then I went to Mack and saw her fucking my dad. The next day you called it off and that's when I killed our baby."

"And framed me for rape," he hissed.

"That didn't come till later. I wanted to hurt Mack first. Our finals were coming up and she wanted me to pass so that our future wouldn't change, but I couldn't stand to be near her. Every time I was, I swear I could smell my father on her. I don't know how I didn't notice it before. So, yes...I set her up," I stated. "I knew you would turn us in because you're a fucking asshole, so we lost everything, our plans, and our future...you should have seen my dad's face when the school called him to tell him what we had done," I snickered.

"He was livid with Mack and me. It's the first time I saw disappointment spread across his face when it came to her, and it gave me pleasure. I wanted to hurt him, to humiliate him to his friends and co-workers that his daughter was a cheater, a fraud." I put my hands in the air shaking them. "Oh my God! Gianna Edwards, Kyle Edwards' prodigy is a liar. Our name was tarnished at the country club, and though I did feel bad for my mom because she didn't deserve it, I also did it for her... and that gave me the last bit of courage I needed."

He nodded. "And how did I get involved in all this?"

I shrugged. "I wanted to hurt you. But I didn't think it would go to the extent that it did. We were both eighteen," I justified.

He chuckled. "See, that's the thing about rape, Miss Edwards. It's against someone's consent, and it's a fucking crime. I was your teacher...it all adds up, you know?"

I nodded. "I'm sorry. I know it doesn't change anything, but I am sorry."

His eyes widened and he stood up. "Get up!" he roared.

"What?" I asked, confused. How the hell did he do that? Go from one extreme to the next.

"Get the fuck up!"

The tone of his voice made me jump. I quickly sat up and it made me lightheaded. He was over to me in four strides, yanking me by the hair and bending my body forward.

"It's time to play," he half-whispered.

He dragged me into Mack's room to demean me; he wasn't done playing with his toy. He wanted to show me that he didn't care about me, that I was nothing to him.

Mack was coloring with a yellow crayon on the wall and she seemed disoriented, completely out of it. I looked around the room and there were drawings all over the walls colored in yellow crayon. What the fuck was going on? What had she been doing in her room this entire time?

"Tell me, Mack?" he asked, bringing my attention back to him. "What happened that night you guys claimed I raped you? You came to my house and Gianna went bat shit crazy on me, but what happened when you left? I want to know that…" he interrogated, not letting up on my hair.

She started explaining what happened, but I remembered it differently.

I was mad when we left his house. He wouldn't listen to us, even though Mack barely did any talking. She thought we went over there to talk about our finals, hoping that he would give us another chance. That's not why I wanted to go over there, I wanted to hurt him, scream at him, and have him feel something, anything. I wanted to know that he did love me, that I wasn't just some game to him, and that there was actual love and he wasn't lying to me. That we shared something powerful and all consuming.

I was beyond livid that he didn't give me anything; he didn't show me any remorse, kindness, or love. It had all been a game to him. I was just another one of his conquests. I went after him and hit him with everything I could muster. I took out all my frustrations with Mack, my dad, and him right on his handsome face. Mack pulled me away from him and we left his house. He didn't give me one ounce of regret for how he treated me, for getting rid of me like I was yesterday's garbage. I was blinded by fury and hate for the three people that I loved more than anything. So I turned my frustrations on the only other person I could, McKenzie.

"I want to get fucked up! Let's go get completely hammered and find a guy and fuck with him," I cackled.

"What?" she asked.

"Let's go to a bar downtown."

"Gia, you're not making any sense. What is going on?"

"Nothing! I just want to not feel anything right now. Let's just say fuck it and throw caution to the wind and go with it."

She sighed, "All right, let's do it."

It was fairly easy to find a guy, they were everywhere. He fed us some shots and the more I drank, the better I felt; it started taking all the pain away. When he told us to come out to his limo with him, I grabbed Mack's hand, knowing that she would be nervous and possibly scared. I told her everything would be all right and we were just going to fuck with him and have some fun. I could see the trepidation all over her face, but she agreed with me anyway.

Mack went in first and he closed the door behind me.

"You guys are trouble aren't you?" he boasted.

"Absolutely, you wouldn't be here if you weren't looking for some trouble," I reminded, making him laugh.

"Take off your clothes," he huskily ordered.

I looked over at Mack and she looked bewildered, but I nodded my head and she followed suit.

I wanted her to feel like a slut and like my bitch. After all the years I felt inferior to her, I wanted one night where I felt superior. That was the point of all this, I didn't care about fucking some random guy. I wanted to show her that I was better than her, that I was a vixen and she was nobody. I belittled her as much as I could, making her feel like she wasn't a goddess like I was. Like she couldn't ever be in charge with anything, and that's why I always needed to take the lead. She was a child and that's why my dad fucked her because he could control her, not because he loved her. I wanted her to feel pain, embarrassment, humiliation, and shame.

Everything I felt times ten.

Mr. Nichols said he wanted to play a game. He hauled me backward by my hair, sitting me in front of his lap with my shirt pulled up to my waist and my legs spread open. I tried to hide the contour of my face in his arm, but he wouldn't let me. He held me by the roots of my hair to stare directly and only at McKenzie. She was told she couldn't look away from me and that she had to answer every question; if she didn't, then he would hurt me. For a second, I saw concern wash over her face. I saw Mack, my Mack, and it made me sad. I hadn't expected to feel that but I did.

The entire time Mack described in vivid detail what happened in the limo that night, Mr. Nichols was hard. His erection was on my lower back, and every time she described the feral acts, he would thrust into my back, making me aware that he was turned on. I would be lying if I said I didn't feel it also. The mere thought of having him inside me again sent me in a frenzy.

Slap! He slapped my pussy with the tips of his fingers. "Are you hearing her, Gianna? Did you listen to everything she said? Huh? Did you enjoy having your best friend lick your cunt? Did you like having her submit to you? Of course you did! You love being the leader…you love controlling everything around you, because you're a manipulative liar!"

Slap! "Look at you, you attention seeking slut! Your clit is swollen waiting for me to touch and rub it. You would let me do anything to you, right here in front of your friend. Because all you've ever wanted is my fucking attention, so hungry and needy for it, you dirty, lost, little girl," he spewed.

Slap! "Are you paying attention?"

I had closed my eyes, not wanting to look at Mack. I wanted to escape the situation I was in; I didn't want to play his games anymore. They were getting out of control. I felt trapped in that room, in that location, in my life, with no way out. I had no one to blame other than myself. I tried to organize my thoughts because they were solely being run on emotions and I hadn't experienced that in a long time. All of that was new to me. I wanted to scream, I wanted to escape and run, but I couldn't…

Mr. Nichols wouldn't let go of me. How much longer would he keep us there? How much longer did I have to endure his cruel words, cold and distant demeanor one minute, and loving James eyes the next…I focused on the task at hand, trying to relieve the ache that his hand had created. I rubbed my legs together, wanting to move away from him. It was impossible; he kept holding me tighter, firmer, never wanting me to feel anything other than being his play toy. I had always been his toy, his doll. He used me when he wanted to play with me and that was it. I let it happen over and over again. It was easy for him because I allowed it.

"Gianna..." he sang, bringing me back to the present. "Don't tune me out! You know how much I hate that. You're going to behave, do what your told, and play my game." I opened my eyes and found Mack coloring on the wall. What was she doing?

"Look at her, Gianna. Look what you did to her. It's all your fault! Everything is your fault. You shatter anything that's around you."

Slap! "Answer me before I really make you sorry."

"No," I quickly replied.

"No, what?"

"No, I'm not happy. I want to go home," I stated in a desolate voice.

He cocked his head to the side and looked down at me. "You want to go home?' he mocked.

"You don't have a home, Miss Edwards. Where does princess G want to go?"

"Stop! Please stop! I can't take any more. Just fucking kill me if that's what you want! I can't do this anymore. Please," I begged.

He deviously laughed and his eyes lit up. "Whose pussy is this? Whom do you belong to?"

"No one," I replied through gritted teeth.

He flipped me over and I never saw it coming. He held my arms above my head and a knee on my lower back. I saw Mack's face filled with fear as he held me down.

"Stop hurting her!" she screamed across the room. "She doesn't like it! Stop it!"

"Oh no, McKenzie; Gianna is a pain slut, she loves this shit. She's been begging me to hurt her since she got here."

He smacked my ass repeatedly until I was screaming and thrashing around, trying to get loose and away from him.

"That's not the right answer...what's the right answer, Miss Edwards?" he patronized.

"Fuck you!" I spit at him and it landed in his eye.

"Still…not the right answer…" he smacked me one last time and then lowered his arm to my clit. He roughly and determinedly moved his fingers, making me scream because he was going to make me do it. He was going to make me come, just to show me that he could. To show me that he still owned me, that he could do with me what he wanted, and it only made me scream louder and with more hatred.

"Stop it! Stop it! Stop it!" Mack yelled.

"Take one more fucking step and I will make you really sorry. I'll hurt her and don't for one second think that I won't. Now sit your ass down and watch the fucking show, McKenzie," he ordered.

Mack did as she was told, concern and sympathy written all over her face.

"Now…where was I. Oh yes! I was making Gianna scream. Should I continue making her squirm or should I just fuck her and have you watch, Mack? Maybe you could lick her pussy again, seeing as I got to miss out on the show the first time. Why don't we reenact everything you just described?"

His fingers moved faster as did his grunts and groans, and I couldn't hold back any longer. My eyes rolled to the back of my head and my pussy squirted from the most intense orgasm I had ever felt.

When I came to, Mack was crying and it took me a minute to even figure out what the fuck just happened.

"That's exactly what I thought, Gia." He finally let me go with a growl and I subconsciously whimpered at the loss.

What the fuck was wrong with me?

Mack shook her head back and forth, grabbing the crayon and went right back to coloring on the wall.

I couldn't take it anymore. "What the fuck, Mack? Snap out of it! Stop coloring on the wall!"

"No, no, no, no…I have deadline. I promised Cara that I would have this done for her."

"Cara? His daughter? What the fuck are you talking about, Mack? You're not making any sense!"

"Yes…Cara, she's sleeping and all this shouting is going to wake her up. She is going to start crying and be very upset. I need to make her happy, I need to make it okay. I won't let her be sad ever again, I am a good mother. I am a good mother," she repeated.

I looked over toward the mattress. "The doll?" Mr. Nichols nodded.

I got up and grabbed the doll from the leg, holding it up.

"AHHHHHH! You're hurting her! WHAT ARE YOU DOING? YOU CAN'T HOLD HER LIKE THAT!" she screeched at the top of her lungs.

I backed away from her with the doll and put my hand up in a surrendering gesture. "Calm the fuck down, Mack, it's a doll. This is not Cara, it's a doll. It's fake! Look," I rationalized, pulling off her arm.

"AHHHHHHH! NOOOOOOOO!" She ran at me and knocked me onto my back with such force that it knocked the wind out of me and I saw stars.

"Why? Why would you hurt her? She didn't do anything to you," she bellowed, trying to hit me all over my face. I covered myself as best as I could.

I removed my arms to look at her. "It's a doll!" I shouted.

"No, it's not, it's Cara!"

She grabbed my hair, brought my head forward and slammed it back to the ground over and over again.

And then everything went black.

Chapter Twenty-three

My eyes fluttered. I was lying in a comfortable bed and my head was on a pillow, I had forgotten what it felt like to have a pillow. I pulled the soft silk sheets to my chin and breathed in the smell of honey, it was all around me. I remembered that smell. It was same scent that I wore in high school. Was I home? Had it all been a dream? I cracked one eye open and then the next. It was dark outside, really dark, but soft lighting surrounded the room from a few candles. I leaned forward, hissed, and immediately grabbed the back of my head.

"Are you okay?" I looked to the right where I saw his shadow. The cast of lighting made him shimmer. He looked translucent, wearing clean clothes.

"Yeah…what happened? What's going on?"

"Well, McKenzie kicked your ass and then knocked you the fuck out," he said, laughing.

"Thanks for you sympathy," I sarcastically stated.

He grinned. "You're fine. You just have a nasty bump on the back of your head."

I nodded. "Why do I feel like I'm waking up to my last supper? Is this where you tell me to choose a meal? I mean, I'm clean and in some sick, twisted version of a romance novel."

He chuckled and moved to the edge of the bed. I scooted back till I hit the wall and covered myself with the sheet; it was the first time he was allowing me modesty and I took it.

"Are you afraid of me?" he question with an amused expression.

I cocked my head to the side. "Not scared but cautious. I don't understand the games you're playing and I'm not going to pretend like I do."

He threw his head back and laughed. Fuck! He had turned insane like McKenzie; I was stuck with two crazy people in the middle of nowhere and now I was the last one standing.

He came toward me quick-like and I put my hands up, surrendering. "I'm not going to hurt you, G. I want to check the back of your head and make sure the bleeding has stopped."

He was back to calling me G. He was like Dr. Jekyll and Mr. Hyde; instead, he was Mr. Nichols, and James.

"Oh…okay," I whispered, tilting my head forward so he could check me. His hands were soft and tender; he was examining me with concern. I waited on pins and needles for the other shoe to drop. Why was he being nice to me?

"Why are you being nice to me?" I blurted.

He sat back down in front of me. "I think it's funny that you're covering yourself with that blanket, considering I just bathed you completely."

I shrugged.

He sighed. "I honestly don't know why I'm being nice to you. All I know is when you were knocked unconscious, my first thought was that she killed you. My heart literally stopped until I felt your pulse, after that, I moved in auto pilot, trying to revive you. You went in and out of consciousness and babbled incoherent things. But you kept asking for James, your voice was pleading and painful to hear," he agonized. "I cleaned you up by the lake and you were so helpless, I could have done anything to you without your recollection. When I had you in my arms, I felt whole. I remembered the feel of you. I hadn't thought about that in a long time…I didn't want you to wake up in a filthy bed." He paused. "It's just some sheets."

I sat there wide-eyed. I couldn't believe what I had just heard. Was this more games?

"I can't explain, it but I wanted to take care of you and make sure you were okay. That's all."

"Did you care about any of that when you sodomized me and left me in a dark room for days?" I sadistically questioned.

He shook his head. "I checked on you the entire time. Every time you passed out."

"What about the other thing?"

"I make no excuses for what I did. I also don't regret it and I would do it again. I only feel remorse that I hurt you. But not that I was inside you again."

Neither one of us spoke after that. I lay down and flinched when he came to lie next to me. We both stared at the ceiling. I thought about how I found myself in a situation like that. If I hadn't found out about McKenzie and my father, would I have reacted the same way? Would Mack have been able to calm me down before I let all the emotions fuel my hatred for everything that had happened? Or would I have still wanted to hurt him?

But isn't revenge supposed to make you feel better?

"If you prick us do we not bleed? If you tickle us do we not laugh? If you poison us do we not die? And if you wrong us shall we not revenge?"[12] I recited Shakespeare back to him.

He turned his face to look at me. "I think that's the first time you've ever quoted Shakespeare to me," he laughed, amused.

I continued to stare at the ceiling. "The entire time I planned it, I thought about that verse. It repeated itself in my head like a broken record. I couldn't get it to stop. I'm not trying to make you feel bad for me, but what would you have done? I think if you put yourself in my shoes for a minute, maybe you could relate. Sending you to prison was not part of the plan. I was young and stupid and I didn't think it would go that far. I just thought you'd be fired and sent away. I didn't want to see you anymore and I wanted you to go away," I informed.

He hadn't moved either, and I didn't know if he was listening or tuning me out so I kept going.

"Mack hurt me and I never thought that would happen. Not once did I ever think she would betray me. Especially not with my own father. It didn't matter all the lies that I had hidden from her, because I was the bad guy. I was perfectly okay with being the bad guy and put her up on this pedestal where she could do no wrong. She was the perfect one. All the years of jealousy, it never crossed my mind that she would betray me and have secrets of her own," I reasoned.

"How could we have been best friends, sisters…and not known each other at all? I don't understand. I would have died for her. And the sick thing is that I would still die for her. How do I love someone so much that I also hate? I can't fathom how after all these years, I still love her. I don't want anything bad to happen to her, but I caused her so much damage. She would never want to hurt me, I know that now, and I guess I knew that then. But it didn't stop me from wanting to ruin her. She screwed me and I fucked her. I couldn't let it go. Revenge spawned an endless cycle of retribution for me. I fucked up my life as much as I did yours and Mack's, so in the end, nobody won. Most of all, me," I rationalized.

"For what it's worth, even if it's nothing–" I turned to look at him "–I am very sorry. But you've seen who I am. You can't imagine I am happy? I'm not living the life you thought I would be and neither is McKenzie. Nothing you evoke can change that. We punished ourselves far worse than you have or could have done."

I sat up, still looking at him. "I think you know that and that's why you hate us. Revenge isn't so sweet anymore, is it? It's much better in the package."

He placed his hand on top of mine and I looked down on them. "I don't hate you, and that's what I can't fucking understand." I peeked up at him through my lashes. "I don't hate you and I have every right to. I can't. I never could. I thought bringing you here would help and it hasn't. I'm completely obsessed with you, just as much, if not more than, I was years ago. You're the fucking plague and it's in my blood, there is no cure from you. I have looked for it." His hand slowly moved to my hand that was holding up the sheet.

"I have always been able to see right through you," he divulged, lowering my hand to bring down the blanket.

"And now all I can think about it sinking into your sweet pussy. It took everything in me not to do it the other night."

His hand grazed my throat and I moaned at the thought of him choking me again, but I stayed still, waiting for his next move.

"You enjoy pain, don't you?"

I nodded.

"When did that start?" he asked as his hand moved toward my breasts.

"I don't know. After everything that happened with you, I guess. Jake didn't know how to handle it. I barely understand it." I nervously chuckled and his hand backed away.

"You're with Jake?"

I shook my head. "I was. We got divorced a really long time ago. I don't even remember being married to him. I was drunk half the time. It only lasted about a year and a half."

"The other night... I thought you were enjoying it, G. You've been wanting me to hurt you this entire time and I finally hit my breaking point and I wanted to hurt you. However, I thought you were enjoying it. When you turned around and looked at me, I've never seen that look in your eyes. It nearly killed me. The mere thought that you felt like I violated you...raped you...made me fucking sick. As soon as I left the room and locked you in there I threw up," he admitted.

"I locked you in there not to punish you but to punish myself. I couldn't look at you and see the harm that I caused. All I thought about in prison was to hurt you. Both of you. I wanted revenge and the moment I saw you lying tied to the bed, I knew I couldn't go through with it. I've kept you here for four weeks because I wanted you close to me. And that's the God's honest truth. I've been fighting my demons and that's you. You're the forbidden fruit. You're still mine and that scares the shit out of me," he whispered the last few words as if it pained him to say them.

"What happens from here?"

He sighed. "I let you go. I let you both go. There's nothing left here for me, for any of us. It was a mistake. And in a fucked up way, I think everyone can leave with some peace."

"What if I don't want to go?" That caught his attention, he looked right at me, but this time was different.

"Why is that?"

"I have nothing to go back to."

"And you do here?"

"Yes," I hesitated. "I have you."

He reached for the blanket and pulled it away from me. I was exposed to him in a much different way than I had been since I had gotten there. My guard was down and so was my flag.

"You're still so goddamn beautiful," he praised, with a sincere tone.

"Spread your legs for me, G." I slowly parted my thighs and opened them in a V with my knees bent.

He made a noise that came from the back of his throat. He pulled me in hard and kissed me with his tongue, tasting every bit of my mouth, with one hand at the back of my neck keeping me close to him where he wanted. His face turned to taste me deeper. I moaned, moving my hips to get some undivided attention to my ache. I could feel him smiling at his recognition of my subtle request. He suddenly grabbed a fistful of my hair; I yelped at the sudden intrusion, his indirect way of letting me know that he was still in charge.

My pussy throbbed.

He kissed and licked his way down my neck to my breast, bringing my nipple into his mouth and sucking hard. Once it was a pebbled stone, he made his way to the other one and I held onto the back of his neck, wanting him to move lower. He nipped at my nipple, reminding me that he was in control. He broke away, making his way down to where I needed him the most. Grinning, he pushed me back and I fell against the pillows, he grabbed the backs of my thighs and leveraged them upward toward the ceiling. My pussy was right in his face and he inhaled my scent.

When his tongue reached its destination, he took my clit into his mouth and lightly sucked. My head fell back in pleasure. It had been entirely too long since he touched me like that. No one could make me feel worshipped like he could. The closeness of his mouth to my most private area was a feeling that had me grabbing the sheets in a frenzy, and he had barely even touched me yet. I expected him to be rough, but he was being gentle, taking his time to devour me and make me wet.

"Oh God," I whimpered in pleasure.

He licked me one last time and then stopped. "Tell me what you want. Beg me for it," he huskily urged.

"Please…" I responded on edge.

"Please…what, G?" he goaded.

"Please make me come."

He growled and returned to lapping at my folds, making me go crazy with passion and desire. Feelings that only he produced. He licked me from my anus to my opening and then back to my clit. He sucked, and when he moved his head up, down, and then side to side, it was my undoing and I came with such force that had my back lifting off the sheets and my eyes rolling to the back of my head.

He didn't stop sucking on my clit and held my legs apart when they tried to close from the sensitivity. I screamed from ecstasy and it made him suck me harder, making me come apart again, hard. I shook the entire time, my legs felt like they were going crazy. He released me with a pop. My legs fell forward from weakness, still shaking when he dove forward, attacking my mouth. He loomed over me as my tongue licked my come off his mouth, face, and chin and he hummed in pleasure the entire time.

I licked my way back to his mouth and I looked right into his eyes, they held everything I wanted to hear. He bit my lower lip pulling it into his mouth before softly kissing me again. His hand grabbed the back of my neck and we kept our eyes open the entire time, not wanting to lose the connection. We both wanted to get lost in the moment. Lost in each other.

"Of all my loves this is the first and last. I could give all and more, my life, my world, my thoughts, my arms, my breath, my future, my love eternal, endless, infinite, yet brief, as all loves are and hopes, though they endure. You are my sun and stars, my night, my day, my seasons, summer, winter, my sweet spring, my autumn song, the church in which I pray, my land and ocean, all that the earth can bring. Of glory and of sustenance, all that might be divine, my alpha and my omega, and all that was ever mine,"[13] he repeated the exact words to me from the first time we made love, and it made my heart yearn for him.

The love collapsed right down into my soul. The only place he existed. Eyes falling shut, he pushed into my channel in one thrust spreading me completely open.

"Don't close your eyes. Let me see your eyes." I immediately opened them and he gripped at the back of my neck firmer and lifted me up a little. Our foreheads rested on each other with mouths gaped open. I hadn't realized I was shedding tears until he caught one with his thumb.

He fucked me with anger, he fucked me with passion, he fucked me for all the pain and punishment I put him through, but most importantly, he fucked me with love. Right into my soul where he was forever engrained.

For so long, I fought with who I was–G or Gia–but in that one moment of clarity, he fucked life back to Gianna Edwards. Gianna was finally whole and he brought meaning to my empty soul. He was my light. And I was his. In that second I saw Gianna Edwards in his eyes. Felt it in my bones and it resuscitated its way into my beating heart.

That's all it took for me to shed G and embrace Gianna, my true self, no longer in the dark, hiding behind lies and secrets.

"Oh my God," I moaned as I felt him balls deep.

"Fuck, you feel good. How does your pussy feel this good? Fuck me," he huskily stated, not thrusting harder. "Yes, yes, yes," he repeated.

He grabbed my left leg and placed it on his shoulder. That angle was much deeper and my pussy tightened around his shaft, which earned me a growl. He never once let up on holding the back of my neck.

"Ahhh...more...more..." I murmured.

He continued to move in a hard and delicious pace that had me weakening beneath him. Making love isn't about movements or caresses, it's about feelings and emotions. I felt every last one of them. I cherished every sound, thrust, touch; I wanted to bottle it up and take it with me. The familiarity of our bodies, our breathing, our minds, and especially our hearts.

"Fuck me," he grunted. "I fucking love you. Please believe that. If things would have been different, you know, if you would have had the baby. I would have been there. Somehow, I would have."

"Jesus, James," I panted, rotating my hips; my leg on his shoulder made it easy for me to take him deeper. I was close and so was he. We were both on the verge of going over and I wanted to do it together.

"I'm close," I cried out.

"I still would have been there," he groaned. "Tell me, G. Please tell me what I've waited eight years to hear. Please," he shamelessly begged.

I grabbed the back of his neck. "I love you. I never stopped."

And I meant every word.

Chapter Twenty-four

We lay there breathless, surrounded by love and truths. My head was on his shoulder and his arms were wrapped around me, keeping me close and safe.

"James," I half-whispered.

"Hmmm..."

"Were you with her? Please tell me that I have something she has never had."

"McKenzie?" he asked, taken aback.

I nodded.

"No, baby, I didn't touch Mack and you were there when I did. I was going to but I couldn't. Deep down I knew I couldn't do that to you, as much as I thought I did."

"I'm glad you brought us here," I admitted.

"Us or just you?"

"I'm relieved that Mack doesn't have that reporter job to go home to. I want her in my life. Does that make me an awful person?"

He laughed. "Maybe a little, but Mack didn't have her reporter job when I found her, she was renting some dump in Florida, a small town barely on the map."

I sat up. "What?"

"She hasn't been there in almost a year. She ran when I was paroled, you think she knew that I was coming for you guys?"

I shrugged.

"Shhh...go to sleep. How's your head?"

"Sore, but okay," I said, closing my eyes. It didn't take more than a few seconds before I was passed out. Happy and contentment, two feelings I hadn't felt in eight years.

The light coming in woke me in the morning. My eyes fluttered opened and I didn't feel James' arms around me. I turned, extending my arms, expecting to find him there, but it was cold and empty. My eyes immediately opened and I sat up, taking the sheet with me. I was shocked to find him sitting in a chair watching me sleep.

"What are you doing?" I smiled. "Come back to bed it's still really early."

"I haven't slept all night," he stated.

"What? Why?" I questioned, not understating where that was coming from.

"Because I wanted to look at you one last time."

My head shot back like he had slapped me. "What? I don't understand," I expressed, trying not to cry.

Fuck! Was he doing this to me again?

"You have to leave, G." He said the words so easily and they flowed off his tongue like it was nothing. I winced at the fact that he called me G. I didn't want to be her anymore; I didn't feel like I was her anymore.

"I can't keep you here. I can't keep either of you here. You need to go. We all do, it's over now."

I backed away from him and pulled the sheet to cover my body. Standing up near the edge of the bed, I bellowed, "So what was last night? Part of the plan? A joke?"

He got off the chair and walked toward the door, leaving me behind him. He paused before he got past the doorway. "It was closure," he announced, never looking back at me.

He started to walk away from me.

From us.

I couldn't take it anymore…

"Your wife made me do it!" I screamed.

He immediately stopped, taking in my words. "Did you hear me? Your wife made me do everything! She was behind it all! She's the fucking mastermind and manipulator, not me!" I yelled at the top of my lungs.

I had never told anyone that. Nobody knew but me.

I found out I was pregnant and all I wanted to do was share it with him. I honestly thought we could finally be together. That our child would make everything right, but when I drove to see him and saw him with his child and then his wife in the front yard, it nearly killed me. I watched them walk into their home together like I had never existed.

Their home.

After catching Mack with my dad and then him crudely dismissing me after class, I needed answers. A few days later, I found myself in the playground of the same park that James and I had our first intimate time together. And that's when I saw her; she was with Cara, their daughter. She was swinging her on the same swing her husband went down on me a few months prior. I couldn't help myself and I went to her, I was hormonal and pregnant and I just wanted answers. I didn't have the courage to face James yet, and his wife was standing right in front of me, so it gave me a reason to find out the truth.

She saw me walking up to her and looked at me like she knew. I watched her whisper something in Cara's ear, and the little girl just took off to the other side of the park, far away from us.

"Hi, Gianna," she greeted and took a seat in the swing.

"How do you know my name?"

She cocked her head to the side. "Oh come on, you think I don't know the name of MY husband's play toys? ALL your names," she viciously spewed.

"What the fuck? What are you talking about?" I angrily replied. I didn't know if I wanted to fight or cry.

She rolled her eyes. "You honestly think you're the first one? You honestly think there aren't more? My husband has a problem keeping his dick in his pants. Why do you think we left? We had to get away from his last mistake, but he promised me he wouldn't do it again. And of course, I believed him."

"You're lying!" I yelled.

Thank God it was only us in the park.

She shook her head. "I always wondered why James likes to pick them so young. I guess it's because you're stupid and easily manipulated." She shrugged, not caring that my heart was literally breaking.

"I don't believe you."

She chuckled. "Then why are you crying?"

I wiped away the tears with the back of my arm. I saw her reach into her purse to take out her phone, and then she threw it at me. I caught it mid-air.

"Check out the pictures."

I swiped at the scream and hit the picture icon. I was smacked in the face with a picture of the young girl, probably my age. She had brown hair and blue eyes, she was really pretty.

"That was the last one; go ahead, keep swiping, I think there are like five or six of them in there," she revealed.

With each swipe my stomach turned and my hands got clammy. I felt like I was going to pass out.

My hand grabbed my stomach and I rubbed it back and forth, it gave me some comfort.

"Are you pregnant?" she asked with a tone like she already knew.

I looked up at her and nodded. "How do you know?"

"The way you're holding your stomach. It's a mother's touch. I did it all the time with Cara, and I've been around enough mothers to know what the glow looks like," she explained. "Wow, you're the second one he's knocked up. God! I'm going to have to get myself tested again. Damn it, James," she stated to herself.

"You're going to have to get an abortion." My eyes widened.

"I can't–"

She stood up and walked over to me. "What are you going to do, huh? Raise the baby by yourself?"

"No. I'm different. What we have is different. I just have to tell him; once I tell him, he will choose me, he will choose us," I sobbed, not being able to control my emotions. "He loves me! He tells me all

the time. I know he does! We're going to be together. I'm sorry but you don't know! You don't know what we have!" I yelled, my voice breaking from the emotions.

She looked at me with concern and sympathy all at once. "Look at the text messages." I looked down at her phone with dread.

I clicked over the screen and hit the text icon. One text after the other...

I love you.

Let's make this work.

I miss you.

I'm sorry. I'll never do it again.

Please forgive me.

No one can replace you.

The phone fell out of my hand and before it even landed on the ground, I jolted forward, throwing up all the contents in my stomach. She rubbed my back as I hurled my entire life away. It all happened so fast and in a flash, I watched it all being taken away from me.

She went into her purse and handed me a baby wipe. I spit the last of it out and then wiped the residue off my face.

"We've been trying to work things out since he moved here, he has been begging me to move back home and I finally gave in. We're getting back together, Gianna."

"Why would you take him back after all this?" I asked her.

"I'm in love with him. And you know what it's like to be in love with someone. We're going to go to counseling and we have Cara. I don't want her raised in a broken family," she responded. "I'll give you the money for it. Your parents would never find out."

I didn't care about my dad finding out but it would destroy my mom, especially if I would be doing it by myself. I couldn't raise a baby by myself; I could barely take care of myself.

I lost Mack.

I lose my dad.

I lost James.

And now, I would lose my baby.

Our baby...

I had no other choice, so I took the money and she made the appointment.

I went to the appointment three days later.

I was sitting in the waiting room, waiting for my name to be called. All different types of women sat there, waiting to get rid of something that was supposed to be so sacred. I wondered if they were like me, did they get lied to and betrayed? I felt some relief that they all looked diverse, there were no set type. No stereotype, it could happen to anyone.

"Gianna Edwards," the nurse announced and we walked through a long corridor where I was taken into a room that had an ultrasound machine and an examination table. The nurse asked questions about my medical history and other personal questions that I imagined were standard. When she was done, she told me to put on the gown with the opening in the back. I was sitting on the table by the time I heard the knock on the door.

The doctor came in, followed by the nurse. She explained to me that she was going to do an ultrasound to find out how far along I was. I laid back on the table with my feet in stirrups as she pushed a wand looking instrument up my sex. I didn't feel anything until the sound that was produced through the speakers almost knocked me on my ass. It sounded like a heartbeat, a really fast heartbeat. She moved around the instrument and told me I looked like I was seven weeks along. The uncontrollable tears slid down my face and the nurse grabbed my hand in sympathy.

They were extremely understanding and reassuring, telling me over and over again that there was no judgment. She explained the procedure and the aftercare. I nodded the entire time, feigning listening. They proceeded with the normal process of getting blood and taking my blood pressure. I was given Valium, which didn't take long until I felt its effects, and a pill that was some version of another birth control. I was taken back into the procedure room and I barely remember any of it. It happened in less than five minutes. All I knew was that I cried the entire time. When it was done, they took me into a comfortable room with leather recliners and I sat in one for a few hours.

I didn't think about anything; I was numb. When I was allowed to leave, the same cab that dropped me off picked me up. I sat in the car and stared out the windshield. I didn't know how long I sat there, staring out into space. I was beyond zoned out and hadn't realized he was driving toward James' house until we were parking a few houses away. I must have told him to go there. There were no cars in his driveway and I realized it was only 2:00 pm; he wouldn't be home for another hour.

I needed to talk to him and tell him what I had done. I needed to have him forgive me, even if I had to beg for it. I killed our child. I wanted to hear his answers and have him tell me why he lied to me if all he wanted was to use me. I needed explanations; I was at least owed that. I used the key from under the mat and let myself in. As suspected, no one was home.

I hadn't moved from the couch and when the clock struck 3:00 pm, I waited for the door to open. I heard the doorknob turn and my heart sped a beat, expecting him to come waltzing in. I never expected his child to come running in. My heart dropped to the floor.

"Cara!" I heard her shout. I didn't know what to do so I ran into the nearest closet, closing the door as I heard her footsteps coming inside.

"How did you get inside, little girl? Huh? Did daddy forget to lock the door?" She giggled and I heard her little footsteps run through the house to what I imagined was her bedroom.

The house phone rang. "Hello," she said. "Yeah, I'm home... Okay...yeah, I'm waiting. I'll see you soon."

Home...she said.

I heard the garage open minutes later and I snuck as far back into the closet as I could go. I covered myself with the hanging clothes and boxes. I hoped no one could see me if they opened the door. I tried as best as I could to labor my breathing, but my heart was beating out of its stomach. I swear they could hear it.

"Hey, baby," he said, and the term of endearment broke me a little bit more.

"Hey, babe. It's nice to be home. I can't believe how long this has been going on. I miss you. I miss us."

"I know. I miss you, too. We're a family and we need to work this out. I don't want to be a part time dad, I can't handle it," he stated.

I couldn't believe the words I heard coming out of his mouth. Everything was a lie. Every last thing he told me. Every touch, every caress, every sonnet, and every I love you. All of it was one big lie.

"You think we can fix this, James?"

"I know we can. Where is Cara?"

"She's down for her nap, she was thrilled to be back in her room."

The next minutes of my life went in slow motion; I heard him kiss her, I heard him touch her, and I heard him bring her to orgasm right on the very door in front of me. They eventually made their way to their bedroom, the room we had made love in countless times. How could he do this to me?

I quietly left the closet and stood in the hallway, contemplating going in there and confronting him. But what would it matter? I had already lost everything that meant anything to me. I was truly alone and confronting him wouldn't change that.

I hated him.

My legs moved on their own accord as I walked to their bedroom door. I heard the moaning and movement, I wondered if he was touching her like he touched me. If he whispered that he loved her. Did he think of me as he thrust in and out of her? Was I even on his mind? I believed everything that he said to me, every last word. He played me just like I played everyone. Was this my punishment?

Tears fell down my face as I pictured them naked together. I touched my stomach, wanting to feel a part of him. But I didn't feel anything because I had killed it just like he had killed me. I was part of one big lie. I stood there and heard him bring her to ecstasy as our baby bled out from me. I started to feel the cramping of our child dying as he moaned, "I love you," to someone who wasn't me. I couldn't take it anymore and tiptoed back out the front door, and then walked in random circles around the neighborhood while waiting for my cab. I had never felt so empty and hollow. I had my whole life ahead of me, a bright, beautiful future, exactly how everyone described it to me. But the underlying secrets were always my companion, sitting right next to me as I brought total emotional devastation upon myself.

When I made it into my room that night, I went straight into the shower. As I watched the blood slide down the drain, I reached below, grabbing some blood on my fingers. I brought it up to my mouth and I kissed it.

I kissed goodbye our love.

I kissed goodbye James.

I kissed goodbye our baby.

I kissed goodbye my future and everything I believed in.

Chapter Twenty-five

He sat there on the edge of the bed with his head in his lap as tears streamed down his face. I couldn't help but feel satisfaction; he needed to know what I went through. I was done lying, it ended that day. We were all going to walk out with the truth if it was the last thing we did.

"Jesus Christ, I had no fucking idea," he bellowed, not looking at me. "I was never with those other girls and those text messages were fake. She must have grabbed my phone. All those pictures, everything she told you was a lie, G. It was all a fucking lie," he roared.

He stood up and was over to me in four strides, grabbing me by my arms and lightly shaking me. "You have to believe me! She lied to you. You have to believe me!" he repeated over and over again.

"I know," I concluded.

And it threw me right back into that night.

"Do you think he loves her?" I questioned, never taking my eyes away from their interlocked hands. He was carrying his daughter; they looked every bit the happy, loving family. I envied her. But most of all, I hated him.

"What the hell are you talking about? Of course he loves his wife. I mean, look at them, they look like a Brady Bunch episode," she said, pointing to them.

"Where is she going?"

"Looks like she's going with her parents or his. They kissed goodbye so obviously they're going their separate ways. Stop hogging the bottle, give me some." She took it out of my hands and chugged some down.

"Let's follow him, Mack. Let's try to talk to him. Reason with him. He has to understand. We can't lose everything we have worked so hard for, we can't let him win."

"Gia, as much as I want to do that, I don't think it's a good idea. We could get in a lot of trouble," she rationalized.

I turned to look at her. "More than we are already in?" she shrugged.

I put the car in drive and tried to look like I was tailing him. It didn't matter, I already knew where he lived, but I couldn't let Mack know that. We followed him all the way back to his house and I parked my car behind the bush of his house.

"Come on." I said getting out of the car. "Bring the bottle."

She sighed but followed me to the front door.

I knocked on the door and grabbed the bottle out of Mack's hands, bringing it up to my mouth and taking down huge gulps. I needed to be G now, I needed to be her and only her. It took him exactly forty seconds to come to the door; his face said it all when he answered.

"What are you doing here?" he asked, confused.

"That's not very nice, Mr. Nichols. Aren't you going to invite us in?" He took the bottle out of my hand.

"Get inside before my neighbors see you," he beckoned us inside and the house looked completely different. Scattered toys were everywhere and new portraits of them were hanging on the walls. I wanted to throw up and scream all at the same time, and it only fueled my hatred for him.

"Mr. Nichols, we came here to plead with you to help us. You know Gia can't lose her scholarship. Please, is there anything you can do?" Mack requested.

He shook his head, not looking at me. "You know I can't do that. You girls blatantly cheated."

I laughed. "Oh come on...haven't you ever cheated before? I mean done something you weren't supposed to? I know you have...I can smell it on you," I mocked.

"Gianna..." Mack whispered, trying to get me to calm down. I just ignored her.

"What's wrong, Mr. Nichols? Did I hit a nerve?"

He narrowed his eyes at me. "How much have you been drinking?"

"Enough to make me forget. Don't you want to be bad? It's so much fun, why don't you let me show you."

"Gia, what the fuck? I'm sorry, Mr. Nichols, I don't know what's gotten into her. Yes we have been drinking. We shouldn't have come." She grabbed my elbow and jerked me toward the door, I didn't want to leave, I wasn't done with him yet. She opened it and he shut it fast, as if reading my mind.

"You're not going anywhere. You're sobering up and then you can leave. Go sit on the couch and stay out of trouble while I make you some coffee," he ordered in the same tone my father used with me. The exact same tone I heard him use with Mack, it made my skin crawl just thinking about it. I moved myself away from her, I had to. Just the thought of my father and her together made me want to hurt her. I sat on the opposite end of the couch. I didn't want to drink coffee, I wanted to keep drinking and it pissed me off that he took it away from me. He kept taking everything from me.

"Hey, Mr. Nichols, can we take a shower, too," I stood and provocatively walked closer to him while unbuttoning my shirt, his eyes followed my hands all the way from behind the counter in the kitchen.

"I mean, since you're being so hospitable and all," I teased as I took off my shirt and threw it on the floor.

"Miss Edwards, put your clothes back on."

"I like it so much more when you call me G." I pouted. I didn't have to look over at Mack to know she looked at me like I had lost my damn mind.

"Put your shirt back on," he demanded in a stern voice.

I laughed, "Anything you say, Mr. Nichols. You need to loosen up a little bit. Maybe you should take a drink, or better yet, give me back the bottle and I'll do it for you."

"Jesus, Gia, are you out of your mind?" Mack observed. I could feel her trepidation.

This scared her? Why didn't fucking my father scare her? It took everything in me not to turn around and unleash on her. She was a fraud just like Mr. Nichols, just like everyone in my life, including me. All of us hiding behind secrets and lies, betraying each other every fucking day; it made me sick.

"Mack, stop being a pussy!" I shouted, looking right at her. Her face showed concern but not remorse, never remorse. Was she using me all these years just to get close to my dad?

I shook my head, trying to rid myself of my dad touching her; I could still hear him bring her to orgasm. I could still hear the way she told him she loved him. My poor mom...how could she do this to me? I was supposed to be her sister!

I turned and took my anger out on him instead. I fucking hated both of them.

"He's already failed me and ruined our lives. You should be angry with him, not me. He's the one that has stopped all our dreams and plans, come on, Mack, tell him how fucking angry you are! Tell him how much of a son of a bitch he is! How much we hate him!" I shouted looking straight at him.

His face didn't reveal a fucking thing, not one goddamn emotion and it further pissed me off. I wanted something, anything to make me feel like he cared about me, like my words were having some effect on him.

"Miss Edwards, you need to calm down."

"Fuck you, James. Stop fucking calling me that!" I shouted and Mack gasped, bringing my attention back to her. "I'll calm down when you help us. I'll calm down when you do something. I'll calm down when you show me anything other than nothing! That's when I'll calm the fuck down!" I screamed as Mack's eyes widened in shock.

He walked from the kitchen to Mack and gave her coffee and then came to stand right in front of me.

"I will not allow you to disrespect me in my own home, Gianna. I am your teacher and you are my student. Sit down and drink your coffee," he scolded, handing it to me.

I grabbed it and took one look at it before throwing it across the room, shattering it against the door.

"Make me," I provoked.

He grabbed me by my arm and I tried to get out of his grip, but it made him grab me tighter. I pushed him in the chest and he grabbed my other arm, dragging me to the couch. I screamed and tried to shove him away.

"You need to calm down. You're acting like a child."

"That's all I am to you, isn't it? Just a fucking child! I hate you. You ruined me. You ruined everything. I fucking hate you!" I kicked him in the shin and that's when all hell broke loose. He tightened his grip and I brought his arm up to my mouth and bit it. I latched on until I tasted blood; once the metallic taste was in my mouth I bit down harder. He yelled and shoved me on the couch, my back bounced off from the impact. I seethed and went right after him, pushing, kicking, and hitting anywhere and everywhere. And then I went after anything I could see. I threw the portraits off the wall; I pushed the lamps over, and threw every ornament that was breakable in my vision. Mack came up from behind me and tried to grab me.

"Oh my God, Gianna! Calm down. Everything will be all right. We will make it work, I promise. We will make it work," she begged.

I calmed down enough to make her let go of me, and that's when I went after him again. I punched him in the face and tried to kick him in the balls, but he blocked me.

"I hate you! I hate you so fucking much. You'll pay! I promise you, you will pay!" I threatened and grabbed Mack's arm, and then we got the hell out of there.

We went to the nearest bar and found the guy who took us in his limo. I wanted to hurt Mack but I also wanted to take any scent of him off of me that still lingered. I wanted to fuck him out of my system.

I enjoyed every second of it, and when we made our way to my car, I could tell she was upset, devastated even. I took the long way home through a dark and abandoned road, wanting to have Mack wallow in her misery of what had just happened. I relished in that feeling and I didn't see the car coming up behind us. I swerved at the last minute as it hit me on my side, making me do a one-eighty on the dirt road. Our heads hit the door windows and I saw stars through my fluttered eyes.

"Mack? Mack, are you okay?"

She touched her forehead. "Yeah..."she replied, immediately opening her door and stepping out. "What the fuck is your problem! You could have killed us," she screamed.

It was then that I noticed the white truck and it all happened so fast, like a domino effect. I saw someone dressed in a black hoodie come out of the truck at rapid speed, it was so dark that I couldn't see the face. My headlights were off and only the truck's were on, facing the other way. The driver was in front of Mack in three seconds flat and that's when I noticed the bat, swinging and knocking Mack out. Her body fell to the ground with a thud and I lunged over through the passenger side and fell face first next to her.

I immediately checked her pulse. "Oh my God! Mack! Wake up, please wake up! Please!" I screamed to no avail.

She had a pulse but her head had a nasty gash, and when I reached for my phone in my back pocket to call 9-1-1, the phone was backhanded out of my hand, knocking it away.

I looked up and saw her face.

Sarah.

James wife.

"What the fuck! What did you do? What are you doing?" I shouted.

She closed her fist and punched me straight on the cheekbone; I fell to the ground, immediately dizzy and disoriented, clutching the side of my face.

"Get the fuck up!" she roared.

My head was spinning and felt like it weighed a hundred pounds. She sat on top of me and started pounding on my face and body. I tried to cover myself as best as I could, but I was too disorientated from the crash and her hitting me. She beat me like she was a two hundred pound man. I could feel my body go into shock and that's when she stopped hitting, but not before spitting in my face.

"You stupid cunt! You fucking ruined everything. He was never going to leave me until he met you. He was happy with me! We were fucking happy. How can you live with yourself? How can you break up a family!" she seethed.

I rolled over, spitting blood and curling into a fetal position.

"Get the fuck up or I swear I'll kill you. Better yet, I'll kill her."

I watched through bruised eyes, trying to keep them open but they were swelling fast. She raised the bat right above Mack's head. "You have five seconds. Five, four, three, two, on–"

"STOP!" I screamed, finding strength to stand on one leg and then the other. I immediately slouched forward, spitting out more blood, and limped to the side of the car door to hold myself up.

"That's better," she stated, lowering the bat to her side.

I finally breathed out and sucked in air from the pain in my ribs.

"Look at me. Fucking look at me, G," she mocked.

I angled my forehead on the car and turned.

"That's what he calls you, right? G...awe, how fucking pathetic. You're so fucking easy, so gullible. Just like he is...the second I told him I was pregnant he believed me like a fucking idiot. You should have seen his eyes light up. Ugh! Like I would ever get pregnant with his fucking spawn again. He believed every word I said. It's actually kind of comical...did you actually think that there were others?" she laughed. "There weren't other girls, you stupid fucking cunt. You were the only one. He does love you and it makes me fucking sick. But it doesn't matter because I already killed your baby, and now I just have to kill him," she threatened.

I tried to understand what she was saying, but my mind couldn't process it fast enough. I think I had a concussion. I convulsed and fell to the ground on my hands and knees. I flipped over and leaned onto the car for support.

"Look at you. What the fuck does he see in you? I can't actually kill him. But I can do something way worse, and guess who's going to do it. The love of his life, G, that's who. Get your big girl panties on, darling," she sang.

"I have it all planned out. See, that's his truck, which you know because he's probably fucked you in it. You dirty whore. Anyway, Mack is knocked out so you're going to say that I am him and he raped

you and Mack. She won't remember anything, thanks to my trusty old bat here," she stated, hitting the bat back and forth on her palm.

"You're going to send him to prison, and if you don't do it, I'll kill her. And don't for one second think I won't fucking do it. I'll do it and frame you for it. I mean, she is fucking your dad, God that's disgusting, not that your dad isn't a handsome man...he very much is. Is it all clicking? Do you understand? There's motive, baby! It's fucking genius," she said in the same singing tone. "All right, you aren't making this as much fun as I thought it was going to be. Maybe I need to give you some initiative."

She backhanded Mack across the face a few times and then fisted her hair knocking her head into the ground.

"Please...please stop...you're going to kill her! Please," I half sobbed.

She put her hands up in a surrendering motion. "Okay...if you insist."

She walked over to me and crouched down in front of me on the heels of her shoes.

"You don't look so good. Come on, G, I know you want to get back at him. I mean, he didn't really fight for you," she taunted. "I mean, granted, I did manipulate him and tell him I was pregnant so I kind of conned him into it. Oh well...beggars can't be choosers. But in all seriousness, I would have expected him to at least struggle a little and he didn't. Plus, you guys are eighteen so I don't think he would get into that much trouble. He may serve some time, but mostly he will just get a slap on the wrist. I just want to make him hurt...just like he hurt me, just like he hurt you. He's not a good person," she asserted.

"I gave him everything and it was never good enough, and then you go and parade your pussy around like goddamn gold and he's walking around with his tail between his legs in love with you. So yes...I was a little jealous, and what better way to get back at him by having his soul mate betray him. I think it's fucking awesome," she shouted, throwing her hands up in the air like she was dancing.

"Like I said, it's very simple, I've already done the hard part, really. All you have to do now is say that he raped you guys. I think you can use your imagination and conjure up something good, I've set

it up perfectly, you just fill in the blanks." She clapped her hands together. "Now... if you could so kindly get up, I'll help, of course, and we can go put some of your blood in his car, so I can go. I need to take the car back and pick up Cara from the sitters. I'll hand you back your phone and you can call 9-1-1. They will come to your rescue and all will be right with the world. Justice served for women everywhere," she clarified, grabbing my arm and putting it around her neck.

And the rest is history...

There were no words to explain the look on his face when I tried to reach for him. He backed away from me.

"Don't," he warned.

"That's the whole truth," I retorted.

"I can't be near you right now."

I sighed. "What the fuck did you expect me to do? I never thought you would get in that much trouble! I thought because we were eighteen that they would slap you on the wrist or something. She beat the fuck out of me and almost killed Mack, and then threatened to kill her if I didn't do what she said," I angrily explained. "I was backed into a corner, but I swear to you on my parents' lives that I NEVER thought you would go to prison. It got out of hand so quickly, and the media blew it up as soon as they got wind of it. I'm so fucking sorry," I wept.

I got down on my knees, right beneath him and grabbed at his pants. "You have to forgive me...you have to forgive me, James. Please! I didn't know! I swear to God I didn't know," I sobbed uncontrollably, slouching forward. "I didn't know. I swear...you have to forgive me."

I just sat there, crying for I don't know how long until I felt his strong, solid arms engulf me.

"Shhh...shhh...shhh..." he whispered, rocking me back and forth.

He just held me as I cried away my sins. I really was a monster and I had ruined the love of my life, and I had ruined Mack. I was responsible for everything; all of it came back to me.

"I love you, I've always loved you and I can't go back and be that person anymore. I don't want to die and I don't want to punish myself anymore. I want to be normal. I don't want to drink to forget or to not feel. I'm sick of being this person, James. I don't want to be G anymore. I fucking hate her, she ruined my life," I revealed, knowing that it was the truth.

"I know. I know, Gianna," he grumbled, and that's when I realized he was crying.

We both sat there, holding each other, just crying. It was the most liberating and healing thing I have ever done. To sit in the arms of the man you have loved and hurt so badly and to have him feel every pained emotion you're experiencing is a feeling like none other.

We wept for the past, we wept for the present.

But we did not cry for the future.

After what felt like hours, we stood and I dressed in some cotton shorts and tank top he had stored. It felt weird to have on real clothes. Neither one of us spoke; there was silence everywhere. But when he grabbed my hand and we walked out of the room together, it gave me hope that all was not lost.

We made our way into Mack's room but it was empty.

"Mack, Mack, Mack!" Still no answer and I instantly panicked.

"Fuck! Mack where are you?" I screamed to no one.

I turned. "Oh my God, where is she?"

His eyes widened in fear and he lowered his eyebrows. "Shit."

"We need to find her," I said and he nodded.

I followed him as we searched for her everywhere in the asylum, only to find her nowhere. She wasn't anywhere. I followed him outside and hours had gone by with no Mack.

Until that old, familiar demon roared its ugly head and I fell on my hands and knees and started throwing up.

"Fuck! Not now," he shouted.

"I can't help it!" I screamed in between dry heaving.

"Goddamn it. Are you okay?" he questioned, rubbing my back.

"Don't worry about me. Go find Mack. I'll be fine. Just go find her." He sucked in is lip, not wanting to leave me but finally obliged and nodded.

"Stay right here. Don't move," he ordered.

I dry heaved for a few more minutes and fell onto my back, right next to my own vomit. My vision started to go blurry and I started shaking uncontrollably. This was it. I was dying. It had all caught up with me and this was my finale. It was time to meet my maker.

I closed my eyes and prayed for forgiveness.

Chapter Twenty-six

What's all that noise?

Beep, beep, beep, beep…

"I think she's waking up." I heard a voice I didn't recognize. "Miss Edwards, Gianna, it's time to open your eyes. Open your eyes for me, I know you can."

I squinted my eyes from the brightness of the room. "Water," I requested with a hoarse voice.

"I'm going to elevate your bed to have you lean forward. Tell me if you're uncomfortable."

I took in my surroundings, I was in a hospital room. How the hell did I get there?

"What am I doing here? Ho–" I cleared my voice. "How did I get here?"

"You've been through quite an ordeal. Do you remember anything?" she questioned as she handed me water in a foam cup. I grabbed the straw and inhaled it all.

"More," I requested.

She poured more and handed it to me, "You're very dehydrated. The doctor will be here in a few minutes. He will be able to answer all your questions. You are very lucky to be alive."

The last thing I remembered was looking for McKenzie. "McKenzie, is she okay? Where is she?"

"She's fine. She's here," I threw my head back against the pillow, relief taking over.

I looked outside the window, it was dark and gloomy. I watched the drizzles of rainfalls and the sounds of the machine were soothing. What a combination to make me tired. I was exhausted and felt like I had run a marathon. My bones were aching and my stomach was queasy.

"Miss Edwards," an older man said, holding a clipboard by my bedside.

"Don't call me that," I quickly disapproved.

"Oh, I apologize. What would you like me to call you?"

"Call me Gianna. My name's Gianna," I informed, taking pride in my name for the first time in my life.

"All right, Gianna. I'm Dr. Longhand. I am the attending physician who has been looking over your case. You have been through hell and back, huh?"

I nodded.

"Well...your friend is in much better shape than you are. I'm sure you're aware of that. How long have you been drinking?"

"A while." I shrugged.

"How long is a while...a few months, years?" he asked in an agitated tone.

"Years." He nodded like he expected me to say that.

"You're pancreas is extremely inflamed and it has caused a kidney infection. Antibiotics can cure that, however, your liver, Gianna," he sighed, shaking his head. "I haven't seen a liver that damaged on someone your age, well...it's been a while. We need to discuss sobriety because if you continue to drink the way you have, you will experience liver failure and you could die," he explained, looking at me like a concerned parent would.

"I understand," I replied.

I didn't want to drink anymore. I had left that life behind me. I was done being that person.

"How long have I been here?"

"You've been here for three days. We've kept you sedated to keep your blood pressure down. We have you on Valium for the tremors and shakes, some Zofran for the nausea and a banana bag IV for hydration and nourishment. Your withdrawals shouldn't be as uncomfortable as they would be. We are medically detoxing you. This is best place for you right now. We will monitor you for a few more

229

days and I'm going to request you talk to a therapist before you're discharged. Do you remember anything?"

"Where's Mack?" I asked, ignoring his question.

I needed to talk to Mack; we weren't getting James in trouble for this. I was done putting the blame on everyone else.

"She's been asking for you as well. The sheriff would like to speak to you, to both of you." I nodded.

"I need to speak to Mack before I speak to anyone."

"I'll see what I can do."

He proceeded to check my vitals and provide me with all the information of what they would be doing for the next few days. I complied with everything he said and suggested. When nightfall approached, I took a few bites of my dinner but mostly just drank my juice, trying to shake the thought of vodka in it. It wasn't going to be as easy as I had hoped. The triggers were everywhere for me. It was very quiet with the lights dimmed in the hallway. I could tell most of the nurses went home because there was no chaos. All was calm. I listened to the voices that came off the TV, not even paying attention to what I was watching.

I must have fallen asleep at some point because when I woke up, James was sitting in the chair sleeping. I sat myself up a little and the tray table skid across the floor, waking him up. He brushed the sleep off his eyes and cracked his neck.

"What are you doing here?" I asked.

He smiled, relieved that I was awake and talking. "I've been here the entire time, Gianna. Who do you think called 9-1-1? I found Mack pretty close to where I left you. She was passed out with a nasty gash on her leg. I carried her back to you and I found you foaming at the mouth and talking incoherently. The paramedic said it was a mild seizure. They brought you both here immediately and I rode with them."

"Oh," I stated. "What did you tell them?"

"I told them I was hiking in the woods and found you guys. They haven't asked many questions. I think they're waiting to talk to you guys."

"Don't worry, James. I have no intention of turning you in, and I'm sure Mack feels the same way," I clarified, not wanting him to stress.

"I know. They haven't been able to get ahold of your parents and I think that's why they've allowed me to stay with you. I haven't been told much information though. I'm assuming you're all right. You look…better," he stated, leaning forward and putting his elbows on his knees.

"I feel like shit, but the medication is helping. I'm not concerned with what happens now; I'm scared of what happens when I leave. All I can think about right now is how bad I want a drink. Even after the doctor has warned me about liver failure, I'm still jonesing for something to take the edge off," I confessed, playing with the ends of my hair.

"It's over," he observed.

He knew I needed to hear it. "I forgive you. I forgive both of you. I'm free, Gianna. I can start my life fresh now and you can, too. You both can. You don't have to live with the remorse anymore. No more blaming yourself. We all ruined our lives and it's time to move on. You're a beautiful girl who deserves a fresh start. You need to try."

"I know. It's not that easy though. I have no idea where to even start. I've numbed myself for so long."

"I understand. It's scary. Trust me, I'm terrified, too. Maybe you and Mack can work on your friendship, you can be in each other's lives again."

"Right. I know I would like that," I related.

"I'm sure she would, too."

We stayed silent for a while. Both of us lost in our thoughts on what to say next. I was dreading what was to come. As much as I wished it could be different, I knew better than to give myself false illusions.

"What happens now, with you? Am I ever going to see you again?" he shrugged and cocked an eyebrow.

"I'm in the same boat you are. I have been filled with revenge and hate for the last several years and now it's my turn to start over. My father died a few years ago and he left me quite a bit of money.

231

I'm thinking I may start a business or something independent. It will probably be difficult for me to get employment. I'd like to buy a house on a lake, maybe. Something quiet and away from the chaos," he said.

"With a woman? Have a family again? Is that in your plans, too?" The bitter tone in my voice was inevitable, but I couldn't help it. The thought of him being with someone else who wasn't me made me want to drink. I had to stop thinking like that.

He scratched his head. "I think it's a little early to start thinking about that. At least for me..." I turned my face to look out the window. I didn't want to have this conversation. I didn't want to say goodbye. I said goodbye to him once and it nearly killed me. What would it do this time?

The moon was bright. All the stars in the sky made me think about when I was a child and wished on that shooting star. If I saw one right then, I would wish there was a world where James and I could be together. Where our love would prevail and it was all or nothing. I wanted to get up and open a window, I felt like I was suffocating. I didn't know what I expected. How did I get my heart back from a man it rightfully belonged to? I couldn't watch my happiness leave me again. I just couldn't do it.

I knew I needed to love myself before I could think about loving someone else. That was the problem all along. It took eight years to finally figure it out. First thing I needed to do was work on myself. The only reason I was in such a situation was because I wasn't happy as a person and I allowed that to influence me.

"I'm sorry," he whispered, bringing my attention back to him. "You're not completely to blame for everything that transpired. It could have been different. But there's no point to reminisce about things we can't change. It's in the past and it would be better for all of us to just leave it there."

I nodded. "I agree."

He chuckled. "Wow. I thought you were going to argue with me."

"There's nothing left to fight for, James." His eyebrows raised and hurt was evident among his eyes.

He got up to walk over to me, but I put my hand up in the air. "Don't," I pleaded. "Please don't make this any harder than it has to be. We had our closure, remember? Just wish me well and walk away."

He blinked a few times, taking in my request. "Please take care of yourself, Gianna." Concerned and hurt layered his voice.

"You, too, James." He nodded and walked toward the door, turning before walking out.

"You know, Gianna really is a beautiful name," he said, making me chuckle. "I think you should bury G and embrace Gianna."

"I think you're right."

He smiled and walked out of my life for the last time.

I waited for the chaos to erupt the second I heard the door close. I thought the emotions I would feel would have me pulling out my IV and discharging myself to go to the nearest bar. To my surprise, I felt peace. I think that's the best word to describe it…had this whole ordeal been a blessing in disguise? How morbid is it to even think that?

My captor had become my savior…

The next morning I was forced to eat cereal and do laps in the hallway. My stiff muscles were sore before I even made it back to the bed. The nurse gave me a few magazines and I had gotten so lost in the celebrity gossip that I didn't even hear Mack come in.

"I worked at that magazine," she said, making me look up. She looked better, healthier. "Did I miss anything pivotal?"

"Yeah, Christian Donovon broke up with Ashley Mayor," I replied, making her smile.

"I spoke to the cops this morning, Mack. They wanted my statement and I told them that I didn't remember anything. They didn't really believe me, but I wasn't going to turn him in, again. I couldn't do it."

She nodded. "Yeah, I know. He came to my room after he left yours. Are you okay?"

"I think so. I can't get any worse."

She sat at the edge of my bed. "He's just as lost as you are, Gia. I know that probably doesn't make you feel any better. But he's

233

just as lost and confused. I know you still love him and I know he still loves you."

"I hate feelings. They fucking suck," I sighed.

She laughed and gave me a sad smile. "Sometimes you have to walk away from people you love to find yourself."

"You're like the Dalai Lama right now, do you want to give me a fortune cookie, too?"

"Asshole," she stated, trying not to laugh.

"How are you holding up?"

"I'm okay, I'm just tired more than anything. I get discharged tomorrow though. So…" We smiled at each other. It felt familiar and comforting to be sitting with her like we had when we were younger, like nothing had changed even thought everything had.

"Where are you going?" I questioned, not wanting to break the open line of communication.

"I have no fucking idea." We both laughed. "I have a house that I rented when I was having a mental breakdown. I'm pretty sure it's a piece of shit and I didn't really make a wise investment. I can't see myself going back there. I'm done running away. I need to try something else."

"Agreed," I responded.

"Are you scared?"

"Absolutely. I'm terrified."

"I understand, but at least everything is out now," she justified.

I sat up higher. "Yeah…about that, Mack. I need–"

We both turned when the door unexpectedly pushed open.

"GG! GG! GG!" she repeated, running over to me and jumping into my arms. I closed my eyes, not wanting to ruin the moment.

I hugged her tight, breathing in her little girl smell. I hadn't seen her since Christmas. I took a deep breath before opening my eyes. We locked eyes with each other and I didn't have to wonder if she knew. It was written all over her face. I looked back at Abby and I couldn't imagine a life without her or a world without her in it, and that very well could have happened if I hadn't gotten that phone call from AJ telling me she needed a blood transfusion. Looking at her now, you would have never known that she was a tiny, premature baby.

The second I saw her I knew she was a product of my dad and McKenzie.

"Abigail, you don't run away from me like that," he said, just as he turned the corner to come into my room. He abruptly stopped when he saw us.

"McKenzie," he said.

"Kyle," she replied.

And then the peace was gone...

Chapter Twenty-seven

"Hi, my name is Gianna Edwards and I'm an alcoholic. It's been ten months since I took my last drink. I'm receiving my tenth-month sobriety chip tonight. I can't say that it hasn't been hard because it has. My sponsor, family, and friends have been extremely supportive, and for the first time in my life, I'm not scared every morning when I wake up. I have feelings and emotions that I struggle with on a daily basis. I used to self-medicate with anything I could get my hands on; I was a human garbage disposal. I'm not proud of the things I have done, but I have forgiven myself and I try to stay optimistic about the future. I've slowly forgiven myself," I nervously laughed. "Umm…that's all I have to say, I guess. Thank you."

Everyone stood up and applauded, and I can't help but blush and smile. My sponsor was in the back of the room and she called me over.

"You did good, girl."

"That was fun…not really, but look at my shiny chip." I held it up in my hand while she laughed.

"I barely recognize you from the skinny, paled, pathetic girl I met six months ago. You look healthy and dare I say happy."

I grinned. "I wouldn't go that far. I'm joking. I feel good. I just focus on how I feel every day and I take one day at a time."

"Look at you, you're like the spokesperson for sobriety." I shrugged.

"I'm going to let you go celebrate. I'm proud of you."

"Thanks."

I was free of all the lies and I felt amazing. As soon as Mack realized that her child was alive and I knew about Abigail being a product of her and my father's relationship, our rekindled friendship kind of fizzled.

I knew that they were together and although I didn't understand it, I respected it. My dad was very active in my life and that was good enough for me.

As far as Mack, she has her own story to tell and I knew nothing about it. She has her own journey to share with her own mistakes, lies, betrayals, and confessions. Don't we all...maybe I'll hear it someday or maybe I won't. I know there are always two sides to every story and I'm sure she has hers.

Everything happens for a reason and I know that now.

I went into a ninety-day rehab program when I was discharged from the hospital. I almost checked myself out three times. My counselor talked me down though, and with her help, I stayed to live another sober day. They make you write down all your feelings, and I mean everything, especially the real personal stuff. When my parents came in for family therapy, it was one of the times I almost checked myself out. To hear everything I put them through was excruciating. I never realized how bad I hurt everyone around me, most of all my parents. It nearly sent me over the edge, but my counselor reassured me that it was normal.

If I hadn't tried to leave, she would have been more concerned. I also realized how blatantly stupid I was for thinking that they couldn't tell I was an alcoholic. They knew the entire time. One of the hardest things that I have ever had to do was look my parents in the face and tell them that I had a problem, and not only that, but that I was a liar. I divulged all my secrets about James, my childhood, Jake, the rape, every last bit. I never thought I would see hurt like I had on my mom's face. My dad remained strong like he always was, but my mom broke down. I was petrified that they would disown me and I informed them of that. They both just embraced me and we all cried together. It was very spiritual and therapeutic.

I regretted my entire life that day; if I had just been honest from the beginning I could have stopped the spiraling results of all the secrets. I'd like to think that I've lived three different lives in my life. That I've been three different people; Gia, G, and most recently, Gianna. I love Gianna; she's smart and levelheaded and everything I

237

aspire to be. She's the person I look up to and she's the person who saved me. Gia was Mack's best friend and the girl who could never keep up with anyone. She was the liar. Now…the infamous G, she was the alcoholic and the devil. She was destructive and lost.

I know that I said she was also James' soul mate, but she never was. It was always Gianna with James; I just didn't know it until now. I hadn't spoken to James, although he did reach out to me around four months ago. I still couldn't talk to him without being afraid that I would relapse. I placed a lot of blame of my drinking problems on him and it's taken me a while to realize it was never him, it was all me. That was a very brutal and gut wrenching realization for me to have, but as a recovering alcoholic, I have to stop placing blame on others for my decisions. They were mine and mine alone.

I missed him every day and a huge part of me was still with him.

After the first three months of rehab, I was placed in sober living where I currently reside. It was voluntary and I wasn't ready to be on my own, the temptation was still high and I didn't want to relapse, I still don't. My counselor suggested sober living and I signed myself right up. It fit perfectly where my life was at the time, and now I find myself maybe ready for something different. I go to AA at least once a day. I'm working through my twelve steps and they are excruciating but helpful. The peace that I feel in my heart is a feeling that I have never felt before. And even though I am still very much living in the storm, it is calm and serene. The waves don't engulf me anymore, I ride them smooth until they are flat and I have resurfaced.

I sat by the windowsill of the library in my sober living home, finishing my journal entry for the day when I swear I felt him.

James…

"You look good, Gianna," he announced, making it crystal clear that he was indeed there.

With me.

I didn't turn, not knowing what to say.

"You have this glow to you right now. Although, you always had a certain aura about you."

I sucked in air.

"Take all my loves, my love, yea take them all; what hast thou then more than thou hadst before? No love, my love, that thou mayst true love call; all mine was thine, before thou hadst this more. Then, if for my love, thou my love receivest, I cannot blame thee, for my love thou usest; but yet be blam'd, if thou thy self deceivest by wilful taste of what thyself refusest. I do forgive thy robbery, gentle thief, although thou steal thee all my poverty: and yet, love knows it is a greater grief to bear love's wrong, than hate's known injury. Lascivious grace, in whom all ill well shows, kil me with spites yet we must not be foes,"[14] he recited.

I took a deep breath and turned to find him standing there in slacks and a button down shirt.

"Oh my God," I declared.

He was holding the Romeo and Juliet book he gave me all those years ago. How did he find it?

He slowly walked over to me and got down on one knee and my eyes widened. He grabbed my hand and flipped it over, the same arm that had all my scars. He flipped his arm that held his scars and smiled, interlocking them together. He opened his palm and placed the same dried rose petal in between our interlocked hands and I started to cry. He reached into his pocket to produce a new, single, fresh, red rose petal.

"Let's heal each other," he whispered, kissing all over my scars.

I didn't know what the future would hold. All I knew was that in the present, he was kneeling before me.

We were together.

James and Gianna.

And that was good enough for me.

Epilogue

I loved her from the first day of school. When she walked into the classroom I knew we were meant to be together. There was this certain beautiful broken entity about her, from the first smile.

She was mine.

I knew she would be uncertain about our age difference but I didn't care. None of that mattered to me.

All that mattered was that we were going to be together.

She belonged to me.

But she didn't.

Her love was a lie.

A secret.

A betrayal.

I don't understand how she couldn't love me back. Why couldn't I get the same passion, devotion, and love? What was wrong with me?

I knew she was cheating on me with him the entire time. I didn't care because I had some of her and that was good enough for me. I loved her that much, I could love her enough for the both of us. I let her go because I thought she would come back to me. That's what was supposed to happen.

Love is supposed to prevail.

I let her go thinking it was what she needed.

She stole my heart.

So I stole her happiness.

I planned it all.

I told his wife and implanted the seed of making him pay, it was so fucking easy. I thought he would spend the rest of his miserable life in prison. But he didn't. So I came up with a new plan and he bit at the bait. Just like his wife had. All he had to do was take care of Mack and I took care of Gianna. The plan was set in motion. I was behind the scenes. No traces of my physical involvement, I just pulled the strings. The deal was he would torture her and make her pay for her sins. I thought that would have her running back to me, thinking he was a monster. But it backfired, just like before.

I have only ever loved one woman.

I will love her for the rest of my life.

But she belongs to another.

Always has and always will…

My name is Jake Henderson and the truth will set me free.

All's fair in *love* and *war*…

The end.

Connect with M. Robinson

Website:
www.authormrobinson.com

Friend request me:
https://www.facebook.com/monica.robinson.5895

Like my FB page:
https://www.facebook.com/pages/Author-
MRobinson/210420085749056?ref=hl

Follow me on Instagram:
http://instagram.com/authormrobinson

Follow me on Twitter:
https://twitter.com/AuthorMRobinson

Email:
m.robinson.author@gmail.com

[1] Friend definition found at http://dictionary.reference.com/browse/friend

[2] Best Friend definition found at
http://epottergirl27.tumblr.com/post/80066085602/best-friend-via-tumblr-on-we-heart-it

[3] Sister definition found at http://dictionary.reference.com/browse/sister

[4] Broken definition found at http://dictionary.reference.com/browse/broken?s=t

[5] "Shall I Compare Thee to a Midsummer's Day" *Sonnet 18) by William Shakespeare
http://www.poets.org/poetsorg/poem/shall-i-compare-thee-summers-day-sonnet-18

[6] "No Fear (Sonnet 145) by William Shakespeare
http://nfs.sparknotes.com/sonnets/sonnet_145.html

[7] *Romeo and Juliet* by William Shakespeare http://lit.genius.com/William-shakespeare-romeo-and-juliet-act-1-scene-5-annotated#note-2558268

[8] *Romeo and Juliet* by William Shakespeare
https://www.goodreads.com/work/quotes/21823035-romeo-and-juliet-plain-text-the-graphic-novel-british-english

[9] "Why are we thus divided having kissed" (Sonnet XI) William Shakespeare
http://www.sonnets.org/love-sonnets.htm

[10] "In Praise of Beauty" by William Shakespeare http://www.shakespeares-sonnets.com/Valentine.php

[11] Sonnet XLII by William Shakespeare
http://shakespeare.mit.edu/Poetry/sonnet.XLII.html

[12] *Merchant of Venice* Act III Scene 1 (Shylock) by William Shakespeare
http://nfs.sparknotes.com/merchant/page_110.html

[13] "In Praise of Beauty" by William Shakespeare http://www.shakespeares-sonnets.com/Valentine.php

[14] Sonnet 40 by William Shakespeare http://www.shakespeares-sonnets.com/sonnet/40

66544425R00137

Made in the USA
San Bernardino, CA
13 January 2018